ZUDD

or

No Bargain in Debasement

Alan Grossberg

ISBN 13: 978-09779561-4-2
ISBN 10: 09779561-4-8

Publishers Cataloging in Publication Data
Grossberg, Alan
Zudd: no bargains in debasement / Alan Grossberg
p. cm.
ISBN 0-9779561-4-8
Library of Congress Control Number: 2006928914
1. Humor. 2. Love stories-Fiction. I. Title.
First Edition First Printing
Printed in the United States of America
10 09 08 07 1 2 3 4 5 6 7 8 9 10

Cover Design: Michele M. DeFilippo, 1106 Design
Book Design: Desktop Publishing Ltd.
www.bookpublishingservices.com

Man is something that shall be surpassed.
What have you done to surpass him?

Nietzsche, *Thus Spake Zarathustra*

Man grows used to everything, the scoundrel!

Dostoevski, *Crime And Punishment*

Dedication

To those who praised this novel
when it was only a rejected manuscript.

One

"Where's the God damned window?"

Gerald McCord, a Godfearing family man who faithfully attended church and had never before been heard to utter an obscenity in public, had shown no sign of losing his reason until the day he went running from office to office like a trapped bird looking for a window in a building that had no windows.

Seeing a patch of reflected lamplight on a wall he hurled himself at it with a triumphant cry and with such force that he fractured his skull, killing himself on the spot.

In his eulogy The Old Man, Harrison Foote III, tried to remove the stigma of lunacy and suicide from the name of the man who had been his oldest and most trusted deputy. He called it an accident and declared that he would remember his old friend's loyalty and dedication to the Foundation, and to himself personally, for the rest of his life.

Having read these words, he paused, squeezing his eyes shut. The mourners were moved, as were the reporters who wrote of it, and, thanks to them, a national audience. Harrison Foote was over seventy. He seemed to be saying that this death of an old friend had darkened his last hours.

But if old Foote's sentiment that he would remember McCord's devotion for the rest of his life had impressed the country it was for the wrong reason. It was not that, as they thought, his own days were numbered; it was that he had made plans to live forever, or thereabouts. He intended to remember McCord, and everyone else, for a very long time indeed. For that reason he had made himself the majority shareholder of Cryology, Inc. He meant to be not just its most prominent but its only client. And he did not want anything to go wrong.

The tears were because McCord's suicide meant something had gone wrong.

* * *

McCord had been his trusted lieutenant for as long as anybody could remember. Not only was McCord his contact with the company, and the one responsible for setting up the alarm system that would ensure his chief's refrigerated survival, but for nearly forty years he had been Foote's agent for dealing with every awkward situation that arose to threaten his peace of mind.

One was a cousin with whom he had fathered an illegitimate child. McCord sent her to the Pacific Northwest and dealt with every attempt she made to claim her son's rightful place in the family genealogy with a legal and medical offensive that always silenced her. He had even produced an alleged father. When in mysterious circumstances she was struck by a car and her concussion developed a need for a lobotomy, questions that were raised were neatly squelched. And when, in the middle of a renewed effort to clear her name she died of a drug overdose, there were rumors, never substantiated, of a mysterious acquaintance.

Another of his triumphs was setting up Harrison Foote's own personal cryogenics company, with the sole purpose of preserving Foote, and only Foote, in a medically viable condition so that he could be revived and cured of whatever it was that caused his death once the medical profession had reached that level of competence. On his seventy-third birthday Foote, feeling a pang in his gut, had asked for a report, and McCord had asked for more time, which was granted. Now that time was up.

A preliminary investigation revealed that he was frustrated by an inability to master his computer files. A man accustomed to total control in his undertakings, he had literally been driven mad by the latest Windows upgrade.

And, thought Foote, by guilt.

* * *

McCord's department was divided in two, and one of these was handed to a newcomer—to Catherine Harlow. Nobody knew why. Apparently she had performed well enough in the Los Angeles branch to merit the promotion. Or was there a different explanation?

In fact, she was McCord's last service to his chief.

Zudd was spackling and painting the crack in the wall made by McCord's skull when she came to take possession of her office. Her appearance affected his breathing. It was not just her beauty. It was that he had seen her in the lobby an hour ago, talking to an adman, and had thought he would never see her again.

His initial stare gave way to furtive glances, then dreams.

It was not so much the straight features and reddish blonde hair and hazel eyes as what she did with them, added to them. It was the artificiality. His senses swooned at the combined assault of an abnormally fresh skin, insolently high cheekbones, a sparkle in the blackrimmed eyes intentionally hinting at madness, the strawberry waves and curls of her wig, covering her own hair of—he saw by her eyebrows—identical color. Painted fingernails. The capped, perfectly white teeth. From women's magazines and his own discreet observations he knew more about such things than most men. Everything about her cried cafe society. His skin prickling with epiphany, he began—he dared—finally to stop theorizing, and to plan.

In the lobby he had seen her talking to that professional Welshman Tom Hutchins, an apparently important adman who seemed to know her disturbingly well, and was struck by two things: the man's hopeless infatuation, and a look she gave him, Zudd—a glance that became a look that thrilled him right down to his toes. From that moment Hutchins became a rival.

He knew Hutchins and the rest of them on the seventeenth floor, a floor that was always in need of some repair or other. It was fitting that McCord had made his great leap there. For there was a futility about it, a despair in the soft clatter of computer keys and printers creating their electronic magic for the world. The zombies staring at their screens and getting stiff necks and aching backs and carpal tunnel syndrome along with their weekly paychecks. For some reason imagining themselves to be better than laborers or repairmen. Or custodians. They sat like animated mannequins in their facing rabbit hutches, under fluorescent lamps, composing their endless reams of copy, each writer a grenade ready to explode as soon as somebody inadvertently pulled the pin. He could smell the desperation right through the cologne and deodorants and mouthwashes.

When the senior executive suddenly left Zudd's heart jumped at the realization that they were alone. She sat down at the desk, opened drawers, glanced through some papers, lighted a cigarette. He sensed her displeasure at his presence in her office.

"I won't be long," he said, eager to make even vocal contact.

She did not answer, or even look at him except for a cursory glance.

That was enough. Truly this was his ideal woman. One he could worship. He spackled on.

"What happened to the wall?" she asked him, suddenly making the connection.

"Well, you know, it's where Mr. McCord—you know."

"Yes. Was he—I mean, did he just sort of go crazy? I understand he thought he saw a window there."

"So I've heard."

"I mean, how can you think there's a window there? If there were a painting, a picture of a window, or a mirror, or *anything,* but there was nothing there, *was* there? Just wall. None of the pictures is hanging in that particular place."

"Well, you see, Ma'am, there was a floor lamp that throws light off the ceiling, a kind of soft lighting effect, you know, and the lamp's head was loose I guess and it kind of swiveled around and shot its light off at a crazy angle, onto the wall here, and he saw that and I guess he thought...what he thought. He wanted a window, and so he thought he saw a window. We all want something."

He had no idea why he had thrown in this last sentence. But he was glad. It expressed a part of his thought. He longed desperately to express the rest of it, but her expression told him this was not the time. It had got somehow personal. Bad. Wrong. But useful. He sensed he had insinuated himself into her consciousness. There were rings under her beautiful eyes. She too wanted something. Now, if only she could be made to want what he wanted. What a symbiosis that could be!

"I wouldn't know about that," she said in an arch tone, putting him in his place. "I just hope it won't *show*."

"Oh no, I'll take care of it. You'll never know it happened."

She glanced over, saw him smiling at her in that cocky way of his, and looked away flustered. The nerve of him! She flicked ash brusquely.

"Couldn't you come back later, when I'm out?"

She spoke with distinctness, in a courteous tone, as always with business associates and social inferiors, and with her dates until the fourth martini ambushed both diction and courtesy. It was an accent drawn from that of the more ladylike Hollywood actresses—Joan Crawford, Bette Davis, Audrey Hepburn. Even now, with this *janitor*, she took pains to be cool but gracious, aware of the effect she had on men of his social level.

"I'd have to start all over," he explained. "It won't take but a minute."

"Yes all right," she said fussing with some papers.

He had a way of moving, easy and confident, as if it were his office not hers. With that laundered chocolate uniform of his with the gold Foote insignia on his shirt pocket, the folded ruler sticking out of his back pocket, the ring of keys on his belt loop. The pomaded tightly curled black hair. And that sneaky suggestion of arrogance in an otherwise deferential manner, like that of a prisoner contemplating a breakout.

He finished and left without another word. And without immoderate haste. Definitely too much of the arrogance, not enough of the deference. She pressed her lips into a malicious smile. That, she reflected before she caught herself, was his mistake.

But she did catch herself. What are you thinking? she demanded. A *janitor*? It was not that she was a snob, it was that any chance he might, just *might* have with her could only be as a supplicant. Her last black, a waiter she had met in Haiti and who had come to New York to find her, had won her that way, by trembling uncontrollably. This one, this janitor, was in for a surprise if he had any such notion. A *janitor*! She would enjoy watching that cocky confidence wither before her eyes.

Still, there was something unusual about him. Where did he get that confidence from? Maybe he had not always been a janitor. A European nobleman, maybe, down on his luck? In the society columns one read about titled chauffeurs who spoke English without an accent. It might be interesting to study him, discreetly.

There was little work on her desk. Her portion of McCord's workload was still in the organizational stage. She had been given to understand that her responsibilities, along with her importance, would very soon reach a higher level.

Leaning back in her executive swivel chair she blew a smoke ring and crossed her legs and thought of Tom Hutchins who she was convinced was as truly infatuated with her as he claimed. She enjoyed toying with the idea of commencing an affair with him. The challenging stare of the janitor intruded. Startled and annoyed, she nevertheless found herself thinking that she had never tried a janitor. The thought excited her, which in turn annoyed her. He was becoming a pest. What *was* it about him?

As one moves from downers to uppers, so she often slid to thoughts of Tom.

The trouble with Tom was it was hard to get a line on him. An advertising man. Did that say it all? As a lover she pictured him as...okay. Just okay. Neither wimpy nor masterful. Certainly not masterful *enough*. A little weak—not the kind that rises to the top. Some personality, in moderate dosages; too much character. Lots of principles. Charming in his way, but soft. Something half-assed about him. She suspected he might be a loser. The kind that intends to do *better things*; that prattles about *integrity* and *hypocrisy* and all that. Which was a waste. That kind had the talent to do creative things, make a contribution, create a fabulous TV commercial or something, but instead went on and on about honesty and prostitution and "selling out". God! To them everybody who made it, who was a winner, was selling out. The minute you did anything that got you anywhere you were selling out. Generally speaking she had found them to be educated and cultured and idealistic, but all they could do was drink too much (well, *everybody* did *that*) and perform below their capability—grudgingly, for the paycheck. Losers. Would-be dropouts, who failed even at *that*.

Her eyes kept returning to that fresh plaster on the wall, still gray and glistening. That was her one great secret fear. Windows, insanity. So often she had pictured herself standing frozen as if lost in time, then stepping through an open window like a ballerina. It wasn't the dying that frightened her, it was the going insane, the losing her wits.

Her therapist in Los Angeles had the peculiar theory that she would be all right once she reached thirty. She only had to reach thirty. He explained it with abstruse references that she thought really boiled down to instinct, a hunch.

Her New York therapist said the problem lay in her inability to achieve orgasm.

Both were convinced her natural father was at the heart of her disorder, for having deserted her; that everything followed from that and from the succession of stepfathers.

A simple prescription: reach climax, make it to thirty.

Oh, and avoid open windows.

Swiveling to her computer, she began lightheartedly typing out a note to that effect, to herself. The phone rang.

"Ms Harlow? Mr. Foote asks could you come to his office if you have a few minutes to spare?"

To spare? Mr. *Foote*? Such quaint courtesy! Who said chivalry was dead. She thrilled with a sensation of opportunity knocking, of boats not to be missed. Mr. *Foote*!

* * *

Harrison Foote, III was over seventy—how much over, nobody was sure. A frail looking man of medium height, with a few strands of gray hair that he wore artistically long, but not too long, he was almost embarrassingly courteous and considerate for such a powerful personage. Not only was he the honorary president recently retired of the advertising agency that bore his name but he owned several important newspapers, a radio station, a TV cable channel, a stable of racehorses, and a great deal of real estate including the ground the Foote Building stood on, besides being the scion of one of the most respected of New England families which itself had a long pedigree of bankers, diplomats, presidential advisors, university presidents, philanthropists. The best kind of WASP, in a word.

His office had an unused appearance. He dropped in from time to time—literally, by elevator, from his penthouse apartment. Soft lighting, lots of leather upholstery and wood paneling with recessed shelves for books and plants and *objets*, the thick carpet.

He surprised her by greeting her not from the position of power behind his desk but from one side, from beside a potted palm only slightly taller than himself. He seemed unoccupied, unpreoccupied, casual, mildly bored, bemused. Casually dressed in jeans, loafers, open neck shirt, a tweed jacket. His shoulders slightly rounded despite an athletic stance. His smile held a trace of melancholy. She felt immediate sympathy, eager to do something to cheer him up.

"Coffee, Ms Harlow? Or would you prefer a drink?"

He indicated a discreet bar with various bottles and glasses. His manner suggested that he expected her to go for the drink. Two bottles caught her eye: an old Glenfiddich, and an even older Napoleon Cognac. She chose the Scotch, while indicating with an apologetic smile that she fully realized what she was passing up.

He handed her her drink, and poured a glass of white wine for himself. "It's an ingrained habit, I'm afraid," he said, raising his glass to her before sipping with closed eyes. "L'apéritif before lunch." He tasted, swallowed, and looked pleased. "Are you happy here, Ms Harlow?"

"Oh yes, very," she said fluttering the long eyelashes.

"I'm glad. I don't normally like to uproot my people, but at the same time I do like to reward good performance by...rewarding it," he finished with a chuckle. Kit smiled. "So I had you transferred here because...well, for several reasons. Your very good work in our L.A. branch was brought to my attention and I thought, here's a young woman whose talents need greater scope, a sort of creative elbow room, if you see what I mean."

"It's all I ask," Kit said with a surge of emotion, the adrenaline flowing fast.

"To see what she can do. And New York's the place for that, isn't it. In fact, aren't you a New Yorker, born and raised? And I remembered seeing you at the company anniversary banquet in Dallas, and it struck me—Do you know, Ms Harlow, you have an extraordinary resemblance to a picture I'm painting—a muse, the artist's inspiration, in a Grecian robe—She's exactly you! It's really the most fantastic thing. The hair, the eyes, the mouth , the cheekbones—your features exactly. Everything—shoulders, the lines of your neck, your bust, your waist—It's the most incredible thing."

Kit had a strong desire to cross her legs, but they were already crossed. She sat stiffly, tensed as if for action, her thoughts in tumult. So he had had his eye on her? But, for what, exactly? She expelled twin jets of smoke from her nostrils—no ordinary smoke, but that of a gold-tipped Sobranie which he had proffered and personally lit, though he himself did not partake—with well-rehearsed sophistication, bending her wrist back. Were palatial doors about to open for her at last? Keeping a smile at play on her lips she listened hard, careful to show intelligent interest, quiet creative power, and, above all, trust.

"I should explain, my dear. I am an amateur painter."

God! Just the way he spoke! Amateur without the ch. His British pronunciation of the word made him, well, *professional*. Tom said it like that, but then he was British and they all did it there. But Mr. Foote—now *this* was *class*.

Foote took a delicate sip from his glass. "The painting of serious pictures, large ones, in oil...That, Ms Harlow, is my passion." His faded blue eyes looked at her in a pause for effect. He went on with a conspiratorial smile as if confessing a sin that required absolution, "I've been doing it for years *and* years. (The darling man, she thought.) We old fellows of my circle, we have a club. (God, what club must *that* be! There were clubs *and clubs*.) And every year we have a dinner at which we show our work. All of us. One work." He sipped, swallowed, sighed. "I'm afraid mine's not going very well this year. I won last year. Nobody has ever won the prize back to back. I thought this might be my big chance—I felt so inspired for a while, but...It's dead, lifeless. My imagination has deserted me. Photographs won't do it, not at this stage. Not any more. They don't inspire me." Another sigh. "Only a live model can save me now." He gave her a look that managed to be seductive, rueful, and bashful, all at once. "Do you see what I'm getting at, Ms Harlow."

She thrilled at his way of asking questions without asking them, dropping instead of raising his voice. Seated in his own soft leather high-backed armchair across a generous expanse of thick, turquoise carpet and with soft light filling the room from a mysterious source, surrounded by what might have been his family of busts and paintings, he smiled. It was a gentle, solicitous smile, the compassionate smile of the supplicant.

Kit too smiled. It was so easy, in his company, in the company of a true gentleman, a true aristocrat. Not your phony aristocrat of the kind that showed up at every social event in winter and every rich and stylish resort in summer, with their skis and tennis racquets and golf carts. Nothing pushy or grasping here, no thirst for public attention, no trying to seduce and suck you dry and leaving you for the buzzards—the playboys, the man-about-town cocksmen. This was a different level. And an artist. Of course! Here was where your real culture was. These were the ones who kept the flame alive. Watching him and listening to his anxious but cultivated intonations while sipping her ambrosia, Kit believed. That this was a good man. From a good mold. That nothing bad could come from such a man. To touch one was to induct magic through one's fingertips. To be near one, sitting in identical armchairs of soft leather, was to absorb by osmosis the spiritually excellent things of this world.

But she too had striven, and perfected, and polished. And in the compassionate tone of voice she had mastered, and used exclusively with men, she said, "I think I do."

And like a suitor in a Victorian novel declaring himself, he said in a rush, "*Would* you consider posing for me, Miss Harlow?" She found the Miss charming: for all his sophistication and power, he had, in his agitated state, forgotten himself. It was known throughout the vast organization that The Boss prided himself on keeping up with the latest societal innovations, and had been among the first to address his female employees with the title Ms. "You would be doing me a great favor. I'd be most grateful."

With the gracious, motherly smile of a benefactress (so many smiles! like a business deal between Orientals!) she nodded eagerly. "I love art," she said. "I mean, *real* art."

"Bless you for saying that, Miss Harlow! What a joy that is, in these times. Oh I do hope you'll decide to do it after thinking it over, I do hope so. It won't be too hard—perhaps an hour or so, maybe twice a week if you could spare the time. Do think about it. I pay five hundred dollars an hour—no, no," he protested as she produced an embarrassed demurral, "I must be permitted to express...you understand...my gratitude. I insist on a certain, um, formality. In such matters. A *friendly* formality. This after all has nothing really to do with your regular work, we mustn't confuse the two, must we... Perhaps I can find a way to make it tax deductible for you...So then you *will* consider doing it? Thank you so much for your open mindedness and...understanding. I see you're not at all an ordinary young woman—but then I knew that. And I want you to feel free to come to me with your personal problems. If you so desire. I've seen something of the world, and I'd be glad to advise you if ever you should feel the need for the judgment of an older, rather more experienced person of...my gender. Of course, this must all be in the strictest confidence. I'm sure you understand the need for...discretion."

Kit smiled reassuringly: Surely he did not take her for a common blabbermouth?

At the door he repeated his hope that she would "consider my proposal". It disconcerted her. She had been willing from the first. He seemed to not want her to consent too quickly, as if that would compromise her virtue, or in some way betray the private image he had of her and that he meant at all cost to retain.

"Do think about it and I'll call you in a day or two my dear."

Thoroughly alarmed (was there a competitor?), Kit fell back on her one sure prop, the smile. And that other trustworthy tactic—the brisk exit.

The last seductive picture of the office that she took with her as the elevator began its return to the nether world was of perfection—the decor, his diction, his appearance, his manner. Even his teeth, that looked natural enough to be his own—although, having worked briefly as a dental assistant, she knew they weren't.

Why was he so insistent on not letting her accept on the spot?

She had sensed very strongly that if she had blurted out an acceptance it would have destroyed something. Might it still fall through? Five hundred dollars! For nothing! An hour's posing! Oh the *magic* in this glass and steel mountain! (Magic? Mountain? The words echoed inside the "Culture" file in her brain, and died for want of a Famous Movies or gossip column cross-reference.)

That Greek robe. How quaint! Did he mean for her to change into it? Or slip it over her clothes like a graduation gown? She could wear tight clothes to accommodate that. What a sweet little man. An amateur painter, an artist, with Greek robes, and a little banquet with his circle of old dodderers at the end of the year to win some prize—ha! She could think of a prize: The winner gets *her*, rising naked out of a big cake and giving them all a heart attack. Greek robes! How sweet. How…*traditional*!

On her seventeenth floor the custodian—*that* custodian—was on a ladder fixing a neon light. Did the man have nowhere else to go and fix something? He paused to look at her—for just a little too long—and, again, it flustered her as she looked away, feeling his eyes on her body. It made her conscious of her walk. But she was used to that. She turned it on, giving her hips a little roll. Eat your heart out, sucker.

* * *

Tom Hutchins was waiting for her in the twelfth-floor cafeteria. He sat at the bar with a highball, not watching the door. Even so, he spotted her immediately.

She watched the switch from nervous frown to relief to pleasure.

She too was pleased to see him. She always was. That was the thing about Tom. And Lord knew she had few interesting lunch dates these days, just the usual swingers and chasers with their flippant, ever so casual nothing-ventured-nothing-gained phone calls. Mostly people from her pre-LA past who could not accept that a fling was just that, a fling, and it was over. Like Katz. Although that was different—at once more ridiculous and less regrettable. She still did not know what had possessed her in that one. Broad as was her taste in types of men he was not one of them. It was her usual condition that was always to blame, of being unattached, uninvolved, at loose ends. Loose ends were her nemesis.

What she wanted, what she really wanted, was a man of taste and culture, not one who faked the first and played at the second. All the men in her life had done that. She wanted the real thing. Wasn't that why Marilyn Monroe had gone for Arthur Miller? And why so many famous actresses and Hollywood beauties, once they'd arrived and could disdain the casting couch, married writers and thinkers when they could get them?

Tom led her to a table in the Saratoga Room, in which battle a Foote ancestor had participated. Large oil paintings of both dominated the wall space.

Sipping her dry martini she observed him. It was a nice face, almost handsome, round with a kind of permanent baby fat but with a solid chin and a straight nose, cute rather small white teeth that went endearingly with his dimpled smile, when he smiled. (He tended to sulk.) Dark deep blue eyes, their bright idealism dulled by years of forced accommodation with reality—or, as he put it, the enemy. Or of being on the losing side, as *she* put it.

What he was was a critic—of himself, society, modern civilization. It was his single most perceptible characteristic, that you saw only after you got to know him and he stopped trying to suppress it and actually turned cheerful. In their few encounters he had already managed to express disapproval of her way of life, and contempt for his own. An interesting sort of loser. Reminded her of Sam Katz in a way.

Not really. He was better looking and more intense. Far less sociable, too. She was not sure why she liked that. It seemed somehow romantic. Lone wolf kind of thing. Independent and iconoclastic. And much better educated.

But, like Katz, he was dead set on marrying her and straightening her out. They wanted to save her. Well, once was enough, thank you.

Yet it was this that bonded them together. Because she *wanted* to be rescued, even if it was not clear from what. The window? Tough as she was, she felt vulnerable.

In her heart she knew she was not the cerebral, highly educated, cultured, efficient player she pretended to be. (Who was? She had scarcely ever met a colleague, never mind how illustrious, who did not turn out to have feet of clay.) She had behaved irrationally and used poor judgment more times than she cared to remember. That was one problem.

That she had never committed herself—no burned bridges—was, according to every lover and counselor she had ever had, the engine of her self-doubt. The thought scared her. *Was* she too cold, as more than one disappointed lover had declared?

The accumulation of accusations troubled her enough to bring on the occasional migraine. What was the good of being all those enviable things with capital letters—Beautiful, Smart, Chic, Seductive, Frank, Responsible—if she was also (that horrid word) Frigid?

What a cruel irony that her passion, when she did unleash it, brought only frustration; that however hard she tried, she was unable to reach, actually *reach* this tantalizing pinnacle of all sensation that she was assured by an army of experts and researchers was her natural right.

Sometimes, too often, she felt all alone in the world, and these two were like family. Like older brothers. It was comforting to know she could trust them utterly, to know that this Welshman in front of her was incapable of telling her so much as a little white lie.

The trouble was, with that reassuring honesty came its twin: brutal frankness. As in that first dance when, in the middle of a not very impressive two-step, he said, "I think what you need is nourishment."

"Too thin?" she said.

"I don't refer to the physical. (That quaint Welsh structure, along with the music of his inflection, had disarmed her from the start.) It's your soul that I mean. You are starving yourself."

"To death?"

"Who knows?"

"And what do you suggest, doctor?"

"A different lifestyle."

"But I like my lifestyle!"

"Do you really"?

The combination of those words and the look that accompanied them had firmly installed this serious bore in her life and, worse, her thoughts. She got emotional at that point, almost angry. It had cost her much time and many hard knocks to acquire that lifestyle. But she'd had an inspired retort.

"First change your own, Mr. Hutchins. Then let me know how it went."

That had gone right into him. He stopped dancing. His face showed strong emotion. It startled her. He looked as if he were about to go to pieces.

"I want to! My God I want to! But I can't do it alone! Nor can you! We must do it together! Together we can...." His voice faded.

She'd laughed a desperate laugh, not really relishing the victory. The laugh succeeded in putting paid to that particular interview, thank God, but it left her troubled. What kind of therapist was this, that himself needed guidance? They all did, of course, but still. Shades of Sam Katz! Like St. Bernards they were, or pretended to be—big comfortable protective facelicking dogs that themselves needed petting and reassurance; that kept watching you and trying to figure you out and gave a disturbing growl from time to time and never gave up trying to rescue you.

She scanned the menu without interest and laid it down. She wasn't hungry.

"So, you say you're happy here," Tom said swirling the ice in his glass.

There it was, that dangerous thoughtful look.

"Very."

The waiter brought another martini, just as she was thinking maybe she should have stuck with Scotch.

"I wonder why you were transferred," Tom mused.

With a modest smile she shrugged. "Good workers move up. I guess they wanted somebody with my particular abilities."

"Yes, of course. By the way, what are your particular abilities?"

She gaped. This came close to open insult. Even Americans did not do *that*. Even New Yorkers.

"Come off it, Tom," she said, controlling herself, "don't be so...*pedantic*. I know good art when I see it, I mean commercial art. I was an independent agent for a while, you know."

"I know."

"You knew?" She couldn't remember having told him. In fact she made it a point not to mention it to people. It could make you look like a loser. "Then why the question?"

"Just to...Why did you quit that, the independence? Was it too hard going it on your own?"

"Oh, I wasn't doing all that badly. But...well, the tax rules are so complex, and I was always a bit short of funds and, um, well, *time.*"

Tom smiled his understanding. "Couldn't get up in the morning? Dark circles under the eyes?"

"Something like that. I'm not sure I like the way this is going, Buster. What's on your mind?"

"What I said. I'm wondering why you were moved to New York. I meant no offense."

"I answered that question."

"No. You didn't. *I* asked for you."

"You what?"

"I asked for you to be brought here from LA."

"You?"

"That's right."

Shaking out a cigarette she said almost angrily, "So if you know everything and it was all your doing, why the secrets and why the third degree? And why did you ask for me? And who *asked* you to do me that favor? I might have wanted to stay where I *was*. I had a life there, you know." Tom nodded in abject contrition. "And since when are you in a position to make personnel recommendations to Mr. Foote?"

"He socializes with some of us from time to time. And he rather likes the British. Including the Welsh. So I gave it a shot. I made the recommendation to Terry Tarantino, that's the personnel man, and followed it up with a memo, citing things that, well, that really had nothing to do with anything. I was amazed when you showed up. I was never told. I still don't understand it."

"What's to understand? But *I* still don't understand why you *did* it."

"That little chat we had in Dallas, at the company dinner. It may not have meant very much to you, but to me...I couldn't get you out of my thoughts."

She remembered that. She had liked him. She remembered thinking what a pity it was that they were on opposite coasts. "I was not entirely unaware of you either." But her thoughts were running all over the place. At what point had the old gent's own eyes taken over? Lighting up with a snap and a click she drew in smoke and blew it over his head, staying cool. "Even so, presumably my performance in California had *something* to do with it?"

"That's just it. They need good workers there more than here. My recommendation went astray. It came back to my office and before I could send it up again here you were!"

"I see!"

"It wasn't my fault. It just got lost somehow." Kit's smile maintained its jeering edge. "So I repeat," said Tom, "why are you here?"

Handling the glass expertly with the same hand that held the cigarette, Kit took a sip and said with a frivolity calculated to annoy him, "You're glad, I'm glad, everybody's glad, so—" with a pretty shrug—"why look a gift horse in the mouth?"

Tom scowled at the tablecloth, struggling for tact, and looked up again. "That's all right for pretty girls, but you see, I'm not a pretty girl, and at the risk of being a frightful bore, I've learned to look gift horses in the mouth, and what I've seen has hardly ever been good teeth. Yes of *course* I'm glad you're here, I *wanted* you here, I'm very *glad* you're here, but my question still stands."

Everything that was wrong with Tom Hutchins, and at the same time everything she liked about him, was right there. He'd learned to look gift horses in the mouth.

But that question. Still standing. How agreeable it was, knowing she could knock it over with a word—one precisely enunciated name. The sensation emboldened her to strike with wild subtlety and wit.

"Maybe somebody up there," she smiled (nearly laughed), raising her eyes towards heaven, "likes me."

"If He did," replied faked-out Tom, "He would not have sent you to New York, in spite of my prayers. But they say the Lord moves in mysterious ways."

"Oh go on," said Kit, now thoroughly enjoying herself, "I'm sure you're really crazy about New York. You're just one of those people that like to grumble about it. And when they leave they can't wait to get back."

"Try me."

"You want me to send you away?" she teased.

"I won't go without you. With you, in a heartbeat."

A new pattern in their relationship was set. She would jolly and joke and tease, neither encouraging nor discouraging him. He would grin and be intense and ironic and serious and sad, and intelligent, and weakwilled, and wise. A mistress and her favorite (educated) water poodle. Fetch the encyclopedia, Tom, there's a good dog.

Two

Locking an office door after a job, Homer Zudd took the staircase down and stopped to look out fondly through the glass wall at the courtyard twenty stories below. Let the old bastard have his penthouse panoramas, this was *his* visual delight, that he loved just *because* it had no sun that shone in, no air that moved except for the occasional whirlwind, nothing but smog and soot. And it was walled in, like a prison yard.

His brown sharp eyes turning soft he contemplated this yard that was his, all his, that he owned because the other custodians and the cleaning women shunned it as they shunned the basement levels that were his home. This was his beloved environment of cold clean cement, and pipes—overhead asbestos-wrapped steam pipes, water pipes, drain pipes, sewer pipes—and the great plates of glass, the walls of sheetrock and plasterboard. And his playthings: the sprays and detergents and disinfectants and deodorants and rat poisons. How happy they all were to leave to him the jobs that meant being sucked into that underworld, thinking they were cleverly exploiting him. So he had it all to himself—three levels of basement and a courtyard—to wander in, free as a desert lizard, free but driven, and plotting. Plotting, like Moses and his children of Israel his and his species' salvation, plotting a metamorphosis, laying out a whole new trajectory for a stupidly uncomprehending, robotic human herd.

One of those great vaults was his living quarters. Opening the door he flicked one of two switches and was awarded a quiet, sophisticated ambience for guzzling, snacking, goofing. Soft lighting, quiet semiclassical music. Sweet. Seductive. Ms Harlow would like it. But the second switch.

Smiling an angry smile as he pictured her cool condescending face he flicked it (so hard he hurt his finger) and the big room jumped alive in a paralyzing *son et lumière* of startling sights and deafening sound—colored lights turning, whirling, revolving, a panoply of planets and suns and moons and darting comets while new and old musical noise pounded and blasted and screeched. Jesus Superstar. Heavy metal. Rap, featuring every savagery—Rape the women! Kill the pigs! Smash Whitey! Burn! It's our turn! Videos on a preset TV screen presented karate killers in action against Mob cutthroats. On a wide movie screen a gaucho in black leather whipped a naked blonde girl (not really beautiful, but the hard Nordic features pleased him) who writhed in ecstasy. This gave way without plausible transition to another sequence in which she whipped him in return after forcing him to undress—he did it with a leering grin—, whereupon his ecstatic writhings imitated hers exactly.

In a corner, a great ape sitting on a platform against a jungle backdrop paddled a naked female mannequin. Her happy surprised pretty face was turned upwards, the graceful hands fluttered. But the ape's head was not right. It was not an ape but a man. The blond hair was parted on the side. The eyebrows and nose and teeth and jawline were model perfect. Ivy League. Jack Armstrong.

It was the best he could do. That was the way they had come in his nocturnal foragings. He found them at auctions and in the trash bins behind department stores, in the sidewalk displays of SoHo's homeless merchants, and on the street—discarded, or fallen from a truck. In junkyards and pawnshops.

The ape's right hand, that held a sawed-off paddle, was raised as if in salutation. Too bad the human face was, well, almost effeminate, Jack Armstrong or no Jack Armstrong. But the ape proper was a humdinger. He had found it at a carnival auction. It was mechanized. Pressing another switch would make it paddle the mannequin. Zudd did not care to press it, just yet. He wanted Catherine Harlow.

On the floor were the supplementary heads and figures to go with the dummy and the original fierce primate head. And a flagellator whip, a stout walking stick, a baseball bat.

Tacked up all over the walls were his erotic posters, each featuring a position, a temptation, a taboo. Stills from movies, mostly, that he had captured on his VCR and enlarged.

Not enough. He needed the right woman.

It was all waiting for her. Wall to wall carpet. A big bed. A big kitchenette on one side and an elegant bathroom on the other. Mahogany furniture. Leather armchairs discarded by Foote's decorators. A small bar. And all that psychedelic action—the colors, the drums, the sensation of menace. Mirrors everywhere, around and over the bed. What more could a woman's secret eroticism desire? This lure was his masterpiece. Catherine Harlow would love it, when she saw it.

Somehow he must get her to see it.

Zudd now performed a daily rite. To the sweet mustiness and dank cement smell he added deodorant powder, pouring it down the drains to release a rank odor of flowers. He sprayed the room with an insecticidal scent of pine. He swallowed a dozen pills from an array of bottles he kept behind the bar. Then he sat in an armchair and drank a wine flavored cola called WineDrink and smoked a cigarillo of hybrid tobacco through its plastic mouthpiece. He was contented.

On the TV screen a kindly doctorish looking man with wire rim glasses and silvery hair extolled a product. "And we don't want to eat foods that have been sprayed with carcinogens, do we," he said with smug serenity.

"Speak for yourself, asshole," Zudd said and fingerpunched the remote control to a different channel.

He leafed through a fashion magazine, went on to a comic book that featured glamorous and indestructible supermen and superwomen, then sank back into the mock leather and watched the two screens simultaneously—one, grinning flagellators and their ecstatic accomplices; the other, snarling killers at war with sadists. He watched until his body began to stiffen. His eyelids drooped, his breathing deepened.

He rushed to the mechanical ape and pressed a button. With a symphony of clanking, clattering, grinding, wheezing sounds the ape fell to beating the female mannequin that lay on his knees, paddle to pink plastic posterior, while Zudd watched dreamily.

But he was dissatisfied. He substituted a female human head for the ape and a male mannequin for the female being spanked, and watched that for a while. Still not good enough. In a spasm of impatience he dropped his pants and threw down the mannequin and put himself in its place. He writhed and groaned with simulated ecstasy as his bare buttocks received the blows. Suddenly he threw himself to the floor and began to masturbate.

But without consummation. At the climax, at the moment ejaculation was imminent, he stopped, clenched his fists, screwed up his face, quivered, fought—and finally relaxed as the terrible moment passed. He lay with his eyes closed, smiling at yet another victory as, slowly, his breathing returned to normal.

A few minutes later, zipped up and his hair combed, he switched everything off. He was famished.

His meal was simple and frugal—a stew of marbled beef he knew was full of hormones and antibiotics, that he spiced with preservatives and additives, seasoners, sweeteners and artificial ingredients such as warmed his heart. The biscuits were his own confection—his favorite recipe. The heartburn did not bother him any more ("Man grows used to everything") but he took an antacid anyway because he liked the chemical taste.

He sat smoking his cigarillo and was contented again, until his eyes wandered to the ape. Again he pictured the beautiful Catherine Harlow, the straight features, the bitter laugh lines, the cool cordial voice, the long legs, the strawberry hair. He imagined her in black leather, whip in hand, a terrible, imperious look in her lovely eyes, commanding him with the haughty disdain of an empress. Man grows used to everything, except when he lusts.

Or could he grow used to that as well? Was he becoming contented with his power of abnegation?

It was something to worry about.

* * *

Kit was late to work, having overslept again.

It did not seem to matter. The few assignments that had shown up on her desk were neither urgent nor important. Even so she told herself, again, that she would have to mend her ways and start arriving on time. It had already been a problem in Los Angeles. No matter how much sleep she got she always wanted more.

That janitor had been in the hall again. He always managed to be in the vicinity of her office doing something or other when she came in and went out. She was starting to expect it, to take it for granted. And there was always that look, that for all its arrogance was beginning to have something piteous in it. That had not been there before. Well, she thought with a smile, let him learn to grovel—or anyway tremble, like the Haitian. Then we'll see. She gave herself a merry little laugh. She would invent a tremblometer! And compare them—the Haitian, the janitor, Katz, Tom. Eliminate slackers!

What's this? A note from Mr. Foote? She grew serious.

Could she spare a moment?

That dear man. Always so courteous, so, well, yes, deferential. Almost timid. So much for power brokers and the upper class. Once you got to know them and fluttered your eyelids they were just as human as anybody else. She fixed her face, touched her wig here and there as if it were her own hair, and went to the elevator in a simmer of anticipation.

* * *

"The Scotch or the brandy, my dear?"

"I'd love to try the Cognac, Mr. Foote."

"Lovely—I will too! Cigarette?"

She hesitated. But he already knew she smoked. An instinct told her he liked it, for some reason. For the accompanying gestures? The cool blowing of the smoke, the cigarette between the fingers, the *je ne sais quoi*?

"Thank you," she said graciously, Princess Graciously, as she accepted the proffered Sobranie cigarette with the gold tip.

And the ceremony of The Lighting of the Cigarette. By him. With a lighter of gleaming gold. She leaned back blowing a stream of smoke, practically quivering with happiness.

Wonderful how no telephones rang, no secretaries interfered.

You would never guess he had a valet and a private secretary and a whole staff of servants. And this bird's-eye view of Manhattan. How many people had all this from sunrise to sunset, and in the middle of the night too? And this was only the office! She had never seen anything like it. Not like this. Those pictures on the walls in their heavy frames—originals, for sure. Van Gogh, Renoir, Matisse—and one that was different: a young woman on an antique chair, the kind you saw in gallery windows and decorator magazines. Dark velvet drapes behind her. It looked like it might be a Foote.

"I did the one you're looking at," he said with endearing diffidence. "I'm afraid it represents the very best I can do."

"But, it's very good, Mr. Foote!"

"It did win the club's prize that year. She was an excellent model, one of the best I've ever had. Lovely girl."

"I can see that," Kit said, her eyes narrowing critically.

"Of course I was younger then—in my prime."

"Oh I'm sure you're still in your prime, Mr. Foote. After all, what exactly is prime?"

"Bless you, you're wise beyond your years, my dear. And you're very kind. And you might just possibly be right, there *are* times when I feel very, sort of, confident. It's when I'm inspired for some reason. But then…That may actually depend on you, Ms Harlow. Have you thought about my proposal?"

"Yes, I have, and yes, I will model for you, Mr. Foote." She felt herself blushing at her determination not to let him weasel around any longer. "I mean, I don't mind doing it."

"Splendid! How very generous of you." He sipped his Cognac and watched her pull on her cigarette and tap the end over an ashtray. He seemed to be making it a point to visibly esteem every gesture of hers. "We ought to set up a schedule of some kind, something convenient for us both. I'm very pleased. A bit more Cognac?" (He pronounced it very French.) It is nice, isn't it. (Tom too said nice when he meant good—another Britishism no doubt.) Old things do tend to improve—if you don't mind my making a little joke. Would this evening be all right?"

"You mean, today?"

"Just a suggestion. It happens to fit my schedule. But, of course, if it's inconvenient...."

"No," she said trying to think fast, "today is fine."

"Excellent! Say, six-thirty? Good. Now, let me tell you what to do. There's a small entrance on the south side of the building, very much a private entrance, you'd scarcely notice it, it says 'Bis' over the door—b,i,s—a French word that means repeat, encore, or half a house number as I'm sure you know, a little joke of mine. You simply press the button and say your name and the door will buzz open. There's an elevator, a private one, it will take you straight to the penthouse. Just press the P button. I'll be waiting for you."

She smiled.

"Have you ever posed? I mean, for artistic purposes? Well, no matter, I'm certain you'll make an excellent model. No need to rush off, do finish your cigarette...I saw you admiring the Matisse. Isn't it a lovely painting? My own style of painting is rather more plodding and classical, I'm afraid. I simply haven't the patience for the modern technique, shall we say."

When she left—insisting in a tone dangerously close to familiarity that she did have work to do—she said to herself (again), what a sweet gentle old man, a real aristocrat, in the truest sense of the word.

In the elevator she found herself thinking of her father. Again.

Every refined man reminded her of her father because he was the opposite—a loudmouth salesman who finally ran off and was succeeded by an alcoholic cop, a very religious man when he was sober, who from the time she was a girl of eleven was waylaying her on the stairs and the landing outside their rooms every time her mother was out, once trapping her in her room and scaring her half to death before ejaculating on her stomach. (Funny, she hadn't screamed, though she'd wanted to.) Her mother, that prim Norwegian lady always worrying about her children and never doing anything about anything, leaving them to make their way as best they could through the succession of stepfathers (four) and house moves (six) like punt returners with nothing more than her moral counsels and useless instructions to block for them...An apt metaphor, and one which occurred to her frequently, since football figured so importantly in her early life, her first lover having been a high school football star who all but raped her the first time and continued on in the same ignorant unfeeling violent way thereafter and one of her two younger half-brothers being the star quarterback on *his* high school team, with some big college scouts after him, and the other a florist who lived with another man and despised football and his own brother the quarterback irrationally, claiming he was nothing but a big dumb insensitive jock, which he wasn't, only a jock and big, but he was a very nice, very sensitive confused kid, and she wished she could help him...But getting loaded and kissing him on the mouth like on New Year's Eve last year and embarrassing him was probably not the way.

The fourth husband? Well, he seemed okay, certainly the best of the lot, which wasn't saying much—Norwegian like his wife, with a construction company and season tickets to the New York Giants football games and a drinking habit, an invulnerably stiff man who tried to be friendly, and probably drank for that reason, and who told jokes nobody ever caught on to. Despite occasional gifts of money or liquor and invitations to a home cooked dinner "with your own family" it was not somebody you tended to call Dad.

With your own family. What other family did he think she had, or would ever have? She longed for an intimate binding relationship—for marriage, in a word. But the sex—that S-word. What if orgasm continued to elude her in marriage, what then? What would she do? What would he do? The thought of a helpless imprisonment inside a sexually unproductive liaison meant to be permanent horrified her.

Damn! There he was again. Fixing an electric outlet. How did he *manage*! Always something, and always in or around her office. Convinced there was nothing wrong with that outlet she swished her head to show her indifference to him. But she had caught his profile and realized it was not that one. Same chocolate uniform, same curly black hair, wrong man. She felt miffed, somehow betrayed, as if she had been stood up.

Three

"You know, you really are a stupid son of a bitch, you wanker," the wanker said aloud to himself.

Tom Hutchins could not bear irrational behavior. When things failed to satisfy his rational standards, as was happening now, he squirmed with restlessness and made threats to himself, the more painful the better. Now he was threatening to leave the United States.

An irrepressible ratiocinator, he could always find some philosophical conclusion to be inferred, some moral to be drawn. Fortunately he had a sense of humor too.

Now he stood at his window looking at a detritus of New York sunset—the paltry bit that managed to sneak through to his fourth floor Greenwich Village apartment through an obstacle course of skyline and smog and one raggedy dying leafless tree—and contemplated his problem.

He was too old; she was too beautiful, too highly prized and pursued. In a few months he would be even older—thirty eight, for heaven's sake. To desire a young woman of twenty five was not only unwise, it was immoral. Surely the gods of propriety would crush him for his vanity. And greed. And lust. But even without his masochistic pining for Catherine Harlow, the sunset alone would have had this effect on him.

It was too beautiful (like her), it was too poisoned and wasted (like her), its quintessential beauty was not properly understood and appreciated (hers certainly was, by every slob in the building, the slut). And he couldn't care less about the sunset.

Calling her slut was a joke, but even so, it troubled him, made him think he was losing his sense of proportion. Really he was going to have to do something about Kit. He would have to either get her out of his mind, *burn* her out, or—win her.

Ah, if he could do that. He would never miss a sunset then. He recalled sunsets he had watched in purer climes—Norway, the Swiss Alps, Ibiza. Together they could make use of things, enjoy things. Then these hothouse addictions and vices would fall away from them like dried scabs. And instead of mimicking, they could create. Instead of destroying, build.

Build what? Create what? Children? A family? Working women her age didn't do that anymore. Not until their late thirties. And where would they do it—here, in New York, in the Foote Building, he as a devoted ad man to Harrison Foote Industries, Inc., inventing copy for Wine Drink and Apple Drink and Peach Drink, those wretched beverages full of chemicals and not a drop of wine or apple or peach? While she, in turn, did whatever it was she was doing and that old Foote had personally thought important enough to have brought her over from California to do?

Should they waste their lives here until the day they went berserk like that poor bastard McCord?

What was keeping him here? Cowardice? Apathy?

The propaganda he and his co-workers spewed out was nothing compared to the brainwashing they themselves underwent every minute of their working lives, thanks to an insidious barrage of pseudopsychoanalytical terms—healthy aggressiveness, healthy outlet for unhealthy aggressiveness, aggressive creativity and so on and on. Everything that was good for Harrison Foote just happened to be good, healthy, normal and creative. But more and more he was coming to believe that for him, at least, good health and creativity meant using that healthy aggressiveness in the opposite direction—in getting the hell out.

But with Kit.

That was what was spoiling his sunsets.

* * *

Penthouse...P.

Smiling to herself, even to the world, since there was no one to see her (or was somebody actually watching the screen on the other end of that TV camera in some shockproof hightech War Room somewhere?), Kit pressed one of only two buttons and rose with startling yet controlled speed towards her latest and greatest Sun God.

He was waiting for her in his working clothes: baggy black corduroy shirt with matching neckerchief camouflaging the flaccid skin of his neck, comfortable slacks (no crease), comfortable loafers (no shine).

Not to be outdone, she was wearing shades and the casual clothes she, for her part, judged correct for modeling—slacks, cashmere sweater, jade earrings tucked into her own natural short-length hair, high pumps. In her bag she carried ballet slippers and the longhaired wig of her own natural hair color, in case he wanted that.

She was in marvelous spirits, lulled by the magic ambience of the discreet rich in full display. It had started the moment the selfclosing street door had cut her off from the dirty, windblown sidewalk and she had found herself in the luxurious vestibule trying to keep her composure in the face of so stratospheric an invasion of her weltgeist. A chandelier in a vestibule? A bust? Original paintings? Plush carpeting? An ornate marble ashtray stand?

In a vestibule?

Upstairs, more of the same. Her marveling eyes forgot how to blink.

He showed her around. Outside the vast windows a mist floated in the sunshine. With a start she realized it was a cloud. Did it ever even rain up here? In a hyperbolic daze at the combination of sumptuousness and antiques and art—delicate vases, burnished chandeliers, exotic (and erotic) figurines and tapestries, huge gold framed mirrors, family portraits, leather bound books, beautiful cabinets and end tables, she followed him meekly to the more casual, more intimate studio.

Here all was functional. Nobody's pictures but his own, presumably. Tubes and bottles of paint and solvents, brushes, easels, paintings facing the wall, paintings not facing the wall, palettes, studio lights, a draftsman's table, rulers, instant coffee jars, a big double-sink. One of the easels was covered. Like a magician saying "voilà!" he snapped off the cloth. Her mouth dropped open.

"Me?"

"Only in a superficial sense, my dear. You see, I started with a vision, then I happened to see a magazine photograph and it was exactly what I'd fantasized, only fuller, richer, and so I used that, you see, for a while. But, you see, it wasn't enough. This wouldn't be you by any chance, would it?" he asked her, producing a magazine cutout. "I understand you did some modeling."

She recognized it right away in a flashback to the five-foot-three photographer and his studio in mid-Manhattan and fighting off his advances afterwards.

"Yes, I remember that one," Kit said, almost laughing, and as she spoke something about his raised eyebrows told Kit that he had known all along, even as he exclaimed, "I *thought* it might be you!"

"I modeled for about two years."

"What an amazing coincidence!" he said. "To have got the very model—What a stroke of luck! You know, I was getting confused, I'd almost lost interest, but now! I feel revitalized, I feel I'm going to do some very good work, create something of real value. The very model! I can't get over it! I can't tell you how happy I am to have you to pose for me, my dear."

He slipped into his painter's smock and adjusted one of the lamps. "Now then! You did bring the long hair, of the same color? Good! Now if you'll just slip on this robe...A bit awkward, I'm afraid. Perhaps if you removed the sweater, too bulky, you see the folds have to be just right—It's very important, you know, a very important element inside the whole concept, you see, what I'm trying to capture, the sense of nubile sort of erotic sensuality with that unflinching aura of maternal, shall we say, the untouchableness of the pre-Raphaelite Madonna. (Get on with it, Kit thought.) Normally the delineation of the bosom should be faintly visible to the eye, we want just the faintest, umm, suggestion...Here, let me adjust that fold just a little, do you mind?..."

Taking off the sweater was awkward—She was not wearing a bra. But he was worldly, and a painter, and an old geezer anyway, and she was a model, and there was the robe, and he was very cool and professional, and the moment passed without serious embarrassment. In fact he arranged the robe and her pose without nervousness, in the most natural way, while taking care not to touch her too much with his sensitive, manicured, aristocratic fingers.

He started painting. He did look every inch the artist, the professional, she decided, with his paint-stained smock and palette and brushes and the rags stained with every possible shade of color. He was very involved in his painting and, yes, she saw absolutely no reason to suspect the intentions of this perfectly courteous and honorable old gentleman.

"Tired?" he said when she made a slight move. "Let's take a break."

Kit had thought he would never notice a tiny fidget. Nothing wrong with his eyes, anyway. It surprised her, too, that he could stop working so abruptly. She expected artists to be more, well, temperamental. Especially old ones. What a refreshing change from those pseudo-artists she had encountered on both coasts, with their pretentious poses and mannerisms and taking themselves so seriously. What a lovely man to work for.

This is my chance for freedom! she thought. And did a double-take.

Freedom?

Was she not free? Of course she was free! Free and independent, utterly. What on earth was she talking about?

She became aware that music was playing, over a loudspeaker, here too. But it wasn't classical. It was Sinatra. She listened to the words, and finally knew the song: "The One That Got Away." And she realized she had heard it before, many times, in this building. It must be somebody's favorite, because, whatever the combination of songs, this was always one of them. And although she knew by instinct that she ought to remain silent while he was working she could not restrain a comment.

"That's a nice song."

"It's my favorite!" he said, in such a rush that she forgot herself and turned her head. No matter, he had stopped working, and was staring at nothing. Somebody got away, once, Kit thought, and he never got over it. How romantic! Who could it be? A high society heiress? movie star? opera diva? ballet dancer? Her head filled with scenarios.

"You mean, it reminds you of somebody?"

"Half a dozen, is more like it."

Afterwards they talked—rather, he talked; she listened. He seemed concerned about her future. It took her breath away. He said his tax situation was such that he could profitably donate thousands of dollars to a charity—or person. And why, he added after an excruciating pause, smiling, should she not be that person?

She could not have agreed more. But she had a moment's doubt. Would that money be a shackle? Would she be tethered to a kind of trust fund? What would he want in return? What would happen to her independence?

Nothing, she decided. I can be just as independent with his donations as without them—more, in fact. How can you be independent without money? If the sweet old codger wants to help me, why should I stand in his way? What would I be trying to prove?

"I could put it in shares in your name, in a sort of trust, so that it—and whatever I might eventually add to it—could serve as a sort of wedding present for the day you decide to marry, or for a rainy day. Are you serious about anyone at the moment, by the way? Or am I being too personal."

"Well, no, not really," she said. "I mean, you're not being too personal and I'm not serious about anyone—I mean, not really serious."

"You understand," he said, "this has nothing to do with your posing for me, or the payment—that's a separate thing. After each session you'll be paid the going rate, that's nothing to do with anything else, with any interest I might take in you in a personal way. And I must say I'm very pleased with your work. You know, I'm just beginning to believe this is going to be my year again. I think I'm going to win that prize again. I really do."

He was gazing critically but approvingly at the canvas. They were through for the day. She stood uncertainly in her robe, waiting for him to dismiss her, in what she knew would be the most courtly and considerate of ways.

"Would you like to freshen up a bit in a sauna, Ms Harlow?" he said with the unobtrusive insistence of a sommelier pushing a specific wine. "Shall I call you Catherine? Only here, of course. You'll find a rather complete sauna bath right through this door. I'll show you the controls. They're not very complicated, even I can manage them. It's a wonderful way to relax. I think it might help those migraines of yours."

Migraines? How did he know about her migraines?

He had not invited her to call him by his first name, as she had half expected. A startling touch of intimacy did occur, however, when he suddenly entered the sauna as she sat sweating nakedly and emptied a bucket of water over the woodburning stove, smiled, and went out. Then when she was toweling and preparing to dress in the changing room he reappeared casually with a fresh towel in case she needed one? And pointing out the fact that the shelves in front of her nose offered a fabulous variety of exotic powders and waters and perfumes, in case she hadn't noticed them? And went out again. He did it so naturally she had no time to be disconcerted.

When she emerged, feeling refreshed and fragrant and ravishingly beautiful, he had hors d'oeuvres and champagne waiting. He opened the bottle himself, trapping the cork in a towel expertly, and poured. They chatted pleasantly. She had a dizzy sensation that she was at an informal cocktail party with distinguished people scattered about in nuggets of power, and she in hers. She could almost hear the smattering of background conversation from the other nuggets. Her particular gentleman made roguish references to the fact that he enjoyed more than he could express in words the company of so young and attractive a woman, adding that she must be impatient to rejoin her younger more interesting companions. And she laughingly assured him (too much, she thought later) that he was more interesting, and her young men less so, than he seemed to think. After her second glass she put out her cigarette and went to the elevator, letting him pushbutton the doors open for her with his usual gallantry, giddily aware that he kept squeezing her arm while thanking her for being such a great help to him and such a perfect model and such a delightfully beautiful young woman besides as he discreetly pressed folded banknotes into her hand. She was so charmed, it was only halfway down that she remembered to look at the five crisp hundred-dollar bills.

* * *

It was a fine morning. The overnight winds had died and the November sky was clear and sunny. It was unseasonably warm.

The sun? He had no quarrel with the sun. Its rays came from far out and went far beyond. It was not of this earth or its nefarious uses, was nothing to do with that natural bitch Nature and her wretched contemptible sperm crawling over the planetary crust in the evolutionary farce it called Civilization. She seized and used the sun, had made the sun her ally, her comrade in betrayal, preaching survival but driving us like cattle to our death. But *pace*, Sun. The sun was not the enemy. Nature was the enemy.

What she had done, won, let her keep. But she must be superseded. Let her stand aside. The hour for change had come. As Minerva had sprung immortal from the brow of her progenitor, granting prolonged life to mortals, bestowing on them the gift of foresight that enabled them to outlast that progenitor, so he, conceived (I'll give her that) by Nature, would survive her evil regimen, her tyranny of cycles, of voluntary cooperation with decay and rebirth and death and decay—of life on earth.

With several hours free, he threw a pile of plastic containers into the furnace and shoveled out yesterday's harvest. Recyclable! Hateful word, with its jawbreaking atonality. Recycle this! he thought, grinning at the gawky coagulations of twisted blackened doomsday shapes.

Marvelous how they suggested a nuclearized metropolis.

He pressed them into trashcans in the agreeable certainty that the Dept of Sanitation, bless its filthladen heart, would be utterly unable to do anything at all with the stuff. It could not be broken down. It was bio*un*degradable! Indissoluble chancres that he was sending out to cover the earth, doing his little part in the human mission to stymie Nature's powers of absorption, to perplex and baffle her, render her impotent, and finally to disrupt the fatal life cycle—*stop it cold.*

He used to wonder why he, Homer Zudd, should have been the one selected. That was at the beginning, when he had begun to see that he was different from other people. There had always been other individualists and misfits, but it was not the same thing, was it. In him it was intrinsic, organic; in the others it was wayward, blundering, accidental, capricious. And superficial.

He had wondered about his strange powers of survival. His mother had told him about the misdiagnosis of her pregnancy followed by a premature birth—thus he had escaped abortion. And how on earth had he avoided anything worse than shrapnel wounds in twenty-nine months of ambushes and booby traps and a copter crash in Vietnam?

Then the explosion in the boiler room. Five dead. One survivor. Like a nebula condensing into matter he had acquired the perception that he was more than human. He was a new idea, a mutation with a mission. Schopenhauer was his preceptor. He was meant to transform the genetic code and father a new and more durable species of human. There was an urgent need. The present species could not survive in this congested, polluted, overpopulated, overprotected, overly diseased world.

He had his purpose, and soon perceived his method. It would be a gathering-in of the necessary components, a centripetal coalescence of his power until so great a density was reached that only sharp steel would be able to pierce it. Like Mithridates, he was immunizing himself against the poisons, all the poisons of this modern world.

Now he understood his attraction to chaos, to disruption, and his detestation of cycles, his love of cacophony, shrillness, violence, broken rhythms. You had to break the mold!

Harmony was an evil, and must be destroyed.

No need to wonder about his attraction to exploding rhythms, to violence, shock and frustration, to why in sex he caught hold of himself at the point of orgasm and choked it off, broke its back, froze it dead. What a deep satisfaction this painful triumph gave him! The frustration in his female partners, when he had had them, only added to the satisfaction.

They almost never came back, and that was okay with him. They were too hot and soft and compliant, with eager body fluids and a sexual hunger that would have left him limp as a rag had he let his guard down. They hated him. In that moment of interrupted coitus he felt the astonishment, reveled in their frustration, welcomed the turning of molten ardor into confusion and anger, and was truly happy.

But he was tired of them. He preferred his solitary thrills while waiting for his ideal woman who would be as cold and remote as she was beautiful.

With the bags and trashcans all neatly in place (he did favor symmetry) he went off on this Sunday morning to his favorite sources of entertainment: junkyards, empty lots, abandoned Hudson River piers. There he was sure to see wreckage and remains—wrecked vehicles, twisted iron frames, ripped tires, splintered poles and pilings, the burnt leavings of some voracious fire somewhere, some victim's personal possessions scattered on the gaping piers or bobbing on the brackish water. And the dead fish floating.

But here, on his stroll to the river, was an unexpected treat. Not a dozen yards from the curb lay a black and white dog, whimpering and crying. Its hind legs crushed and bloody, it was trying to crawl to its feet.

Zudd stopped and watched, holding his breath as a car came around the corner. But it managed to avoid the dog. Then another came fast and bumped but did not kill it. Eyes gleaming, lips parted, heart thumping, Zudd waited. A truck finally got the job done. The rear double wheels got it. The driver was smoking a cigar. A van and several cars following behind left a flattened bloody hide. Zudd whirled and walked away quickly, laughing to himself soundlessly—a high uncontrolled hysterical giggle that he abruptly broke off as was his habit.

Zudd walked along a line of refrigerated trucks parked along a wall between two piers. A bum investigating a pile of junk looked up as he went by. Smog shaded the otherwise bright sky at the level of the oil tanks across the river. Gulls swooped and swung, riding the air currents.

He looked across at the Jersey shoreline where tankers and freighters unloaded at piers with company names painted in gross capitals across depot walls and felt a welling up of revulsion, he did not really know why. He just hated them. He hated just about everything he saw.

He lit a Tiparillo, exhaled, and turned pale. There she was. Across the street. The cold beauty of the seventeenth floor, Catherine Harlow. With that man Hutchins, Thomas Hutchins who'd been running after her and now there they were together, Sunday morning. Walking on West Street, eyes downcast in thought.

She was in slacks and a long coat and her hair was short and derelict. You could see they had just got out of bed—the same bed.

None of the painted calculated refinements she wore to work.

It looked exactly like one of those stupid reconciliations lovers were always having, based entirely on the fear of being alone.

Zudd turned away in furious disgust.

* * *

It was past nine when Kit had finally called Tom. She was feeling so good after the modeling session with Mr. Foote that she felt girlish and playful, and teased him for a while before finally letting him coax and coerce and persuade her that she was not too tired to meet him and no, it was not too late.

Pleased that she could go straight to their rendezvous at an East Side restaurant without having to go home to her dreary apartment first, she let that and the wine and his infatuation and his wry humor and the Welsh musicality of his speech seduce her into inviting him back to that apartment for coffee and a nightcap.

Who knows, she thought as she waited at the door of the restaurant for Tom to catch up, he might be the one. Maybe all this...*earnestness* of his will do the trick.

There was a hitch. Sam Katz came in just then. There was no way to avoid him. He came right up to them, stubborn mouthcorner grin and crucified eyes and all, grinning his sleepylidded, curly red-bearded grin at her. She had to introduce them.

Shaking hands, Tom understood that this man adored Kit in a manner as shameless as it was defiant. He wanted everybody to know.

Kit was wearing her shades. She had to smile when he tried to get them to have a drink with him, knowing he did not drink or smoke except when he was trying to make out. "Thanks," she said, "but we were on our way out."

"Where you going?" he had the temerity to ask. "Maybe we can all go somewhere together."

Smiling, giving him a kind but determined look, Kit shook her head. Tom felt out of it, reduced to observer status.

Katz refused to let go. A kind of hysteria came into him and he forged a semblance of conversation: He'd called but she was never home; she had not returned his calls, had ignored his messages...He had met some very interesting people he would like her to meet, she would like them, film people, people she oughta know, they could do things for her. Tom, listening to all this, felt helpless in the face of the brazen rudeness of this man who made his impotence into a strength, into a kind of tyranny. And why not all go back to his place for a drink, said Katz. He could call a few girls he knew and also those guys he had mentioned...?

Kit reflected. It might be fun to drag Tom off to a little party when what he wanted more than anything else in the world was to get her into bed.

"No," she said. That was all. Just no. No explanations. (If only she could feel this secure with everybody and not just the smitten.) "Another time," she said with a thin smile.

Sam Katz watching them go with his brown suffering dog's eyes, they went along Third Avenue in the dark looking for gas for her lighter. A corner drugstore was open. They emerged to find Sam waiting for them in the passenger seat of an open red Porsche with idling motor, driven by a wiry young woman with short blond hair and a leather jacket and a scarf so long it had Isadora Duncan written all over it, who looked at Kit as if she knew all about her.

"Hey, come on, it's still early, let's have one drink."

Christ, what's this guy got against me? Tom thought with an incipient desire to inflict a stinging rebuke.

"I'm afraid not, Sam," said Kit in British.

"Why not?" he pleaded. "Change your mind for once. Just one drink, then leave, okay? Why not? Huh? Why not?"

Christ! Tom thought, openly staring.

"No."

Kit still smiled—a thin firm smile. Tom concluded it was a little game they played, over and over.

"Why not? Come on…All you're doing is going home—" he looked at Tom, as if realizing for the first time that he was present, and in fact was the one she was going home with "—You got lotsa time, the night's young, what's the hurry?"

Unwilling to walk away Kit kept shaking her head and there was a silence that stretched painfully until the driver in disgust yanked the stick shift and roared away into the dark carrying off the redbearded lover, his eyes still craned towards her in supplication.

Tom was transfixed. "Wow!"

"Karenin," he said softly.

"What?"

"You know—Karenin, on a motorized sleigh."

"Who? On a what?"

"You know, Anna Karenina's husband?"

She calculated silently. History? Fiction? Movie? TV?

"You remember," Tom said, "in that scene? He's been away, he's decided to be firm, unbending, but it's no good, she's leaving, and he goes off on his sleigh looking pathetically back at her?"

"Oh yes, I was just trying to remember who was in it."

"Oh, is it a movie?"

"Isn't everything?" she said triumphantly.

They lighted cigarettes.

"This guy Katz is really something," Tom said. "Obviously he's nuts about you."

"Get ready for a shock. Funny, your mentioning that, um, husband and wife scene, because, I was married to him."

"You were what? Married?" He stopped walking. "To Sam Katz?"

"He's really very nice, you know. He just sort of has this thing for me, a sort of Jewish thing, he likes shiksas, especially WASP shiksas. In fact I think he's the nicest man I've ever known." Her voice trailed off with doubt. She was thinking, Mr. Foote is nicer.

They moved on.

"I didn't know you'd even been married, for God's sake."

"Only four months. It was a couple of years ago. A kind of crazy lark, you know? Like a roller coaster—not that it was so exciting or anything like that. I don't really know why I did it. I mean, it's not like I was pregnant or anything. I don't feel like I've been married. That makes him furious, to hear that. But I mean, four months. He's just an old friend now."

"So you're a divorcée," said Tom.

"Not quite. It was annulled." She laughed, "Same thing."

"Not quite. He looks annulled, not divorced. Canceled."

"Oh you're so pedantic," she scolded prettily, in a teasing way. Tom, feeling his liquor, thought she looked so ravishing that he stopped again and put his arms around her. Kit's gaze was benign but, as a woman who was utterly proper in public (except when dancing or drunk), she considered this to be in poor taste and primly stopped him with his lips an inch away from hers.

He gave a contrite grin and walked on, thinking, with some heat, I do not understand this woman!

Her apartment was on the fifth floor of a modern building in the East Fifties, not ten years old, with an awning from entrance to curb and a doorman. Not the kind of doorman who opens the door for you but that other kind who loiters like a reformed hoodlum in the lobby with a macho mustache under his nose and a scrutinizing glint in his eyes as he looks you over, drawing cynical conclusions, one about you, one about her.

Inside her apartment she was not the same woman. Tom could not fit her to an apartment, to domesticity. He could only see her as a product of the city, as a woman about town. Kit was New York, New York was Kit. Kit was a bedroom, for sure, but not this specific bedroom. The details—the reality—disoriented him.

In the one-and-a-half-room apartment the kitchen though tiny was complete, gleaming with chrome and tile and stainless steel. The bathroom was all tile and glass, diminutive but modern, with a snub bathtub cum shower with sliding door panel, designed, like the entire apartment, the entire building, to be functional at the expense of comfort, at the same time making a pretense of offering that same precluded comfort. It was a compromise between an executive suite and a homeless shelter.

Wall-to-wall was the decorating theme, from the whole room's carpet to its Culture Wall, a continuous waist-high piece of shelves with nooks for books and TV and radio and VCR and knickknacks and hard liquor, then mirrors from there to the ceiling.

Kit poured two Scotches, with ice for her, water for him.

Still wondering, as he had been all along, if this was going to be his night, and hunting for something to say to cover his anxiety, Tom found he could not get Katz out of his thoughts.

"Why did you decide to annul him?" he said after his first swallow.

"Sam?" She smiled again at that way of putting it. "Oh...It just didn't work, you know?" Shoes off, feet tucked under. They were on the settee that was, he was to learn, also the bed. "I mean it just couldn't work, you know? I thought it might but it was—I mean I thought sexually it would almost have to work, because you know, he's some kind of sex nut, a regular Mr. Fixit—you know, orgies, gang bangs, that sort of thing." She took a double take at Tom's face and added, "Oh, not with me. Though I suppose that would only have been a matter of time...No, on the contrary he kept telling me I was the first girl he'd ever met that he didn't want to, you know, have orgies with. He meant that as a compliment. He meant he was in love with me in a special way that he'd never experienced before. So, like, there it is. Sex was his thing, and when that didn't work—well, what was the point? I realize how shallow this sounds. But, I don't know how else to describe it."

Tom was finding it harder and harder to act debonair. "How do you mean, exactly, sex was his thing?"

"Oh, he's a master. I mean a real pro. I mean it could be his doctorate. Anything he doesn't know about sex isn't worth knowing."

"Uh huh. But you say it still didn't work? By the way, what exactly do you mean by that?"

"I have a problem with orgasm."

She said it in an even, deliberate way that gave him to understand that, one, they were going to bed, and two, it was now his problem too.

"But why be so pedantic," she added crossly. "I mean, why are we talking about Sam Katz, anyway?"

The three-piece settee that sustained a long passionate kiss between the two lovers became a bed as she realigned cushions and pulled out bedding from compartments underneath. He thought he was dreaming and, afraid he might still lose the dream somehow, he made haste in its consummation. He hurried to demolish the last barrier, that nonworking clause with its annulment power, and let slip the puppies of love. His passion for her surged and broke inside her, flooded her, possessed her. Or so he thought.

He woke from a happy comatose wandering through sunny flowery Edens some minutes later to see her smoking as she gazed frowning at the ceiling, having already slid out from under him with a half-remembered shove.

"My darling," he murmured, overcome by her angry beauty and his great good fortune.

She took a puff, then another, and finally granted him a frigid look.

"I hope you enjoyed yourself," she said with her most crushingly precise enunciation.

It took a long walk that ended up in the West Side downtown piers and all the diplomacy and eloquence he possessed to dissolve this obstacle that had sprung up between them in what should have been his happiest hour.

Four

After half a dozen sessions a certain familiarity came to coexist with the initial puritan Old World formality, with the impeccable manners in which she was now a grandfatherly "my dear" or "Catherine" to him, while Kit, although she would not have dreamed of addressing him as other than "Mr Foote," had begun to say it with a familiarity that was almost flirtatious. And this despite the unease she was beginning to feel at certain liberties he was taking.

"Draw the curtains if you like, my dear," he said, as he always did.

So she did and once again looked down at the harbor of New York Bay, at gangs of seagulls attacking some edible in the discolored water and mugging the one that managed to capture it, at two Staten Island ferries passing within hailing distance of each other, a freighter unloading on the opposite Jersey shore, a barge moving downstream, a tanker nosing upriver towards the huge oil tanks that comprised a New Jersey pier. From up here, with the dirt and floating debris and dead fish invisible, it was a lovely view.

"Shall we start? Not that there's any hurry. It is rather beautiful, isn't it."

"Breathtaking! I can't get tired of it." She was repeating herself, but nothing better came to mind. She could not help feeling clumsy and inarticulate alongside this debonair man of the world.

"Yes. One feels quite isolated from, shall we say, the mundane."

He too was repeating himself, but it seemed somehow perpetually fresh coming from him.

He had donned his smock and all was ready. The picture was coming along. Why the unease? she asked herself.

It was because she was looking ahead. During the twenty-minute break there would be the libation and the gold-tipped Sobranies and the surround-sound classical music playing softly and as intimately as if he had a private orchestra behind a curtain, followed by the goodhumored but businesslike return to work. That far ahead she could see, but no further. And it made her nervous, because it seemed to her that Mr. Foote was in a very subtle way getting just a little too intimate.

She was used to it, to having this effect on men (especially men) of all ages. It came with the gift. Still, he was touching her more, and she was afraid she might have to deal, eventually, with something she was not prepared for, that she did not know how to prepare for.

It was that sublime courtesy. The perfect manners. His fear of offending her—his shyness, in fact. She knew she needed only say a word to mortify him, paralyze him. But she never said it. She did not want to paralyze him, not this deferential almost timid old gentleman. When an insidious thought prodded her to wonder if he had intended the intimacy from the start (you know what men are) she had a reflex reply: Not him. His kind didn't behave like that. Her kind was prone to be callous and cynical about people of quality. That was why her kind never got anywhere.

And yet. Each touch of his produced a shiver of dread. She was beginning to anticipate them, while doing nothing to avoid them. She always acceded to his polite suggestions: Would she terribly mind removing her blouse? It was a pretty blouse but its folds threw the robe out of its linear integrity, it lost that delicacy of form…No, it still didn't flow, these things have to flow, you see, a Greek robe had its own voice….

So she was virtually topless, and he painted happily for a while, but by the end of the next session he was vexed again. This time it was the rest of her—The robe was still a problem. Neither fish nor fowl. The purity of line, etc. Of course if she had *inhibitions*…But it would be such a triumph of art and freedom and naturalness if she could dispense with that armor of cloth—not, of course, if it would cause her to feel even the slightest embarrassment or insecurity.

Such words always brought out the Irish in her. Me insecure? Me, embarrassed?

Kit could not admit to any man that she was unsure of herself, nor could she reject one with anything other than a clear, frank No. No shades of gray, no half measures. Thus, whatever was not a no was a yes. She consented, and on only her fifth visit found herself posing in a diaphanous cloth that was off one shoulder and one breast, with the freefalling locks of her wig that he had carefully brushed to one side pointing to her navel. And she found herself wondering, while she posed, what was on his mind.

Because there was more. (Wasn't there always?) There was the solarium/sauna that he insisted she use. Always in the sweetest, most solicitous way. "One does get a bit stiff from posing, n'est-ce pas? And those headaches of yours. My dear, the thing is there, make use of it, it cost thousands, nobody uses it." She found it so hard to say no to him.

And the truth was she loved it. Her own private sun lamps, her own sauna! But it was becoming awkward. Sooner or later she was going to have to draw that line. But where? And how? Every yes seemed to yield so much more than she had intended, whereas a no, rejecting one insignificant little suggestion out of so many, seemed crude, disproportionate, silly. Immature. And besides there was something…you could almost call it exciting, in the shy, courteous way he went about it. She wondered could he actually feel anything? at his age? Anyway what had she actually given up so far? Glimpses of her body. A few touches. Nothing. As a model she was touched all the time.

Wait a minute, that was then and this is now. No more casual touching. You're an executive now. Remember that.

But those oil rubs he insisted on giving her. Her neck, her back. And the talcum powder. His hands did wander. And what about that little joke of his, that his creaky old muscles could do with a bit of a rubdown too one of these days—What would she do then?

"Could you just lower that fold a little so it hangs more naturally, Ms Harlow? A suggestion of hip and belly might be a nice touch—Here, let me do it."

* * *

Zudd was restless. That Catherine Harlow on the seventeenth. Every time he saw her he was more certain she was the one.

He had grown impatient with his whipping machine. It needed *her*—to do the whipping, to be whipped. And she knew it, he could swear that she knew it, he saw in her eyes that she sensed it every time he darted one of his searching pleading looks at her. She was the first woman he had ever wanted so badly, and it was messing him up so much he could hardly think rationally. It made the pounding music and the videos and the ape and the mannequins seem dull, stale, inadequate.

He was not hungry, though it was lunchtime. He swallowed a handful of pills and soda and went out and bought a few fat, salted pretzels at a pushcart. He ate them as he went, throwing bits straight before him to see the hungry pigeons scatter in panic under his feet.

In Bryant Park people with lunch bags sitting on benches and on the grass listened to an amplified classical concert. How he despised them! All sweetness and serenity, the violence in them idling like a tank at a stop light. Why did they bother? They were made for action not contemplation. Heavy metal, not classical. String quartets indeed! He wished for a huge boulder to fall on them, scattering them like the pigeons.

Ah, here was something more like it. A girl, hardly twenty, sitting alone with her back against a leafless tree reading a book, was the object of desire of a lusting Latino with an El Diario in his pocket. Zudd saw him staring at her, clearly beside himself. The reason was, she seemed to forget she was not wearing slacks. Every time she moved her legs, exposing thighs and underpants, his mouth twitched with menace. He hopped around on a game leg and could not take his eyes off her crotch.

Zudd saw he was not the only one observing the potential rapist. A heavyset man, his face the map of Ireland, also watched as the Latino, growing increasingly agitated, hobbled back and forth to keep her in view around intrusive passersby. Curiously, the girl was unaware of him, even though when turning a page she rested her eyes for a moment by looking around at the scene her stalker did not so much as look away.

The Irishman—judging from his clothes and demeanor and the racing form in his pocket he could have been a bartender or a detective—stood behind the Latino. Behind them both, off to a side, was Zudd, finishing his pretzel as he waited in surging impatience, his vision clouding ecstatically with the fantasy of the Latino jumping the girl, and the bartender/detective—maybe he had a daughter her age—subduing him with kicks and blows and a chokehold. Or maybe he was jealous. Whose turf was it?

The music crashed to an end—cymbals, drums, horns—and sudden silence. The girl closed her book and looked around. Then she saw the Latino. Startled, she looked away. But a moment later he was still there and still watching her. She got up, clearly flustered, and went toward the opposite side of the park, to 42nd Street. Limping vigorously, the Latino went after her. She looked back, saw him coming, and really took off, disappearing around the edge of the library. Her pursuer vanished behind her a moment later, limping along in violent haste.

The second man kept watching the spot as if expecting them to reappear. Turning away at last, he saw Zudd and, to Zudd's surprise, burst into a rage not at the stalker but at the girl.

"That little whore, serve her right, throwin' it around like that in everybody's face. They don't give a damn how they behave. Throwin' her legs around like that—I hope he catches her and plugs her a dozen times, the little cockteaser. Let him pull her into an alley and rape her! Why not? She's askin' for it. Readin' books, one leg here, one leg there—Serve her right!"

He stalked off searching his pockets furiously for something that turned out to be a cigar.

Zudd was delighted. He loved this city. New York, New York, it's a wonderful town, the crime rate is up and prosecutions down, haha. He loved it, loved every bit of it. He'd been sure the Irishman was going to voice disapproval of the Latino and empathy (the word du jour), for the girl, along with hopes that she would manage to escape her pursuer. Not a bit of it! Just violent raging at the girl, of all things! Hatred of the girl! Marvelous! It acted on Zudd like a narcotic. He went looking for more action.

At the western end of the park he came upon a promising commotion. People were watching something that turned out to be a drama between an old man, white, and a young man, tall, slim, and black. They had a dull gray block of stone carved with an inscription as a backdrop. The young black wore a shabby coat over a dirty white sweater and, on his face, an expression of superciliousness. He was holding a cigarette that the old man apparently had given him, and was demanding, *demanding*, a light. The old man had to light the cigarette for him. Or else. Or else he was going to punch him out. Destroy him. Break his ass.

But the old man was falling back on a racial characteristic—stubbornness. He was an East European Jew, with thick glasses and an even thicker accent. For some reason he had been willing to give the bullying black the cigarette, and for some other reason he was unwilling to give him the demanded light, whatever it might cost. The fear and the stubbornness had met and married, for better or worse, till death did them part. He was scared but obstinate. You saw that he was accustomed to being scared but obstinate. Besides, there was the audience. Maybe he had a little show biz in him. He was not going to give in in front of all those people, one of whom was Zudd, and another a stocky man wearing a skull cap.

"Light ma cigarette, motherfucka."

In a teacherish manner the old man told him he would give him a light only if he asked him politely. A little unsteady on his feet, the black, himself not unaware of the audience, then described in rich, inner city patois the terrible things he was going to inflict on him if he did not light the cigarette and say "Sir" besides. He was going to cut him, mess him up bad, he would bleed like a sieve. Did he know what a sieve looked like? He was going to bleed like one.

"Only ven you say tenks," the tremulous voice declared.

"You ain't never gonna hear me say dat, motherfucka, not for as long as you live, an' you ain't gonna live 'notha five minutes you don't light ma cigarette an' say Suh, too."

"Only ven you say tenks."

"Listen Jewbastid—"

"Leaf him alone!" The stocky man with the skullcap and long sideburns stepped up to them.

"Who's gonna make me?"

The man gave the black a strong push that sent him tumbling against the monument, hitting his head. He sat stunned.

"Pliss, no violence, no violence," said the old Jew, raising his hands in horror, whereupon the young one, with a Star of David swinging at his neck, gave him a glancing backhand across the face that dislodged his glasses, muttered something contemptuous in Hebrew, and walked away.

Grinning at one another in confusion, the crowd dispersed. Zudd looked back and saw the old man bending solicitously over the halfconscious black and talking to him, handing him another cigarette.

Please, no violence, Zudd chuckled to himself.

The city was full of people like that old imbecile. You saw them everywhere, wearing forced smiles to disarm potential nasties, eager to apologize at the slightest physical aggression and to excuse their assailants afterward. Viveca Lindfors couldn't wait to forgive her streetcorner slasher. Slash me once, I'll forgive you. Twice and you get a hug and a sermon on self-esteem. Three times and I'll marry you, you poor sweet victim of society.

Cheekturners that get walloped on both cheeks. And those smiles! Where Asians and Europeans and Africans used the ritual phrase, Americans, especially New Yorkers, those haters of ritual, used their faces: those wincing smiles. As if a bullet wasn't going to find them from a carjacking or a neighborhood shootout or a mugging anyway, smile or no smile. First the muggers took what you had because they wanted it, then they killed you for having had it in the first place. Or for just being there. Or because a trigger finger abhors inaction and craves culmination. Ha! Show them a smile and they say Who you laughin' at?

What a day! Already excited by the two incidents in the park—in one small park!—he encountered another not two blocks from the Foote Building. And he was in luck, because it was the most violent of them all, albeit the most ludicrous.

Three threadbare, staggering alcoholic bums lurching along the sidewalk in front of him passing a bottle of wine inside a brown paper bag from hand to hand suddenly broke into a fight. It was two against one, and very clumsy. The two shoved the one and when he fell they took running kicks at him, their torn shoes getting him in the head, the neck, the back, the face, anything. One missed and fell down, scrambled cursing to his feet and made another run at him like a field-goal kicker.

Promenaders looked on as they went by, giving them a wide berth. When the most unfortunate of the bums stopped moving the other two staggered off scowling and calling him names and praising each other's kicking prowess. It was never clear what the problem had been.

The *problem*?

Zudd kept laughing to himself. What difference did it make? It was the pretext that mattered. The play's the thing! It was a game, a dance. Any little motivator would do.

A dance....

How could he get her to dance? Oh what a partner she would be! He felt it in his blood. But, how to lure her down from the seventeenth floor? His brain sizzled with schemes.

Five

On the West Side people parked their cars wherever they found a space and locked them, praying they would not return to find them vandalized or stolen, and hurried off in the brash light of street lamps and neon signs to bars and restaurants and theaters.

Hurrying out the door with the unpretentiously snobby "Bis" at the top Kit went looking for a public phone. She had to go two long crosstown blocks before she found one that had not been mutilated, and by then she had put together a credible excuse. It was getting harder and harder to retain her credibility with Tom on the reasons for these broken dates or late arrivals that resulted each time Mr. Foote called to ask was this evening all right and was she really sure it would be no inconvenience to her?

On top of that, poor Tom was now taking a proprietary interest in her as a *whole human being*, discussing things like her psychological scaffolding, her cultural deprivation, and, of all things, her soul. While annoying and amusing her it also found a response in that soul, a silent one. For she was aware that a parallel world existed alongside hers that was all but invisible to her: the world of human accomplishments, the deeper, spiritual world of the arts that Tom, she was not surprised to learn, loved.

Mr. Foote too was of that world, and loved it too, no doubt, though less...ostentatiously? The young made such a passionate crusade out of everything, while the elderly...Love itself seemed different in them. Take Mr. Foote. He had so many other irons in the fire—business, the affairs of the world, his social clubs, his painting, more than she could know. His name tended to show up unexpectedly in the society columns as one of the distinguished guests appearing, and sometimes photographed, at the various social events she hungered (admit it!) to attend. He was not one to throw his life, or what was left of it, into an all-consuming love affair and dreams of reforming and redeeming the object of his infatuation.

Tom, on the other hand, a man who was simple by comparison, complicated everything, and went on and on about how she was failing to realize her full potential as a human being, etc., etc., ad nauseam. Bemused, she dodged and faked him out, jollied him along. But then sometimes she asked herself, Why am I doing this? Why don't I just tell him off, tell him to mind his own business, tell him to work on himself before he starts on others?

Well, she knew the answer: Improvement. To become as good a product as it was possible for her to become. To make it utterly impossible for her to be rejected on any grounds, by anyone. Others made it by accident—luck, or the casting couch. Too risky. Most of those got used and dropped. Passed around.

You had to become unrejectable. Then you could have it all. And you would get to keep it.

So she listened to Tom, and obeyed Mr. Foote. And tried not to disappoint either.

Trouble was, it wasn't working with Tom. No more than it ever had with any of the others. His trying to prolong the act, which she certainly appreciated, had gone and made him impotent. The sexual frustration went on and on. And it was getting worse. Nobody could be expected to be as good as Katz, at least in technique, but she certainly had not expected Tom's temporary letdown to turn into impotence! What a joke! Could it be her fault?

She liked him. She did not want to lose him. But, there it was. The more things change…Suddenly she felt like crying. *Was* it her fault? She lit a cigarette and drew deeply. Adjusting her shades, she dialed Tom's number.

An anxious voice answered on the first ring—"Hello?"

"Hi."

"Where the hell have you been? I've been—"

"Now *look*."

"Where shall we meet?" he said instantly contrite. "Where are you?"

"I'm sort of midtown."

She heard him silently pondering some questions and deciding not to ask them. Fortunately he hated being a bore. "How about The Overflow for a drink? Then we could try the French restaurant we saw the other night that looked interesting."

"The Four Coins?"

"Haha, right, *Les Quatre Cuang*, right. Say, twenty minutes?"

"Umm, better make it an hour."

"Okay. Where did you say you were?"

"Midtown."

"Yeah, okay."

What she liked about him was he knew French and his English was, well, the Queen's English, but at the same time he could say yeah. She liked the fact that he always pronounced his s's and his t's, all very English and attractive, she was sick to death of American linguistic corrosion—and the yeah. That she liked. What she did not like was, she wasn't sure he was aware that she too knew a little French. So, she makes a joke and pronounces it coins and he has to straighten her out. By what cultural paradigm did he assume she did not know any French at all? And just how far did this condescension go?

The thought bothered her all the way home in a cab, actually it was only a five minute ride but she refused on principle to walk more than two or three city blocks. She put the hundred-dollar bills (always new, bank fresh) away with the others—only twelve now; the rest had become a white camelhair coat—and showered to get rid of the feel and smell of the talcum powder.

The Overflow was a dark discreet little lounge a short cab ride from her apartment that the Pakistani driver went past because he had never heard of the place, or any place, and whose principal appeal for them was that they had been to it several times and nothing rude—no insults from waiters, drunks, or each other—had occurred within its tastefully papered walls hung with safe post-Impressionists .

Tom was waiting at a table, unimpressed by the surrounding

coziness. As she examined his face in the soft light she thought, Let him have his French, he needs a victory, and gave him an especially sweet smile.

If Tom's face showed anguish it was because he knew he was losing a crucial battle. With anguish came its mate, confusion, for he did not know why he was losing the battle, or why he should even be fighting it in the first place. But he understood now what she had meant by its not having "worked" with Katz, because now it was not working with him either. He was now Katz.

This impotence that tormented him was a new thing in his sexual life. It went back to that first night, that wonderful but finally inglorious night of his…conquest? and that moment when Kit broke into his happy drowsy reveries with the dry observation that he had given pleasure only to himself.

That woke him to shame and chagrin. He had been impatient, had wanted her so desperately that there had been no thought of self-control. Gulping at her reproach, he thought, "Okay, now I'll do it right," and he began making love to her without waiting for the return of desire. Finding his libido uncooperative and she, in that strange spoiled way of hers, openly unresponsive, he drove himself harder and harder all that night and on subsequent nights—the nights when she, with alcohol blurring her speech as well as her mysterious purposes, yielded to his desires—until he fell back exhausted.

Everything he did—things he had heard about or read about or imagined—pleased her in principle, and there might be a glimmer of sensual pleasure, but nothing got her where she wanted to be. Nothing, however much he tried, sweating and pleading and wondering what had become of that innocence that had once been his companion and mentor—wondering, too, if he was going insane in his passion for this woman—nothing was able to trigger the elusive orgasm. "I think I'm getting close," she said from time to time. That and the knowledge that the great Katz had almost, *almost* succeeded, and the intimation that something might really be occurring inside that pelvic ice house, urged him on to the inevitable emptiness as, in his determination not to selfishly indulge himself while she went hungry, he continually checked himself; so well did he learn this tactic that when at length she relented and gave him permission to release and enjoy his own climax independently of hers, it was gone.

"So here we are again," said Kit in her most accommodatingly gracious manner, "back in our Overflow."

"Yeah."

"Let's ask if that derives from leftovers from other lounges, or my cup runneth over, or what. *I* think it's the kind that can't find a barstool or a table after the theatre."

"Uh, yeah, I think you're right."

"Now what? Can't you cheer up?"

"Why? I'm okay."

"No, you're not okay. A minute ago you were smiling, now you're glum."

"I didn't know it showed."

"It shows."

"Well, damm it, I keep wishing we were in Paris, or Florence, or Mallorca. Or anywhere but here."

Kit sighed, looked desperately for a joke, and finally said with a disingenuous *moue*, looking around as she spoke, "I thought you liked this place."

"I meant New York."

"I know you meant New York."

"We should be on our honeymoon and anywhere but here in this godforsaken city. When are you going to give in?"

"When you stop calling it a godforsaken city."

"It's not a godforsaken city."

"You're old fashioned, Tom. People don't get married anymore in—"

"This godforsaken city?"

"Or any city, godforsaken or not. Will you please cheer up?"

"I'll try. Maybe another drink will do it. Before we move on?" He signaled the waiter.

"Yes, all right." She drained her glass. "By the way, how good *is* your French?"

The waiter came and Tom ordered two martinis, very dry.

"My French? Not too bad. I was in school in Bordeaux for a year."

"I didn't know that. How old were you?"

"Eighteen. I spent a few summers there as well."

"Why don't you speak French to the waiters?"

"They speak English."

Kit smiled. She liked that answer. "I did notice you had a very good accent. With the menu, and the wines, you know, and the way you say *merci*. I wondered why you didn't, you know, do more. I mean most people who know a little French use it all over the place."

"I guess I'm afraid of looking pretentious, or of making a mistake. My French is not perfect—I mean, I wouldn't fool a Frenchman for more than a minute."

"You'd fool everyone else, though."

"That was never my reason for wanting to learn French."

"What was your reason?"

"Well, it's true, I knew it would impress the girls back home. But the basic reason was literature. Molière, Balzac, Flaubert, Racine—I wanted to read them in French. And I thought it might help me vocationally. That too."

"Has it?"

"No. It does look good in the résumé, though, so, who knows?"

"It must have. Mr. Foote is a very cultivated man."

"I suppose he is. But he's more anglophile than francophile. It's his English accent he wanted to perfect. Haven't you noticed?"

"Me? Why should I have noticed?"

"Why not? Everybody else has."

"Well, I didn't."

Tom looked puzzled. "Do I detect a trace of company loyalty here? Devotion to The Boss?"

"Why not? He brought me here and gave me this wonderful job," said Kit, hiding her face behind her glass as she drank.

"What wonderful job are you talking about, exactly? You seem to have an awful lot of time on your hands. Wouldn't you like more responsibility, more...*excitement*?"

Kit studied the question. "I have my work," she said. More than the words, her tone of voice struck her as defensive. Annoyed, she went on the attack. "Look, Buster, what are you driving at?"

"What?" Tom said, startled.

"What are you trying to prove?"

"Prove? What do you mean?" Trying to read her mood.

"What I said. What are you trying to prove?"

"I didn't think I was trying to prove anything. What should I be trying to prove?"

His eyes slipped to one side even as he spoke, as if he thought he might know the answer.

"Well."

"Well what?"

"Nothing."

"What do you mean, nothing? You said I was trying to prove something. What?"

"Let's drop it, shall we?"

"I don't want to drop it. What did you mean by that?"

"Well, you know."

"No. Tell me."

Suddenly there was a chill between them, right in the middle of what had been their good humor. The word manhood lay there like a block of dry ice, though neither had spoken it.

"Nothing," she said, putting her hand over his. "Just because you sometimes think a thing doesn't mean it's true. Of course you don't have to prove anything. You know I think a lot of you. I think you know that."

Removing her hand she kept looking at him, knowing he could not resist the pull of her eyes.

"I wouldn't have to prove anything if you weren't...." He looked away.

"Weren't what?"

"Nothing."

"Weren't what?"

"Why go into all that?"

"Weren't what?"

"You know."

"I don't know."

"Frigid."

After a long silence she said, "At least I'm trying to do something about it."

"Yes, I know," he said in a tone on the cutting edge of bitterness.

"*What* do you know? I don't have to take this from you, Buster! It so happens I'm seeing an analyst. That's what *I'm* talking about. What are *you* talking about?"

"You're seeing an analyst?"

"Not an analyst. Who has the time or the money? A therapist."

"Since when? Why didn't you tell me?"

Kit swirled the liquid and cubes in her glass between puffs on her cigarette. "I'm telling you now. He's Danish and very big-time. And something of a sex maniac if you ask me. I mean, above and beyond the call of professional duty. Not that he's, you know, taken any liberties. But he's into *everything*. He assures me he could induce orgasm anytime I want, through hypnosis. Do you think I should do that?"

Tom shrugged.

"I feel it would be a threat to my...sovereignty, for lack of a better word."

"What's wrong with that word? I agree."

"But then what else is there?"

"That's just it. What else is there? By your own account you've tried Southern Baptists, black militants, Jewish sexologists, total strangers, vibrators, bisexuals, alcoholics and junkies, and nothing worked, so why *not* hypnosis?"

Kit bridled. "One of each, as it happened. You don't have to pluralize. And I see I shouldn't have told you about them."

"I think you should stop transforming that elusive orgasm into the Holy Grail. Can't you just enjoy sex without it? It's like saying you can't enjoy a banquet because you know you're not going to have the dessert. Think about it. The reason you can't have it is you've focused on it so hard. Maybe hypnosis *would* get you over the hurdle—*once*. As for after that, I don't know. I'm not a hypnotist."

"That's just it, I wouldn't want to get dependent on it. That's why he hasn't pushed it. But I wouldn't call it dessert, it's the whole banquet."

"Alas, that's what you've made it into. You've made it the whole banquet."

"So? Isn't it yours?"

Tom could find nothing to say in reply.

"Cat got your tongue?"

"Ah, I just don't understand women. And you least of all."

"What's to understand?"

"You baffle me."

"Baffle-shmaffle. You know me better than anyone. You know I care for you."

"Care for," he repeated, very dry.

"If you want to force me to say I love you, then, all right, I love you."

"Yeah? Then marry me."

"Not tonight," she smiled. "You know," she said, "I think there was somebody came from Wales, or Scotland. One of my mother's husbands had a branch—no, it was my father! That's right! That," she said brightly, "would make me part Welsh!"

"Or Scottish."

"Anyway, I'm not interested in leaving New York, married or not married, honeymoon or no honeymoon." Just her saying those words over and over constituted a delicious tease. This was when she was at her happiest.

"It wouldn't have to be Wales. I don't dream of going back or anything. It could be anywhere—Spain or Cyprus or Italy or... anywhere. Canada, Alaska. Anywhere."

"Doing what?" she said coolly blowing smoke over his head with a little practised lift of her chin.

"Anything. Freelancing. Starting up something, or connecting up with something. I've got *some* money, you know. We'd get by."

"The trouble with you, Tom, is you're not ambitious enough. You know that, don't you? Why did you come to the United States?"

"For adventure. Excitement. Broaden my horizons. This was where it was happening. Ha."

"But if you dislike it so much, why do you stay?"

"I'd leave tomorrow if you came with me."

Saying this, he felt stupid and helpless and pathetic. A Katz.

"You know, I don't understand you," Kit said. "You came here to make it and you are making it. You're moving up, and you can keep moving up. Why not? What's to stop you?" At his impatient frown she went on, "You know what I think? I think you're losing heart.

And that's why I couldn't run off with you, Tom Hutchins. Regardless of how I felt about you. See? Because the bottom line is you're ...You don't want to go for it, do what you have to do to be where you want to be." Leaning back, she puffed at her cigarette, pleased that she had found an intellectual rationale for her confused feelings about Tom, a good-sense justification for not doing what she knew she was not going to do anyway. She blew the blame back to him along with the smoke.

And Tom inhaled deeply.

"You've lost your (instead of you have no) fighting spirit. And you a Welshman! The only native people in Britain the English never conquered."

"It's true I don't feel very aggressive at the moment," Tom said with a sigh. "How did you know that, about the Welsh?"

"I'm not totally ignorant, you know. I *have* read *some* history. Why don't you see an analyst?"

"I would, but there are no analysts, only psychoanalysts, and I have better things to do with my money."

Picturing the patronizing smile of her libidinous Dane when she reported that remark, Kit said, "Suit yourself. It's not my funeral."

"It will be if you don't get away. You're doomed here. But you don't see it, do you."

"You have no right to say that to me!" she said, surprising herself with her vehemence. "I'm happy here!"

"Are you? Sorry," he said with that maddening obstinacy, "but I know better." Then, with surprising passion, "Darling Kit, don't you get tired of crazies suddenly screaming at everyone on the subway train and homeless persons defecating in doorways and cabdrivers who can't speak English and can't find anything and rude waiters and couriers on bikes speeding through red lights and nearly running you down as you try to get safely across the street and calling *you* asshole? Don't you ever long for quiet, polite people and for trees and plants and flowers and clean air?"

"There are trees and plants and flowers at the top," she said. She smiled. "And fresh air. And courtesy. And lots of money. And lots of freedom. To do what you want."

She was thinking of the penthouse, but not only of that—it was a metaphor for the you-can-have-it-all that she was really thinking about, always thought about, therefore she was shocked into near panic when, seeming to stab into her innermost mind, he said with surprise, "At the top? You mean, of the Foote Building?"

"What?" she said, flustered.

"Have you been up?"

"Of course not! I mean, why should I? I only meant, don't they always have flowers and shrubs on those penthouse terraces? The ones *I've* seen do."

"Well, *I have*." Leaning forward, he fixed her with a hard look.

"You have what?"

"Been up there. And you're right. Flowers, plants, miniature trees, shrubs. Very impressive. Provides a little extra oxygen, too—I thought he was joking but he was serious. He has an air filtering system too. Eighty floors up! How about that. Seems you can't get high enough. That hole in the ozone affects him, too."

"So, you've been up there?"

"I see you're impressed. But it was a fluke. It had to do with his family interests, which of course reach very far and wide. He thought I might have some personal anthropological information about Wales."

"And did you?"

"No."

Poor loser, Kit thought. "And so," she said, "that was that? You haven't been back?"

"No, I haven't. Is that important?"

"I understand there are better floors to be on than the seventeenth. It wouldn't hurt to get him interested in you."

He was silent.

"Well would it?" she said with a touch of exasperation.

"Those floors are all the same to me. And suppose I had had the information he was after? What difference would it have made? A cigar and a drink and maybe another ten dollars on my Christmas bonus? Whatever happens, I'm still just another flunkey supplying some little piece of information, some little detail to help him cement his high position in the oligarchy."

"I didn't know you were a revolutionary."

"I'm not. I'm a critical and impatient evolutionist."

"What's the difference?"

"Bloodshed. Look, what are you driving at? That I'm a loser? Is that what you're saying?"

"That," Kit said at his sudden change of tone, "is the wrong way to be aggressive, Buster. That won't even get you to the eigh*teenth* floor."

"I keep telling you, I'm not trying to get to the eighteenth floor, or the eightieth floor, or any floor."

"Well, congratulations, you're a big success at that."

A heavy silence sat like smog while they toyed with drinks and cigarettes.

"Shall we move on?" Tom said finally.

"Where?" she said testily, letting him see she was in no mood for lovemaking, in case he had that in mind.

"You know, Les Quatre Cons."

"The Four what? I happen to know what that means."

"You do?"

"I've known one or two Frenchmen."

"Well, then you know it's really only vulgar in English. Anyway I thought you liked those kinds of words."

"Not in public. And you know that."

She gave him one of her beautiful angry glares. He grinned apologetically. "It wasn't public—nobody heard me."

"I don't give a *shit* who heard you! It's still public!" she said in a fierce whisper just as the waiter arrived with the check. Horrified, she grabbed her purse and rushed out, forcing Tom to overtip as he ran to catch up (she knew he would) and talk very fast to calm her down and save her from having to grab a taxi back to that apartment so early in the evening.

Six

Tuesday and Thursday mornings Harrison Foote was in his spacious office suite on floor sixty-five, scanning the more important accounts and receiving departmental chiefs. As Tom was not a departmental chief he had wondered as he waited in the anteroom why this sudden renewed interest in him. He imagined a great many things but it turned out to be none of them.

"We've come into the possession," Foote began, prim, trim, and slight in his high backed leather chair behind the grand desk, "of a publishing company. Such things," he said with a small smile, "happen occasionally."

I'll bet, Tom thought, returning a hypocritically indulgent, approving smile.

"This happens to be something I'm especially interested in. It's something I think we should give some very serious thought to. Do you see what I mean?"

"Yes, Sir," Tom nodded, encouraged by the we.

Looking out the window at a passing cloud, Foote drummed his fingers dramatically on the desk.

"You can see, from the name, this is one of the oldest and best of the publishers. The world doesn't know about this just yet, by the way." A sharp glance of his aging blue eyes got the desired response—Tom quickly nodded to show he understood the need for discretion. "It is known for its sense of tradition and quality. That fact, you might say, gave me a certain advantage. And I shall not disappoint. We will maintain those standards, while at the same time examining with modern efficiency the causes of its decline. We do have to avoid the conditions that create losses, don't we. Now, I understand you used to do some writing, Mr. Hutchins."

"Yes. Once upon a time. I gave it up."

"Wisely, I dare say, in view of your present position and possibilities for the future. But the interest in literature I trust is still there? You haven't turned sour on what others produce simply because of your personal defection?"

Christ, Tom thought, how did he know that? He began to feel a grudging respect for the man. Maybe he's been there, with his oil painting, and that's how he knows. "If I'd done that, Mr. Foote, I would have become a literary critic," he replied with a smile.

Foote laughed, a rich chuckle. Tom wondered if he ever really laughed. Probably not. No belly laughs. No belly, for that matter. The bugger was in good shape for a man of seventy-plus.

"How would you like to be a book editor, Mr. Hutchins?"

"You mean, recommending novels for publication?"

"I was thinking more of making the final decisions."

"You mean, top man?"

"That is exactly what I mean." He gave an indulgent smile to show that he understood Tom's thrill sensation of career breakthrough.

But introspective Tom's thrill was balanced with questions: What did this mean? Why him? Why this sudden attention? And how was this going to affect his life?

"I don't know what to say," he said.

The old man kept smiling and nodding to show he understood. He always understood. There was nothing he did not understand. That was why he was on his side of the desk and everybody else was on the other side. (Of course, he was born into it, but that was part of the understanding.) He liked Hutchins, appreciated him as a good solid straightforward imaginative advertising man of British stock. However, advertising could spare him—and he preferred Catherine Harlow's lovers and suitors to come from outside the building. Especially this serious one. And this move, which spurred him to self-congratulation, would not only put Hutchins in a different department and different wing but would keep him, especially for the first few months, very busy.

"Of course it means a considerable increase in salary, as well as in responsibility. But I think I have got the right man. And I think you'll find you have the right job. More demanding, perhaps, but more rewarding, too—more...*satisfying*, do you see what I mean. Of course, at the beginning you may find it taking up rather more of your time. So you should think about that."

Yes, I should, thought Tom even as he said, "Oh, that's no problem."

"Good! As I said before, I know I've got the right chap. One thing you must keep in mind. Fiction publishing is a business. It is not a charity. We are getting into it to make money. In any case not to lose money, by that I mean a lot of money—the sort of thing that can't be written off or in some way reconciled by our tax people. Quality, of course, must always have its place, but as in all things one must keep a sense of proportion, mustn't one. Now I have here a portfolio of documents and recommendations and a general description of conditions in the various departments, how things stand at the moment. Including the novels that were being read and considered for publication. There is a certain urgency here. One novel in particular, an autobiographical novel I gather, is about a young writer, a pure-minded, dedicated artist, who wants to write a novel absolutely without compromise, and without money."

"Without money."

"And for the first half of the novel without even a place to live. Obviously nobody understands this young man—editors, agents, friends, family—and he has a very difficult time of it. Can't get into any of the art colonies. When he tries to get a job he can't find one, for various reasons."

"Maybe he has no talent. I mean, for writing."

"He has been published, just once, and with good reviews."

"Is that autobiographical too?"

"So I gather."

"Well, okay, he has some talent. And honesty. Maybe too much."

"Too much honesty?" Foote was temporarily distracted from his agenda. "Is that a bad thing?"

"Well, you know how it is when a story teller gets too involved in accuracy. He loses his audience. Good story tellers don't worry too much about the truth."

"H'mm. An interesting point." Foote reflected that he had been in danger of underestimating his man. "At any rate what we have here is someone with a bad case of...artistic integrity I believe it's called."

"Yes. But I like it. Provided he's a good writer, I like it. I don't know if it will sell many copies, or interest anybody who is not himself a writer—"

"Or herself."

"Or herself. Should I have said theirself? Anyway it could be an interesting novel. Personally I think I like the idea."

"So do I. But there's a problem. He's black."

"Black! But, that's perfect! Given the tenor of the times. It could be a big seller. But I didn't hear anything about racial struggle."

"That's because there isn't any in the novel. He's trying to write a novel that makes no reference to the problems that come with being an African-American writer."

"I guess he doesn't want to limit his field of interest. He wants to be an artist, not an ethnic hero. He doesn't want to be an *important* writer, he wants to be a *great* writer. He wants to embrace universal themes."

"Can an African-American do that in our racist society?"

Tom stopped to think. Was Foote testing him? He was talking like a campus radical for pete's sake. This shoe didn't fit. Oil painting, okay. Grants to this or that liberal enterprise, okay. Money for Mandela and Al Sharpton and Jesse Jackson, okay. But *our racist society*? Harrison Foote?

"Well, ahem," Tom said slowly, trying to think, "I don't know... Is ours a racist society? Granted, blacks don't get equal treatment on every level—but then, neither do I. They get less than me in some ways and more than me in other ways."

"How do they get more?"

He can't really be meaning this, Tom thought. He's sounding me out. Harrison Foote is not a campus radical, or even a coffee shop radical. He can't be. So what is he? The hell with it, I'll go for broke.

"I don't think I would have gotten the millions Rodney King got, whatever I'd done and whatever had been done to me. I'd have gotten what the white Reginald Denny got. I don't think I'd have been acquitted after yelling 'Kill the Jew' at Mr. Rosenbaum and stabbing him and being caught with the knife in my pocket and confessing, and the jury would not have come to a party celebrating my acquittal. It would have been more like what the white lout and his cronies got in Bensonhurst that killed the young black who had gone there to buy a used car. And if I delivered hate-filled speeches at a university, not being black, I think they would have thrown everything but the kitchen sink at me—especially if my tirade was against blacks. When a black does it he's cheered by his supporters and indulged by everybody else—meaning the university administration and the media."

"Hmm." Foote contemplated Tom noncommittally, while Tom watched him wondering if he had cemented or lost the job, squirming with the ineffable guilt of the whistle blower. "Of course, we must have balance, mustn't we. But I think you'd have a problem convincing people that this is not a racist society, in spite of certain areas of progress."

"I know. That's another problem."

"And as for our young author,..."

"What seemed perfect is not," Tom said. "I wonder if I know him."

"His name is Desmond Raines. Do you?"

"Not personally. I'm pretty sure he lives in the Village, though."

"The blacks don't like him. He de-emphasizes race. He approaches Western civilization in the light of its accomplishments, not as an evil. He blames commercialism and greed, not white society, for his hard times."

"Just as if he was white."

"Just as if he were white. Exactly."

"I'd like to read this novel."

"You will. He has his supporters. A few black intellectuals, a few white conservatives. A few literary critics. Not many. The majority of blacks and the white liberals are solidly and I might say vociferously against him, as you might expect. The Village Voice has already attacked him."

"This gets less perfect all the time," Tom said.

"I'm afraid so. I haven't read the novel, but I can tell you this. If the liberal press is against it, it hasn't got much of a chance. I want you to read it and tell me what you think. How good you think it is, and how well you think it will do if we publish it. It could be big, it could be a disaster."

"What it really comes down to is politics," Tom said.

"I'm afraid so," Foote said. "But then, doesn't everything? But let's consider the plot. A struggling artist. Not everyone's cup of tea. Is it anyone's, except for struggling artists? And how many of those are there these days?"

"Why doesn't he just throw in a racial—"

"Artistic integrity," Foote cut in with a smile. "It's useless to try to talk sense to somebody who's been bitten by that bug."

"I know."

"His novel will be panned and dismissed. Or simply ignored. To counteract that—after all, he's not well known—we would have to launch a big advertising campaign to give it any chance at all. Look, I'll be absolutely honest. Personally I see no point in publishing this. But I want your opinion. The trouble here is certain editors. They'll be replaced in time, but the ones who are responsible for the company's financial state of affairs have a tradition of publishing this sort of book. And losing money."

"Then, you want me to reject it?"

"I want you to be a sensible and responsible arbiter. Can you start reading it right away?"

"Sure," Tom said, suddenly cut adrift, unmoored, but thrilled.

"I'll have you moved to your new office."

"Fine, Sir." Unmoored, but thrilled. But adrift. Uncertain.

"Have you any questions? Any at all?"

"I can't think of any, offhand, Sir," said Tom, though his head was full of them.

Seven

"Hi." Cordless phone in hand, Kit shut the door behind Tom. "Fix yourself a drink. I'm talking to Sam."

Not listening he heard the sotto voce flirtation with Sam as effortlessly she turned the poor sucker on, laughing with happy sensuality at the erotic jokes and hopeful suggestions he poured into her ear like Hamlet's uncle. He carried a Scotch-and- water- no- ice around the small upmarket, one-size-fits-all flat, the penumbral half-room with its half-window that she had made into an airconditioned half-office complete with black filing cabinets and a computer workstation that had greatly impressed him until he realized it was little used.

Come to that, why was anything here? Why was the kitchen equipped for culinary events that never took place? She could not cook, did not care to practice or learn the art, almost never ate at home. Yet the equipment was such as a *cordon bleu* graduate might envy.

Twice she had cooked for him. Both times she had overgrilled (burnt) the meat while drinking and talking—once on the phone, pleasantly, and once to him, unpleasantly as she informed him that he could like her excessive drinking or lump it. That second time, she was so angry she refused to eat, and after he devoured both burnt veal chops while standing in the kitchen ("Sure you don't want yours?") she said, "Now that you've filled your stomach you can leave!" And she meant it. Off he went.

The rest of the furnishing was the same—trendy, yuppie, gadgety, mostly left over from her freelance agency days. The whole outfit had been to California and back.

In the whole room (she was lighting a fresh Marlboro, the ashtray beside her already grotesque with long crumpled butts, her feet tucked up on the bed-sofa, cradling the receiver with her shoulder while sipping at her highball and somehow managing also to turn the pages of Elle on her lap) he studied her book collection—a lean compilation of Shakespeare's tragedies, a Great Artists, The Little Prince, a Who's Who, a few modern unread novels (Updike, Vonnegut, Roth) and encyclopedic volumes and some advertising and PR reference books. A dictionary and a Thesaurus were in the office. How he longed to fill her with culture! But all he ever saw her read on her own time were the society and showbiz gossip columns.

He moved to the great triple-sectioned windows and looked out. Nothing there but a gray courtyard and the window-studded wall of another wing of the same building, the windows all with curtains and blinds drawn. You saw so many such walls in this city. And that courtyard! No greenery, no life, not even a bird. Not even a pigeon. No weeds, no ants—just cement. And bricks. And glass. Even dreary, smelly East Side tenements were more sightly than this empty, desolate, sterile squelch of life and Nature. He wondered if any of the other tenants had found a way to give their apartments a lived-in, multi-generational feel, the feel of something personal and individual.

If only they were poor. The poor personalized everything with rags and makeshift furniture and hungry squalling babies. Nothing like that here. Here everybody earned over fifty thousand and owed money on their credit cards and was trying to move up another rung. Everybody. *They* might be individuals, but the rest of it was identical—windows, blinds, elevators, incinerators, apartment design, and the carpeted halls, the living rooms-cum-bedrooms, the state-of-the-art gadgetry. And it was all right there in that dismal courtyard. Though it grope like a hand over a dungeon wall, that was all that the eye could find. One longed to see that inanimate pavement rent by bombs, atomized, and the earth heave up over it, reappropriating it for swift jungle plants and bugs and bacteria.

God! Tom thought turning away, I'm turning fucking perverse!

A psychopath!

"Something out there?" said Kit peering out through a window she had never opened.

"No, nothing."

"The way you were staring I thought somebody had jumped or something."

"No such luck."

"What?"

"Just joking."

"That's not funny," she said with a shiver. "God, you do have a weird sense of humor sometimes. So, what was the important thing you had to tell me?"

"Foote has made me chief editor of a publishing company he just bought."

"Tom! That's *wonderful.* I'm so *pleased* for you. Which one?"

"Harriman Press."

"Harriman Press! That's *big*!"

"Sure is."

"What does it mean? Did it go bust?"

"Search me. But he has it. 'Came into the possession of' was the way he put it. Maybe it's a merger. Somebody always gets the upper hand in a merger, don't they?"

Kit was in thought. "But why you?" she said.

"Well, I don't really know. He seems to know I wanted to be a writer at one time. But why pick a defrocked writer to be your top editor? Anyway, I accepted."

"At a raise in salary, I expect?"

"A big one."

"Tom! That's *wonderful*! Let's have a drink to celebrate."

"We're already having one. Let's go out and celebrate."

"Oh, I can't. I have a dinner date. Oh well, look," she said seeing his face, "I'll call and say something came up, okay? Why the reproachful look? Listen, I'm still a free woman, you know. You don't own me."

"I was thinking, this new job means I won't have much free time for a while."

"Well, advancement has to cost *some*thing."

"I guess so. Hey, why don't we save a lot of rent and live together?"

"And be tied down? I like it just the way it is. This way, we have a quarrel, you go home, I go home, no problem. That way, we can't go home! Let me just freshen up, won't be a minute—oh! I'd better call John first. Chief editor! Harriman Press! How *about* that."

She was very apologetic to John. She promised to make it up to him. She didn't say how, but that teasing tone crept into her voice. Tom looked out the window at the now blackened courtyard. He could see nothing. Reflecting how perfect a silhouetted target he made for the psychopathic snipers that proliferate on urban rooftops (and that unfailingly pick off someone who is moving up in the world), he decided to lower the blinds like everybody else.

Eight

A big collision? On the *river*?

Kit carried her drink to the railing and looked in the direction Harrison Foote, binoculars in hand, was pointing.

"Yes, I see it!"

It really was like being in an airliner. This was not your ordinary terrace, this was a wonder of the world. It was almost scary. How high could you get and still be umbilically attached to the earth?

The tanker he had indicated was not moving. It lay astride the apparent sea lanes. You could see something was wrong. Tugs puffing and blowing labored up and down her length. Tiny black figures ran along her deck. She seemed to be listing. A copter hovered over her. Two fireboats leaving broad wakes approached her from the Jersey side.

And some distance away, nearer the Verrazano Bridge, a gray freighter seemed to have anchored. Something wrong there, too.

"I think they collided in the early hours," Foote said, not entirely displeased, it was like having the best seat in the opera house, or the Colosseum. "This sort of thing simply should not happen. Very costly. For everybody. I understand a flat barge carrying trucks or automobiles just managed to work its way around them...The freighter seems all right, although I did see some smoke this morning. Don't know what the cargo is—But that tanker! Well! That's a horse of another color, isn't it. That could be trouble. Very costly trouble. Would you like a look through these, my dear?"

Lower Manhattan and a good part of New York Bay at the turn of a knob, along with a strip of New Jersey and hazy Staten Island. A lower building obstructed most of the Statue of Liberty but there was a piece of Brooklyn, all of the Verrazano Bridge, and the anchored freighter. And that oil tanker, with its frantic tugboats and worried fireboats.

"Will there be an explosion, do you think?"

"Good gracious, I hope not. I don't think so. There could be a fire if they're not careful, and that could be very nasty but I think the various services will know how to—I talked to the deputy mayor this morning, he said there's nothing to worry about, they are in control of the situation. Of course they always say that. Well! Shall we go in and do a bit of work?"

She had lingered as much as she dared. This was the famous arboretum Tom had mentioned. She had not appreciated it as much as it deserved. The geranium pots and rosebushes and hydrangea and azaleas and lilies of every kind, all the exotic shrubs and miniature fruit trees, a score of beautifully grotesque cactus plants, stunted palms. And orchids. And cyclamens. Her florist's assistant half-brother Stephen would love it here—maybe she could bring him up one day...There were so many things she could do if she played her cards right. A team of three gardeners cared for all this, why not a fourth? And other perks? Once you were plugged into the system, it carried you along like a surfboard!

But those cards she had to play. "A bit of work" now meant forty minutes of posing with nothing on ("I now realize it was the Nude we were after all along, my dear, don't you think? I mean, all that, you know, artificiality and covering up. Not what we want, is it. What after all is more fundamental, more true and beautiful than the Nude. Art history shows over and over—It's not for nothing that historically the great masters have always returned to the basic—You don't really mind, do you, Ms Harlow? You have such a beautiful body. I could hire a professional model but then she wouldn't be you, would she. Of course if you're at all uneasy about it....") followed by two hours of sauna and sunlamp and a scented Jacuzzi bath, assaulted by mirrors and beautiful prefaded Pompeii mosaics and surround-sound Mozart. And the goldplated faucets.

He joined her in the solarium, stripped to a towel. ("Ah, the heat does one good, doesn't it?") Then came the rubdowns—long, unhurried, sensuous ("This will do wonders for your headaches, my dear, you've no idea the tension I feel in your body, you must relax those muscles, the ones you don't know about")—with a fragrant oil. And with her on her side on the massive rubberized mattress he would lie down behind her, behind his Reclining Nude, not touching her with his body though she felt some of its heat as the wrinkled hands caressed her everywhere, almost everywhere, and she sensed his increasing excitement as she waited eyes closed for a climax which eventually came in a confused but somehow systematic trill, an agitation of hands and towel and hard breathing and the odd whimper. Then he would doze off for a few moments while she waited in the heat from the lamps and the serenading of Mozart.

That was now the routine.

But this time he introduced a variation she was not ready for. She had persuaded herself that he was at his ultimate reach, and that he would not or could not presume further. And that she would stop him if he did. But as he was rubbing the oil into her back he suddenly reached around and with gentle but surprising authority rolled her onto her back and proceeded to oil her breasts.

"Relax, my dear, just relax."

So she did. She gave herself up to the moment and let him do whatever he wanted.

With caressing wandering fingers he finally did what with other men was foreplay. And because she was not asked or cajoled, but instead was escorted, guided, invited, a strange thing happened. Gliding in the direction indicated, suddenly she shivered, and delivered, drawing deeper breaths even as she surrendered until she shook out of control and had it, had her climax, had it at last.

On the periphery of her consciousness she was mildly, only mildly disturbed by an awareness that he too was having a damp completion upon her thigh. And as she lapsed into dreamy somnolence, she smiled. It was the wrong man, but no matter, she had done it, she had joined the human race, she was happy.

* * *

Happy as she felt, Kit was not prepared for the happiness of Harrison Foote. You would have thought *he* was the one who had achieved his first ever, the way he carried on. He was like a schoolboy, laughing and joking and baring his breast of doubts and disillusionments and dreams. And plans. Plans for their—*their*! —happiness, their future together.

"Would you like to go to Paris? I'd love to see it again in that mood of...To be in Paris and in love, there's nothing quite like it. I suffered a terrible rejection there, once—I was very young. She suffered too, perhaps worse than I, but she kept saying no, first yes then no, then yes again, but it was too late—Or Rome? The Greek Islands, Cyprus, Istanbul—Oh the possibilities! You can choose whatever you like. I can always find the time, you know. Of course, there will be younger men, very handsome men, they'll ask to dance with you thinking you're my granddaughter—Could you handle that? Separate rooms, of course—but adjoining and with a communicating door. Would you like that? You must be honest with me."

"But my job," she stammered.

He laughed like a teenager. "Are you forgetting? I'm your boss! Your office can spare you, my darling, I'll see to it."

She couldn't think, and retreated into silence, keeping an indulgent smile on her face—an expression that she hoped fell safely between the third rails of encouragement and rejection.

"You know, I've been impotent but I feel certain it's going to change, I'm too young for that, I mean, you know, I—I'm sure it's coming back—You've made me very happy...Are you—are you pleased? I mean, was it a happy experience for you too, just now? And are you just a little bit...No, don't answer, it's a stupid question."

He lay for a moment, their bodies still joined wherever his form found discreet refuge along her curves, then slowly disengaged himself. Imperceptibly her body moved without moving—settled, as in a sigh.

"I'll get dressed, my darling Catherine," he said. He wrapped himself in a towel, and suddenly produced with a gay laughing lilt, "My darlin' Catheryne" He grinned at her to see if she had caught on. "As in Clementine. Get it? Well! Come in when you're ready, and we'll have a glass of champagne, shall we?"

By the time they met in the post-massage room he called his den she had, while showering and dressing, run in and out of every possibility—resigning, disappearing, trying to marry him, becoming his kept woman, suing him for fifty million on grounds of sexual harassment, or going on as if nothing had happened—and he had regained his composure and his urbanity.

His silly sophomore gaiety—the one time she had detected a vulnerability in him—was gone. He was his normal, solicitous, untouchable persona. A bit put out by this, she nevertheless smiled to herself. She knew how to get it back.

She looked for changes in his behavior and saw none. His ever-present staff were, as ever, invisible—at most, she might glimpse a door being softly pulled shut. The champagne and the canapés and gold-tipped cigarettes were the same as always, as were his deferential manner and the five crisp hundred-dollar bills he slipped ever so discreetly into her coat pocket while seeing her to the elevator.

Riding down she did not know whether she should feel triumphant or angry or disgusted or amused. When was her next appointment with the Dane—Friday? Two days. He would advise her exactly what to feel. He had already shown intense interest in her adventures with the old man. (She had of course not given his name—only Katz knew that). After pointing out that even as her therapist there was a limit to how much advising he could in good conscience do, he said he thought she ought to go on with it for the time being, as long as she did not feel abused or debased. In his opinion it was the first mature relationship she had ever had with a man.

Katz, on the contrary, thought it was sick. But what did he know? His solution was a ménage à trois. He said he had a girlfriend who really liked her.

The one she would have liked to talk to about all this was Tom, but she didn't dare. Anyway, these days Tom was hard to get hold of—always working, always tired, hardly ever free. When they did manage to get together for a drink he looked haggard and as if he could use some of that sun lamp treatment himself. He was always running to talk to agents and editors and carried a briefcase full of manuscripts and readers' reports and seemed half asleep. He always had to be some place else. And he had become obsessed about politics.

"*Everything's politics*," he had muttered over and over the last time they'd met. "Everything. And money. The bottom line. Politics and profit, profit and politics." He wasn't fun anymore. There were circles under his eyes. And he was drinking a lot more.

* * *

The question Tom could not escape asking himself was, why me? Why had he been chosen? Why was he suddenly an uncomfortable Winner instead of the comfortable Loser he had been? And why was he the one selected to butt horns with the experienced and well entrenched editors who were now his colleagues? What was the point of all the hard work he was doing, even the good salary he was being paid, when he and they were working at cross purposes, continually vetoing each other? This was a job for a politician, or a bottom-line accountant.

Trying to find a rational argument for publishing the novel, he had gone to see the black author.

Raines lived in the West Village a dozen blocks away from his own flat on Waverly Place. He could walk over.

Desmond Raines was not at all what he had expected. He called himself a rebel par excellence and a disenchanted liberal. He said liberals were not liberal anymore. They were dominant. They had become the tyrant, the bullying, blinkered, arrogant orthodoxy. He really had ideas. He went on and on about political correctness.

Physically too his appearance was a shock to Tom. He had expected this man who was taking on all his opponents literary, commercial and political, to have an imposing appearance, and had found himself introducing himself to a short and homely, bugeyed and balding, very black man in his thirties with dirty eyes and a very wide mouth and an effeminate manner. The only imposing thing about him was an almost palpable determination to be taken seriously. Even his voice seemed below normal strength. But in articulateness he did not disappoint.

He spoke with the polished diction of a Shakespearean actor, the fluency of one who knew his lines.

"I know all about black suffering," he said with wide eyes in his soft, stubborn, petulant voice. "And about human suffering. And the suffering of the artist in our society. So, tell me, which one should I write about?"

"Which one?"

"I choose to write about the artist. Black or white. That is the bigger picture. His being black only clouds the issue. All reasonable people agree about poverty and racism and equality for all, and bigotry. What they don't agree about is art and artistic freedom and integrity. That's where our culture breaks down. Supposedly reasonable people go off on tangents. I'd just gotten used to the commercialism—not that I knew what to do about it—and now, of all things, political correctness has reared its head. Against *me*! So it's a pincer attack—commercialism and PC. What's a dirt-poor black man supposed to do? I want to be the best writer I can be. And they won't let me. They won't even let me try. Between the accountants on one hand and the blacks and their white liberal groupie allies on the other, I'm trapped."

Tom had not heard this before. And from an African-American! His first thought was, he's not an Uncle Tom, so what is he?

"Of course they call me a Tom," Raines went on. "It's the only explanation they can handle. But what would you do if you wanted to write a novel about human beings, black and white, and the human condition, la condition humaine, without racial friction as its primary conflict?"

"What are you saying, exactly?"

"I want to be a human being! Not a black man or a white man, but a man, a human man, a human being! Can you understand that?"

"Of course I can," Tom said. But he was strangely on the defensive, and sensed it, and didn't know why he should be, since he was in total agreement.

"What I don't understand is," Raines said, "why are you here? I gather you do like the novel?"

"I said so right away, when I came in. Yes, I did like it. Very much."

"Oh. I didn't hear. Too busy trying to think what your visit was about. All I heard was you're not sure you can publish it. I missed everything else. What do you want me to do? Do you want me to make changes?"

"Only writers, the literati, will be interested. You forfeit the blacks, so we're stuck with the literati. That means capital loss at the bottom line."

"Unless there are good reviews," said Raines.

"Unless there are rave reviews, you mean. And there won't be rave reviews, that's for sure. The liberals will see to that."

"I'm afraid you're right." He pondered. "Should I compromise a little?"

"Personally I wish you wouldn't. As an editor, though...I can't really ask for a sacrifice so few writers make. I wanted to write myself, once. If I had a great talent, which it's possible you have, I would not ever want to compromise it. But then I'm a hopeless romantic."

Raines made big eyes and smiled. He liked using those bug eyes in that way. That and the pliant mouth and sensitive expression were his sexual weaponry.

"I like the type," he said, not quite flirting, not quite not flirting.

"What are you going to do?"

"I'll think about it. It's a terrible choice. My people and their admiration versus my art and their odium. But tell me more of what you think about the novel. Is it interesting? Did you want to keep reading? I worry about boring the reader."

"I did want to. But I don't know how others...The two editors who have also read it are less sanguine. I don't know why, exactly. I'm finding that you can't leave out the politics. Maybe they read the Village Voice, maybe they don't. I'm sure they read the New York Times, especially the book reviews. They strike me as PC but who isn't, these days? They're Ivy League multiculturalists, they probably voted for Ralph Nader. The best you can hope for is to be patted on the back. But what good would that do? You want more than a marginal acceptance, you want whoopee. Am I right?"

"You're right, but, in the absence of whoopee, I think I would settle for the acceptance."

"Isn't that a kind of premature death?"

"Starving would be a premature death."

Tom started to smile but then took another look around the room and lost the smile. This man was poor. The few dishes, the paucity of cookware, a few pathetic cans of food. One small room, and the bathroom in the hall, no stove, no fridge—Jesus! Maybe starvation was not a metaphor after all, but a real and constant menace. He might be serious. And this was what the novel was about. This was the room in which the hero dies not of starvation, but of poverty and neglect. Of artistic integrity.

Raines seemed always to be reading his thoughts. "Did you like the ending?"

"It's not suicide," Tom said.

"Not quite. He's driven to the alcohol and drugs mix. The rest is an accident. Accidents happen." He shrugged, and smiled, then looked uneasy. "Of course there should be inevitability in the accident. I didn't want him being hit by a car."

"I decided it was the right ending," Tom said. The writer grinned cautious relief.

Sitting in his sprung armchair in a corner of the room Tom slumped in confusion. His own struggles had never achieved this height, or depth. He had talked about garrets, but never actually lived in one. This was a garret.

He had stumbled across a real, a true artist, in the archaic, classical, Romantic sense. But he should have been a white Caucasian, not a black African-American. He should at least have been handsome, athletic, and heroic, with a deep, resonant voice, an Othello. All he was was heroic. Not good enough. The media could easily make him into an icon if they wanted to, as they had done with walleyed pygmy Sartre. But the media had coddled Sartre; here they were the opposition.

"Speaking of which," Tom said, "did you know Bill Welborne?"

"Yes. Very well. I suppose you know he committed suicide? They said cirrhosis, which of course was true, but, well, you know. It was suicide."

"Well, I know he drank himself to death, but that's not exactly—"

"It was suicide," said Raines with a level look.

"How do you know that? After all, he always drank a lot, even when he was happy with his book's progress. Whether to forget or to celebrate, he drank."

"I'll tell you how I know. One time we were in the park, he was sober, and he started coughing. I told him if he didn't lay off the drink, at least for a while, he was headed for an early grave, and he said, 'I want to die.' I was shocked. Then he said it again, just like that, unemotionally, matter-of-factly, 'I want to die.' Looking straight ahead. That's how I knew he meant it."

Nodding, Tom said sadly, "Bill and his big biblical blockbuster of a novel. It became the joke of the Village behind his back. 'Bill and his magnum and only opus', they'd say. But he finished it! He actually finished it! For all the good it did him."

"He couldn't sell it," said Raines.

"No. He took it to every important publisher—you know, he couldn't be bothered with agents—and actually got them to read it, though it always took ages. They all rejected it. Too big, too diffuse, too ambitious, too everything. He was very bitter. But I didn't think he was suicidal."

"Well," said Raines, gazing out the fire escape window, "me neither. But, after twenty years of that kind of dedication, and total commitment, and convinced as he was that in the end it was going to make him rich and famous. I mean, what else did he have in his life?"

"The reason I mentioned him," Tom said, gazing at the same window, "I was watching a documentary about ancient Egypt, and they had something they called a Death List that any Egyptian that could afford it could purchase for passage to eternal life. The soul went through a very long and difficult ritual based on their moral behavior when they were alive, and if they passed, they entered into eternity, or heaven. It named the more important gods, and one was Osiris, and I remember Bill talking about how he was thinking about his story and reading up on things to get his facts straight, The Golden Bough was one, and windows started opening in his mind—Osiris, and how it all tied in with Moses and the Hebrews and The Ten Commandments and especially, in a very direct way, the New Testament. Well, that documentary could have been a review of Bill's book!"

Raines nodded to Tom, and frowned. "You know, my father was a preacher back in Harlem and this kind of thing really hits me where I live. You know that Bill sold the idea and some chapters to Knopf and got a few thousand dollars advance to finish it. They gave him a year. Then those windows started opening and, you know, he would not compromise, and after a few years they got tired and slammed the door on him."

"I know. I know. Anybody who ever bought him a drink knows."

"Have you read it?"

"Parts. I never knew if I was reading a masterpiece or a fancy dime novel with a biblical theme. I never read it from start to finish. I wonder where it is now."

"The manuscript? I've no idea." Raines looked at him. "It would be nice if you could do something with it."

"Yes, it would. God, there's so much I could do. I want to publish you, I want to publish Bill. But I'm not sure how to go about it. I'm new at the job. I don't have any clout. All I can do is make my recommendations, and most of those are ignored."

Raines's homely sensitive little face was eloquent with pessimism. "But you'll try?"

"I will try. Yes. I really will try."

The sad gracious smile. "Thank you."

Tom went away wondering if he was on the verge of becoming one of the legendary editors of American publishing, another Maxwell Perkins. And if so, at what cost.

Nine

Accustomed to figuring people out, especially men, Kit found herself flummoxed with Harrison Foote. Old men, at least, should be easy enough to figure, but this one always left her feeling outmaneuvered.

The next séance had produced nothing—just the painting session. He had not joined her in the sauna. Not a word about anything. Afterward, with the champagne, he gave her, for the second time, a thousand dollars worth of IBM stock, plus the usual five hundred dollars, and that was it. No talk of Paris, no darlings, no euphoria. She was relieved—and troubled. Had she inadvertently squelched him? Shown repugnance by an unconscious gesture, an errant look? Well, the hell with it, the hell with him, the hell with everybody.

In the elevator she felt...*wild.* (Confusion, impatience, a touch of testiness, a spurt of anger, of devil-may-care. Wild.) The usual antidote these days was Tom. (The hell with Tom.) In the vestibule she strode to the door and pushed it open.

She looked out at the gray twilit street, the passing cars and buses, newspapers and candy wrappers blowing in eddies of wind, and retreated. (I don't want to go home.)

Surprised at her own reaction, she looked around. What are you thinking? she asked herself. It's either up or out, and up is out so that leaves out. So out you go. Wait a minute. Where does that other door lead? (I *don't want* to go home.)

The closed circuit TV had nothing to tell her, but she had

wondered about that door. Probably it led to another street. She lit one of her own cigarettes and thought about it. Why not? Carrying her cigarette like a laisser aller she opened the door, peeped in, saw a down staircase. She went on down the stairs and found herself at the start of a corridor.

She followed it, her stiletto heels clicking on the bare concrete floor. The occasional open door revealed shadowy interiors inhabited by giant tanks and furnaces and oil burners and asbestos-wrapped pipes, pipes on all levels, high and low, connecting everything to everything. It occurred to her that she really ought not to be here. But she did not turn back. She wanted nothing that was old or familiar. Or home. She wanted only to proceed on this adventure in this hallway and come out the other side of this great building and see what was there—street? avenue? plaza? Some great restaurant she had been to, or never been to?

And that cab ride home.

The last door, a dead end, was clearly not an exit. It had two locks and a peephole and a frayed rubber mat. She turned the knob and when the door turned out to be unlocked peered in through a discreet gap and saw indistinct shapes in a darkened area that looked as if it might be an apartment. In the basement? A storeroom, more likely. Seeing a wall switch she flicked it on and gave a little cry as the world exploded with violent lights and sounds and the kinetic gestures of amorphous, faintly recognizable shapes.

* * *

On seeing her open the street door, Zudd turned away from the closed circuit scanner and went to shut off a timer. When he looked again the door was closed and she was gone, as always. He went off to check a gauge, and a few minutes later returned to hear, as he neared his apartment, a burst of sound, of music heavy with drums and electric guitars that meant the switch had been turned on. He realized he had not locked the door. An intruder! Even so, he was startled, as he made the last turn, to see one in the flesh—an actual intruder. And even more so when he saw whose flesh it was.

Kit's expression too altered from fright at the commotion inside the apartment to relief.

"It's you," she said. Then doubt crept back in as she saw her only path of retreat was past him, past this strange man.

"You?" he said. "Catherine Harlow? I thought you—But how...?"

"I—I was looking for a way out."

"A way out? From the basement?"

She had no satisfactory answer, and stumbled on: "I was looking for a different way out—Just curiosity. I opened this door—I thought it might be the street door. It was dark, so I pushed the switch—and this happened!"

They could scarcely hear each other over the noise.

"Excuse me," Zudd said, maneuvering delicately past her while she made herself thin so they would not touch and switching it off. Another switch brought a more normal lighting inside what she now saw was in fact a comfortable and lived-in if peculiar apartment.

At his air of deference her own composure returned, and with it, her customary haughtiness with this stratum of worker.

"What in God's name was all that?"

"Well, this is my R&R, sort of," he said.

"Your what?"

"It's how I relax."

"Really! What fun! Do you spend a lot of time in there?"

"It's my living quarters. I live here."

He watched for a reaction, smiling a little. How much had she seen? Despite the smile his eyes gleamed with an intense interest; it gave the smile a shadow of that insolent selfassurance she remembered from the first day.

"So...You live here."

"Sure thing. Can I offer you something? A drink?"

"No, I—" She felt the picaresque sensation of wild fun returning to overwhelm her nervous watchfulness, but had no idea what to do with it or what it meant—"I don't think so, Mr...."

"Zudd," said Zudd.

"Zud?"

"Right. With two d's."

She controlled an urge to laugh. Is he kidding? she thought. Is he real? Is any of this real?

"Homer Zudd, at your service, *my dear*."

The sudden mimicry of Mr. Foote shocked her, stupefied her. He had that queer disconcerting smile. What did this mean? What did he know? She initiated a panicky, haughty departure, and stopped, and turned back. "I'll have that drink."

Zudd threw open the door. She went in looking around. "Have you got an ashtray?" she said holding up her cigarette without looking at him. She was looking at a mechanical gorilla with a human female-bimbo head and a wooden paddle in its upraised hand; and at a confusion of male and female mannequins and their optional replacement heads in a jumble beside it. She turned back with a smile. "Just a simple uncomplicated ashtray."

She meant it as a lighthearted joke but realized it had emerged as mockery. Indeed, she was confused by her reactions to this man. She wanted to escape, and she wanted to stay. She wanted to speak civilly to him, yet felt compelled to mock him.

"I think you'll find this building is a very complicated place," Zudd said slowly, too slowly, handing her an ashtray. "But of course you've already made that discovery, haven't you, *my dear*."

They were dueling with smiles, and Kit's froze again at the Foote impersonation. Part of her confidence drained from her as she said, "I'm not sure I follow you, Mr. Zudd. Are you trying to tell me something?"

The testy question brought a startling response. His smile vanished. Suddenly his face had the intensity of a religious zealot.

"I have many things to tell you, Ms *Harlow*," he said, emphasizing the Ms and her name.

Kit's anxiety was offset by a rush of adrenaline. "Oh?" she said in her haughtiest manner. "Well, okay. Start." But she thought, What kind of nut is he? Am I safe?

His insolent grin returned. "Before the drink?"

Haughtily still, Kit appraised him. Was he the beater or the beaten? "Before."

"Couldn't we hold the glasses, without drinking?" Zudd said. "I sort of need the prop."

Kit blinked at the unexpected hint of charm, then rebounded, "I should think you had enough props here as it is."

"None that I can use here with you, Ms Harlow—yet."

Again her smile failed, again she felt the tremor, and a surge of anger.

"I'm glad we understand each other, Mr. Zudd," she said going to the door.

"Okay, no prop, no alcohol," he said quickly.

She stopped and looked at him. He was pale and, once again, respectful. She liked that—the switch, the easy, casual suddenness of it. And she still had that curiosity. Again she appraised him. The muscular neck. The strong arms. The twitching of a cheek muscle and the movement of his Adams apple as he swallowed, preparing a speech.

"Take off your coat," he said.

In the silence that followed she found herself unable to look away, or turn away. She found herself shaking. Still, she managed to control her voice. "I beg your pardon?"

"Take off your coat," he said with the same tonelessness.

That stare. Was he trying to hypnotize her? Again silence. Still shaking she forced a laugh that merely fluttered in her throat. But it gave her back her own voice and her orientation. And some of her strength. "Just the coat, Mr. Zudd? Nothing else?"

"Everything else."

His voice was low and thick and unexpectedly persuasive. She felt faint with—astonishment? It was that incredible jack-in-the-box confidence. It came and went.

"One thing at a time," he said with that unwinking stare. "Starting with the coat."

Panicking at his temerity she nevertheless screwed the beautiful face (she felt its beauty) into a taunting, malicious sneer. "Sorry, Mr. Zudd, but nothing is coming off. Nothing. Not even the coat."

He permitted one mouth corner to grin. The man was a regular chameleon!

"I know that," he said. "Without the liquor there's nothing doing with you."

"Not for you, Mr. Zudd. With or without. But I have to admit, for a janitor you have a remarkable nerve."

"Oh I'm a special kind of janitor. You can ask Mr. Harrison Foote."

"Congratulations. I'm sure you're his favorite janitor. But you're not mine." Kit turned back to the door. Get the hell out of here.

"No, you're the one to be congratulated, Ms Harlow. For knowing how to get close to your boss. You've managed something none of his other employees has managed except for a few empty headed bimbos who didn't last long." She pulled the door open. "And me." She hesitated. "I have a special relationship with him, thanks to the fact that I happen to be in on a few of his secrets." She closed the door. "Including yours. Oh don't worry, it's safe with me. Though of course, the one who has to worry is him, not you. I still don't know how it happened that I missed the fact that you didn't go out the door and came here instead. I missed that. I thought you were gone, like all those other times. But how was I to know this was to be the day Ms Harlow, the beautiful unapproachable Ms Harlow, after her visit to the penthouse (she stiffened but did not turn around), after those ambrosial wonders of the pleasure gardens on the eightieth floor was going to suddenly come blundering into the underground wonders of my basement?" He went up behind her, not touching her. "And after all those times that I fantasized something like this happening, when it actually did happen I wasn't here! It kills me that I might have missed you. God! You were here and *I wasn't*! Yet I'd *wanted* it, *willed* it. The light switch must have been a shock. You weren't ready for it. Except of course that you *were* ready for it. It's just that it was too sudden, too unexpected, wasn't it. Oh you were ready for it all right."

He moved against her, lightly, their bodies touching now throughout their length.

"You should be part of this. In your soul you already are. I wonder if you know that." He reached around with his hand and placed it on her breast through the open coat. She did not move. He kept it there, warm hand on warm breast. "You," he said in a lowered voice, "are part of the excitement of all these things I've gathered together. But they still need something. Something's still missing. They need a real woman. They need you, Ms Harlow, Ms Catherine Harlow. *I* need you. And you want it. You want excitement. You're bored, you want something new and real that will reach deep inside you, free you from the mundane. You want to be free! I see things in you.

We're attracted to each other. It isn't just sex, there's something else you're looking for, that's what we have in common, I saw it right away. And you sensed it." His hand fondled her breast slowly almost absently as he spoke, through the fabric of her shirt, as if to say this is no mere seduction, there is more at stake. "We have something that doesn't exist in all those others. Why do you keep looking for something over and over in the same places when you know it's not there? Like someone who has lost a wallet full of money? It's not there! You won't find it in the penthouse. I've been waiting for you, a woman like you. For a long time. And I want you just the way you are. Not like others that want to change you, make you over. I think I know that you are a cold woman. I felt it the first time I saw you. That cold beauty comes from something deep, but I like it. I *like* that polar, that...ice-bound furnace that I *know* is in there, deep inside you. You're a frigid woman and I'm a frigid man, as I wish to be—*will* to be. I have a very strong will, Ms Harlow. I will it because it's *good* to be cold. It lets you control yourself, control...*everything*. You'll discover things with me. Oh I've waited for you so long!...Have you ever been beaten? Not in anger but to answer a profound desire? I'm trembling. And so are you. I can feel you trembling. Have you ever beaten a man, a lover? Because he *wanted* it, *begged* for it? Have you ever had a real, honest-to-god slave? Someone completely and voluntarily in your power?"

Violently trembling now he leaned against her with his mouth in her hair—her own fresh-scented wavy goldred hair. He squeezed her breasts with both hands and his voice shook, "We can do these things, Catherine! You and me—Catherine! Come inside!"

A tense moment passed in which everything was possible. Then the room burst, it exploded with revolving lights, the thundering heavy metal beat with jungle primate shrieks and screams and the tomtom attack of gangsta rap and cretinous rhymes and the machines jerking and grinding and spanking...as Kit went rushing off down the corridor laughing without control.

At its end she stopped, half-collapsed at the foot of the stairs. To recover her composure she lit a cigarette, then tossed her hair as she looked back with a wildly silent smile at the disconcerted janitor still trembling in his doorway and doing the only thing he had left to do—look from her to the wall switch she had struck to save herself, and back, with piteous adoration, to his goddess even as she went up the stairs to the vestibule door and was gone.

Ten

Sitting in his oversized office that had his name on the door and a shared secretary out front, Tom was not just tired; he was asking himself, with a catch in his throat, if he was depressed.

He could not see the point of all this hard work he was doing. He was at cross purposes with the staff, they vetoed the novels he liked, offering fatuous, specious reasons, and offered for approval novels he despised. The salary was astoundingly good. But—why? What had earned him this fantastic promotion?

Why was he so suddenly and effortlessly, one might even say involuntarily, a man whose photograph appeared in slick magazines in a group of success stories?

A reporter from The New York Times Magazine had just called to arrange an interview. What did I do to deserve this? he kept asking himself.

He sensed that his life stood on a fulcrum. The elation of his promotion having thoroughly eroded, he felt he could fall either way and that he had no control over it. Foote had picked him, he did not know why, and it was clear that that was all he was going to do for him. There's your job, you'll earn a lot of money, do it any way you know how, just keep your nose clean. That Publishing Realities lecture. Okay, the pay was good, the position was a big step up. But. He never had any time for himself, working away half the night every night and all weekend. Kit on the other hand seemed to have hardly anything to do. Nothing made any sense. He had no time to see her and was worn out when he did. At this rate he would lose her to somebody else, and what good would all this money and status be then?

Now Christmas was coming. He had to get away. Leave all these manuscripts and deals and contracts behind and take a good long Christmas holiday. With Kit. Without her was unthinkable. All the offices in all the wings and departments of the building were buzzing with how many shopping days were left and the office parties being planned and how wild they were last year, plus the old rumors about things going on in the penthouse that would frazzle your hair.

Plus the new rumor that the oil tanker marooned in the bay was in worse shape than the authorities were willing to admit; that they did not know what to do about it or about the oil that was leaking into the bay faster than anybody had anticipated, producing an oil slick that was starting to grab headlines.

The rumor about Foote was just that, a rumor, probably groundless. But the tanker. Wildlife could suffer. The oil could burn. The tanker could explode.

Turning the pages of a book report, he sighed. If only.

If only he could find the time to take Kit up in the Statue of Liberty where, from all accounts, the view of the tanker was unbeatable...Fuckit! Why was he suddenly so unable to do the things he most wanted to do? Why was he so *paralyzed*?

Someone came into his office. He looked up and was almost paralyzed for real. Mr. Foote? Here?

Foote looked pleased that he was doing something unnatural.

"Things coming along, Tom?" he said. "Everything all right? Any red hot prospects? I hope you've not been too distracted by the goings-on in the river. Mind you, I wouldn't blame you. It's a very distracting business to say the least."

All this before Tom could say a word. But that was only the start of it.

"One man dead, I hear." After a pause: "What do you think, Tom, is there life after death?"

"Life after death?"

Foote had not sat down, so Tom was now standing. He stood a head taller, and felt about that much dumber than the old...fox. (Why fox? Well, why not? That's what he is. A fox. That wrinkled forehead, the slow steady watchful gaze—in his case that equals fox. Wanting to know what people think. Watching them think.)

"Well," he hunted around, "there are people, maybe even scientists, who believe we go on in some way. They present metaphysical arguments." Nodding, smiling, Foote waited for more, so Tom stumbled on. "I guess it comes down to how. We go on as ashes and dust—but I don't suppose you mean that. How much are we meant to keep? There's reincarnation, of course. But, I think you mean something more? Like keeping one's identity? One's character?"

"Everything! All the imperfections—everything. The ego—*le moi*, as the French say. The me. What do you think?"

What Tom thought was, Does my job depend on my answer? So he was careful with that answer. He gave it a lot of thought. And then said what he thought. "I don't think so."

Foote looked at him, nodding expressionlessly.

With a look of indulgence and regret—after all, it was clear whom they were talking about—Tom added with just a touch of cruel satisfaction to the man who had everything (to lose), "When you're dead you're dead."

Foote wandered to the window and the somewhat restricted panoramic view of the river. "Maybe," he said. "Maybe not."

"You think there's a possibility?" Tom said, trying not to let the ridicule show.

"Have you heard about cryogenics?" Foote turned from the window.

"Sounds familiar, but...."

"To put it crudely, you freeze the patient and unfreeze him later, when the cure has been found for the ailment that killed him."

Interesting, Tom thought, he says "him", not "them".

"That sounds pretty optimistic," he said. "I guess I was forgetting about scientific genius."

"But that's just it," said Foote with a surprising note of triumph in his voice, his face radiant. "Scientific genius. I prefer to call it scientific discovery. It's there, we just have to find it. And they have found...." He looked happy.

"Cryogenics."

"Exactly."

"Amazing! But, of course, that's not the same thing. What about all those pre-cryogenic dead? Are they out there surviving or not? I thought that was what we were talking about."

"Yes, that's one question. But it does no harm to have an alternate means of achieving the same thing, does it. That tanker is in trouble. It's listing more than it was this morning. There's an oil slick."

Tom joined him at the window. Not much to see from here—part of the tanker and one fireboat and some seagulls. "There is? Is it a big one?"

"You can't tell from here, but there is one. I've had it confirmed."

"Then there's danger of a fire?"

"It could get out of control." Foote moved to an armchair. It had a twin and Tom, still wondering about the reason for the visit, took the second one. Both chairs were positioned to face the desk and each other.

"I understand you want to go ahead with that Desmond Raines novel."

It had the sound of an accusation, and Tom went straight on the defensive.

"Well, you know, I think it's an important book."

"Will it make money?"

"That depends. It could."

"What are the odds?"

"Well, Sir, that would depend on...a few things."

"Politics, in other words?" It was a sort of rhetorical question and Tom sort of nodded. "I see," said Foote.

Wondering just what he did see, Tom lit a cigarette after asking the indulgence of the healthy old nonsmoker, who permitted smoking even in non-public places.

"Go right ahead," Foote said, "it doesn't bother me." Then, putting his palms together as if in prayer, he went on, "I'm a liberal democrat. My voting record is well known. Through my foundation I give large sums of money in charity to universities and social justice groups. I have no wish to antagonize the NAACP or any other minority organization engaged in civil rights and...that sort of thing. And black columnists have made Raines a cause célèbre. They don't like him. If they don't like him, we don't like him."

Tom was stunned. He had not expected such an abject avowal of deference to minority power from this pillar of the establishment. Was this a song of surrender? Was he, Tom, being given inadvertently a glimpse at the real movement of the atoms inside the publishing polity?

Tom read The New York Times every day. Very liberal. But the times they were a-changing. Was Foote behind the Times or the times? More to the point, did he, like all the country's movers and shakers, know things that ordinary folk like Tom simply had no access to? Was he a member of the Kissinger think tank? Did he subscribe to The Oxford Club?

"You're talking about liberal columnists, aren't you, Mr. Foote? But what about the neo-conservatives, and the independent columnists impatient with political correctness? Some of them are black."

"Yes, I know. But they're not as loud as the others. I don't hear them."

"The loud ones are the demagogues. I think the country is turning against them. The elections and polls have been showing that over and over."

"I know, but what did those Republican majorities accomplish? You see, elections are one thing and social justice is another. The good fight goes on regardless of how the last election may have gone. We can't suddenly drop our friends just because of an electoral blip or two, can we."

"Not if they really are our friends, no."

"Are they not our friends?"

"Yes, as long as we have something they want, and continue to want. One never knows how militants will move. Anyway I don't think friendship is the question, I think it's alliances. I think it's fairness. I think it's cultural affinity. I think it's morality. Raines is a moral person. I think we should make him an ally. I think we should publish him and to hell with the columnists and organizations and rabble rousers."

Foote scratched an itch on his face thoughtfully. Tom figured he might just have talked himself out of a job. The Foote Foundation was easily as liberal as the Ford or MacArthur or Mellon

Foundations. Minority and Third World program officers were in every department, doling out the money to their favorite groups. A Welsh wildness was in him. Raines was right, Foote was wrong. Even if it cost him his job this was the time to assert himself with the boss (since he could not do it with his own staff).

"Maybe you're right," Foote surprised him. "We wouldn't want to be...monolithic. Or blinkered. Very well, carry on with it. What's the situation?"

Tom was so surprised, and so relieved, he could not think. He nearly had to remind himself who Raines was. He tried to understand the strange capitulation while at the same time trying to create phrases for his pitch for Raines and his novel—which only now he saw really *was* very important to him. He had to ask and keep asking himself *why*. Was there a political motive lurking behind his own decision to back the novel? In that case, what about its literary merits? And his own integrity—his very credibility as an editor?

"The situation? Well...Raines himself is uncertain what to do. He needs our support, our encouragement. It can't be easy for him. But he knows what's right and I know what's right and—I need to know if you're behind me on this."

"Absolutely," Foote said. "If it's a question of moral integrity, you can count on me."

Tom's eyes widened as if in a spiritual awakening.

"That's such a marvelous thing to hear you say, Mr. Foote. I've been so, you know, confused." Tom realized he was gushing, spilling his guts, being incontinent, but was unable to close it down. "I honestly didn't know if I really wanted this job, to be honest. But your saying that, well, that changes things. I can really go forward now. It's what I needed to hear."

"I'm glad. I want us to be one family here. I want you to know in your heart that you'll never be out on a limb entirely by yourself, not while you're working for me."

Tom drew a deep breath that ended in a sigh—a shivering sigh that, reverberating in his ears, both exposed and emulsified the awful doubts and anxieties that had been tormenting him. He felt energized, renewed. He now had something to *do*. He was going to be *useful*, was going to make his *contribution*. Oh brave new world!

But Kit had to be part of it. He had a wild idea to bring up the subject of Kit in the hope that the old man, this father figure, would produce a happy solution. After all, he needed only snap his fingers for countless Sesames to spring open. But Foote was already on his way out.

"You will keep me abreast of the Raines novel, won't you, Tom? I've a special interest in it," Foote said as he went out.

"I sure will, Mr. Foote!" Tom foolishly called after his already vanished boss. Then he sat back down, disoriented and with a happy imbecilic look on his face.

Eleven

Zudd found himself drawn to the river. He could not stay away for long. He had found a perch on a rotted wharf and looked on with the serene excitement of someone staring into a fire.

Fireboats circled the tanker incessantly, hoses at the ready. The tugs were trying to pull her out to sea or at least further out into the bay. The leakage of oil was a trickle that was widening. To avoid it, the ferries kept changing their lanes. And they were nothing if not crowded.

Even between rush hours. During them, so many passengers crowded the upriver side that the boats actually listed. Loudspeakers dramatically warned them not to throw lighted cigarettes or matches into the oilslicked water. Kids wearing untied sneakers and baggy pants and teeshirts with obscene messages of course did both. One of the teeshirts, worn by a plump gumpopping girl in jeans torn expressly at the buttocks, quoted Wordsworth with poetic license: "Bliss was it at that dawn to be alive/But to be young was fucking heaven".

Every time the tugs got a grip on the tanker and pulled, the flow of oil quickened. When they tried a different maneuver, though it slowed the leak it made the vessel list further. Already the stern was dangerously low in the water.

An attempt to pump the oil into a smaller tanker had to be abandoned. The media offered conflicting reports and analyses by experts happy to be summoned by television anchorpersons, but nobody really knew what exactly was happening or why. There was talk of corruption and buckpassing and incompetence and racism—the dead seaman was a Nigerian—and of Higher Interests.

On day five the last towing attempt was abandoned. The remaining crewpersons (the cook was a Portuguese woman) were removed. River traffic was closed off.

Yet there was a vibrant sense of excitement. Everybody but the police and firemen felt it was a wonderfully exciting thing to have happen in their city. For once, people had something to fear besides their fellow New Yorkers, or a terrorist plot. They stood shoulder to shoulder with junkies, muggers, pedophiles, hoodlums, pickpockets and gaped with fascination at something that might be big enough to hurt them all equally while remaining fathomable, unlike attacks by space aliens or terrorists. There was talk in the media of horrible pollution, fire and smoke, cancerous ecological repercussions. They were glad not to have missed it by being away somewhere. This was special. People would be talking about it for years the way they did about the great blizzards and hurricanes and high-fatality fires. This could be one of the big ones! And they were seeing it in real time, with their own eyes! Breaking news!

Dead fish floated everywhere, oil coated the feathers of seagulls. Compassionate citizens pulled them out and treated them with detergents and chemical washes and rinses, making honest mistakes. It made little difference (except to the ubiquitous reporters and photographers intent on recording absolutely everything), they died anyway.

And Zudd looked upon all this and was enthralled.

He fantasized a sheet of flame running across the water like a beautiful sunflare—burning and charring and breaking every one of Nature's sacred cycles that rose up in righteous preciosity in its path, smashing them to pieces, one after the other…Ah!

Any burning floating object could do it. Picturing this, and the explosion that would follow, triggering a series of detonations that would set this part of the world on fire, his eyes gleamed as if already the flames were there, reflected.

It almost distracted him from his primary concern of how to get that woman back into his apartment. He had let her get away, had her in his power and let her escape! That switch! How had she thought of it? At such a moment! What fantastic cool! He adored her more than ever.

He was sure she wanted to come back. But she would have to be pushed. How? How to lure her back in?

Twice since that day she had been back to the penthouse. The first time, he waited behind his corridor door and listened to the well-oiled doors of elevator and street open and close with scarcely a sound. He looked into the vestibule half expecting to see her but saw only the remains of a goldtipped cigarette blithely burning away on the ashtray as if jeering at him. And smelled that post-sauna French perfume.

The second time he caught her. He thrust open the hall door as she was about to reach the street door. He thought the sound might stop her. He saw a hesitation, no more, and it was only when she was outside that she turned and shot a look back at him from those beautiful eyes that pinned him to his empty vestibule, empty corridors, his empty basement hi-tech pleasures.

He saw her every weekday—in the halls, the cafeteria—as he prowled her most frequented floors with just that hope. Weekends were a torture. And when on Monday she went by without more than a glance and a perfunctory smile he was almost happy, just to have her back. The rest of the week her manner tormented him, but no matter. He drew solace from her haughty indifference. It seemed to be reserved for him, only him—she was friendly enough with everybody else, including custodians.

He stared so hard sometimes, so desperately, he was sure he had drawn attention to himself. He must not antagonize that old rat up in the penthouse, or cause any trouble. Catherine Harlow was his, she belonged to him. But nobody must know it.

What was holding her back? Fear of compromising her relationship with the old bastard? She didn't *seem* the kind to shrink from risk—on the contrary, she seemed to crave it. And she *wanted this*—he was sure of it! Had he not felt her trembling against him, even as he too had trembled? He knew what she was waiting for. She was waiting for The Lure. The lure that would trap her. Laughing at him and waiting. Daring him.

And there was Tom Hutchins.

Once she had gone all the way over to the other wing to visit him. Sometimes they met in the cafeteria for coffee. Apparently they were not seeing very much of each other these days.

That too was an interesting development, that transfer of Hutchins to another department. Night after night he was one of the last to leave. The old boy certainly knew how to go about things, you had to hand it to him. His mother had never been able to resurface after his birth, once the Footes had cranked up their legal-political-financial engine and seen to it that every one of her claims and charges was ignored by the press and ridiculed by high-profile lawyers and spokespersons. Well, he was going to take care of daddy in his own way, in his own good time. There was no hurry. Catherine Harlow was more urgent.

Then he had his idea. He was a chip off the old block, all right! It was sure to work. If not the first time (Hutchins might not be in his office when he called, or at home) then the second.

Zudd was so excited he went straight to his apartment and threw the master switch. With the pretty blonde mannequin head substituting—not for long, he hoped—for the beautiful Catherine he placed himself with lowered trousers across the furry lap and gave himself a good spanking. So great was his ecstasy that he waited until it was almost too late before choking off the tremendous release that gathered in his loins to strike, serpentlike.

Twelve

The loudness of the music surprised her because it sounded loud without being loud. And it was classical. She had always meant to get better acquainted with classical music but had never found the time. Tom was an addict, and Katz played it on his radio sometimes as background music, and now Foote. The loudness reminded her of that music in the basement apartment of that weird, strangely interesting, oddly attractive, even fascinating Homer Zudd (and what kind of name was that? Was it his real name? If so was it Anglo-Saxon, or some crazy Balkan name?) But where that was earsplitting loud, this was a quiet, controlled kind of loud. During the first break she asked Mr. Foote what it was.

Harrison Foote raised his profile and listened. "I believe that's… Rameau? Handel? Telemann? No…I know! it's Praetorius— 'Terpsichore.' Dances. Do you like it?"

"It's beautiful. What gets me is, well, how loud it is without being loud. Do you know what I mean?"

"Yes, and bless you, my dear, that's an excellent observation. You *are* an extraordinary young woman, Catherine! And very charming. You do have unsuspected qualities."

Patronizing. She would not have taken that from a younger man, or a less elitist one. She never forgot that she was dealing with a Foote. She even found herself blushing at the flattery. "When you compare it with today's music, which is so *loud* loud," she said.

"The heavy metal and the punk rock and the gangsta rap," he sighed. "Still, it's your music, isn't it—I mean your generation—You don't mean you prefer this?"

"Well, not *prefer*, but, well, I'm glad this is here. I'm glad it *exists.*"

"I'm so happy to hear you say that. One hears that so rarely from the young. It sometimes seems as if the younger generations want our classical culture to simply disappear."

"I know there's a debate going on in the universities about Western civilization and multiculturalism and all that," Kit said, hoping not to have to expound. She knew this because Tom had talked about it, and that was as much as she remembered of his peroration on the subject. He had gone on and on until he noticed her stifling a yawn.

"Does that mean you're tired, or just not interested?" he had said in his petulant way.

"It's not that I'm not *interested*, but, well, that big fight between liberals and conservatives is just not something I want to get into. Just tell me who won when it's over and let's get on with it."

"With what?"

"Life. You know. What we're trying to live."

Tom at that point had surprised her by talking heatedly about his new black author. Which surprised her because, one, changing the subject wasn't like him, and two, she perceived him as a rebellious anti-revolutionary type, so what was he doing championing a black author, who was undoubtedly one of those black revolutionaries, unless he was an Uncle Tom, and Tom would never support an Uncle Tom. And what would the black author have to say about this? Black leaders as a rule defended and were eloquent rationalizers for their inner city *brothers*. They had found their political voice and were not about to give it up, whatever some maverick author or some quixotic Welshman said. Politics! Her alcoholic father, who played around, was a rightwing Republican, and her promiscuous mother, who drank, was a leftwing Democrat. So much for liberal or conservative—choose! She herself was determined to stay on the side of pragmatism. Sorry, alcoholic dad, I have to go with promiscuous mom. She's winning, and anyway hers is, allegedly, the humane, compassionate, caring side. How can I oppose that?

"Dear Catherine," said Foote, "I'm glad it exists and I'm glad you exist. I have a great weakness for beautiful things, and you and the music are two of them." With a gesture toward his painting: "Well, what do you think of it now?"

"It's gorgeous. But who is it? I mean it does look like me but there's something about her eyes and her mouth...I think she looks a little *hard*. That's not me."

"Bless you, you are perceptive. You've uncovered my secret. It's Lady de Winter. You know, 'The Three Musketeers?'"

"I've seen the movie. I seem to remember she was a bitch."

"No, you're an angel, and, yes, she was very wicked, a villain. We used to say 'villainess', you know," he added with a chuckle, "but a magnificent and very beautiful villain. I've always felt attracted to her. There's *some*thing there. I like to think she looked like you."

"Really!" Smiling, eyes wide, she gazed at the canvas, trying to recall more of the story. D'Artagnan loved her. His new friend, the Musketeer, who was a count, had found out about her after they were married, and he branded her and thought he had got rid of her. She bewitched everybody. She had murdered. Kit recalled thinking how stupid men could be with a woman like that, a real femme fatale. How they longed to be made into innocuous pets. Lady de Winter! Now how would a movie billboard put it? Catherine Harlow is Lady de Winter. The image gave her goose pimples.

The posing was easier after that.

If only it weren't for that half hour in the solarium.

After the sun lamps and sauna, and the revulsion that started with the rubdowns and did not end until he lay on his back dozing with his monogrammed towel over his middle and his outflung hand not three inches from an intercom with a red button she had always thought must be his direct line to the stock market, she lay on her side clenching into a fist until it hurt the hand that had given him his thankfully unseen pleasure behind her.

Slowly the repugnance filtered out and she forced herself, once again, to start counting: the money, her blessings, her possibilities.

It was always at this point that she decided not to tell Tom, at least not yet. How could he understand? What did a man know, with his priapic drives and his purity obsessions? Experience—and men's horrifying confessions—had taught her never, never to confess. *Never.*

This old man was not an elitist lightweight. He had ideas. He talked to her. Sometimes he betrayed his own instinct for discretion and spoke about things she thought he withheld from his colleagues and friends, maybe even from his family. (What was she, then? None of the above? *All* of the above?) His wife, who like a royal consort was in the media as much as he was but rarely at the same events, was never mentioned.

He talked mostly about his siblings. There was a Foote who lived in Paris and wrote about food in the New York Times. There was one who was running for the Senate in Florida. Another was an anthropologist rummaging in New Guinea. He told indiscreet stories about them, of sexual adventures and divorces and adulteries. She had seen it all in the newspapers, or most of it, but to hear it from him. It showed her, once again, that one thing the rich were not was straightlaced. There was one about a myopic cousin who had taken a society lady home from a party, given her a drink, and proceeded to undress only to discover, when he had replaced his thick glasses, that she was still fully clothed and had no intention, moreover, of following his lead. Foote laughed a lot while telling that one. Then there were his prep school and college days, his early trips to Europe. Everything reminded him of something. He would look away smiling and recall an incident.

Then they got back to work.

The posing and the talking were the fun part. That was one Foote. The activity in the solarium, that followed, that was the other one.

And she was unable to reconcile the two, the one that amused and impressed and delighted her and the one that repelled her.

That second one was like the myopic cousin, and she the party lady except that that gal had known how to keep her clothes on. Face it, she told herself, this particular Distinguished Old Gentleman, of Best Families and Exclusive Clubs and no need to ever go about with vulgar cash on his person, this sensitive old man with beautiful manners who doubles as the satyr of the solarium is putting something over on you. He is having his way with you. He is buying you. Well, isn't he? No! It's not like that at all!

At this point, with depression threatening, and a migraine

waiting for her in her apartment, the daring thought always came to her to pay another visit to the man in the basement.

The last time, she thought, smiling, he had actually caught her, had thrown that door open just as she, aware without looking, was going out the street door laughing to herself. What would he do this time? The savory thought came to her that she could probably have him fired with a word to Foote. A mere custodian! Or was there in fact a special relationship between them, as Zudd had claimed?

It might be fun to find out.

But no, that hardly mattered. She had a direct line of attack. She had enough power over him as it was. She had felt the power pulsing that time, and all the times she had run into him since. The question was, did she want to use it?

I just might.

Descending the eighty floors silently, afloat with champagne lightness, she composed herself, lighting a cigarette and setting her face with the expression of arch but empathetic cool she reserved for all her suitors, high and low, and prepared herself mentally for any impertinence the custodian might present on her brief walk to the street door.

There was no one. She reached the door. "Ms Harlow?"

Smiling to herself she threw her routine glance at the man in the chocolate uniform while continuing to turn the doorknob.

"Tom Hutchins is out there."

Kit released the suddenly electrified door knob and stared at Zudd.

"I thought you'd want to know," he said, and vanished.

* * *

With no way of knowing when the desire to see her was going to overwhelm old Foote, Homer Zudd had to be on the lookout. Which was easy enough, since Foote never summoned her during working hours, and the street buzzer that announced visitors to the penthouse sounded in Zudd's apartment too. But her visits had, he had noticed, a not-so-casual twice-a-week pattern, and this time he was ready. As soon as she had stepped into the elevator he called Tom

Hutchins's office and, telling his secretary he did not want to disturb Mr. Hutchins, left a message: His fiancee wished urgently to meet him across the street from the Heavenly Haven Bar at seven sharp.

"Fiancee?" the surprised secretary said. Zudd hung up.

Then he waited, and felt the ravishing adrenaline pulsing in his veins with every minute that passed, until he could hardly bear the pleasure of the pain.

At seven he caught glimpses of Hutchins walking in impatient circles in the twilight, carrying a thick briefcase, staring at the sidewalk and continually looking east and west to see if she was coming.

Zudd smoked a cigarillo until the buzzer informed him the elevator was about to function. When it had performed its mission, and she had emerged, he made his rehearsed move: "Ms Harlow? Tom Hutchins is out there...I thought you might want to know."

Returning immediately to his apartment—having been careful not to sound exultant and to close his door without waiting for a response—he turned one of the black armchairs to face the closed circuit screen, as well as the door that stood wide open upon the hallway, and waited.

On the screen he saw her looking around for a way out. She opened the street door a bit and peered out, and quickly shut it again. Trapped! He saw her biting her lip, trying to think. Then he saw her coming to that other door, the door that led to his apartment, and vanish from the screen.

Now there she was again, descending the stairs, in the flesh. And she saw him. She stopped, thought for a moment, and came on. Christ but that woman knew how to walk, a voluptuous coordination of waves—of hair and unbuttoned white camelhair coat and sashaying hips. Then she was in his doorway, leaning against the door jamb with exquisite arrogance. And a touch of mockery. That and the legs and the sensuous curves of her figure, the erotic contours he knew carnally, *he had felt them with his hands, with his body pressed against hers,* and the shadowy eyes that he could not see, yet knew better than his own, that and the mockery made him nearly swoon.

Her face expressed conjecture, bemusement. Her hands were in the pockets. Her leather handbag hung from her wrist. Everything she did, everything about her had that effect on him, made him feel faint. And he knew she knew it. The two-way awareness, endlessly reverberating like Chinese mirrors, swelled this delicious sensation of ravishment and rapture to its bursting point.

"You wouldn't have something to do with that, would you?" she said.

Zudd, entranced, but also wary, made no reply.

"What do you know about me and Tom Hutchins." It was not so much a question as an accusation, and he stayed silent. "So you've been spying on me?" she said. Then, still directing her remarks as much to herself as to him, she said, "His being out there right now does sort of come in handy for you, doesn't it."

She did not appear to be angry. Nevertheless Zudd sat stiff and mute, waiting it out, taking no chances. He could lose her again.

"Well," she said finally with a little smile, "I willl have that drink."

Jumping up, Zudd indicated his bar: an end table with glasses, a bowl of ice cubes, a pitcher of water, and a bottle of Chivas Regal.

The movement got him his voice back.

"Very old," he said. "I know you like old Scotch whiskey."

"On the rocks."

Zudd poured her drink. As he was bringing it to her she flicked the master switch. In the explosion of noise and gangsta rap and marauding colored lights he stared at her, while she took it all in without haste—everything: the lights, the huge TV offering a detergent commercial, the blonde ape dummy paddling the air, the several mannequins. What held her finally was the movie screen, where a blonde in black lace lingerie and calf-high leather boots whipped in slow motion a darkhaired hairychested muscular man shackled to a bedstead. Except for an athletic supporter he was naked, and although the whip fell repeatedly across his buttocks no welts appeared on the skin. Yet he writhed, seemingly with pain—or ecstacy. After a moment he altered his writhing slightly, moving his head in a different way, and she changed her stance, reversing the position of her feet. Thus the camera doth make actors of us all. And the dummy with its incongruous blonde head and its pretty, haughty, expressionless face that looked as fresh and modest as a schoolgirl's kept whacking the air. Kit hit the switch again and silence returned.

Zudd waited for her next move.

With an abrupt laugh Kit walked into the apartment. She sat in one of the leather armchairs crossing her legs and took out a cigarette. Raising her chin and lowering her long false eyelashes she gave him a smiling speculative look. She lit the cigarette and blew a long white curler of smoke towards him. She laughed, a soft, mocking laugh, and saw him start to tremble.

Her smile faded as her satisfaction deepened. It faded because, though now she knew her power, she did not know what to do with it. He watching her like a dog and trembling, his eyes, like those of a dog, soft and brown with adoration. But there was not the attentiveness, the watchfulness of a dog, only the submission.

She held out her hand for the glass. He brought it to her and stood quivering. Without removing her eyes from his face she took a big drink of the whiskey. She put the glass down. She too was waiting. She was waiting for an idea to come to her. She felt in no hurry. Tom was out there prowling the sidewalk. She had lots of time.

"Hadn't you ought to shut the door?" she said, using a British construction borrowed from Foote. It surprised her that Zudd, for all his resemblance to a dumbstruck slave, did not leap to obey. Puzzled, exasperated, she smoked and waited for clarification, trying to understand what he wanted. She took another swallow of the whiskey.

Suddenly she knew. Asking him if he should close the door was off the mark. He needed to serve, and obey. *Commands* were what he wanted.

And she had *known* that, known it all along! *Sensed* it. And desired it! He wanted to be despised, humiliated, mistreated. And beaten. He had hinted as much. He was *begging* for it.

Uncertainty gave way to the clearest of illuminations like shafts of clarity breaking up a cloudbank of ignorance. It sundered and scattered what was left of her innocence. For some time she had thought of flagellation as an optional accessory of love play. After initial shock, she had accepted it, in theory, as normal—though she would not have accepted it in her own lovemaking any more than she could accept such other strange and apparently "normal" aberrations as lesbianism and promiscuity and—Katz's favorite—sex with multiple partners. But with this man it went deeper, to an uncharted underworld. The excitement she felt at this perception manifested itself in an unexpected way—in serenity.

Her features, already irradiated with an awareness of power, now relaxed with something even more powerful: understanding, the knowledge that before her stood a human being who was utterly helpless and at her mercy, because only she could supply what he craved.

Her features softened with an instinct of responsibility, of protection and compassion, a precognition of love that made her able to do what she now understood she must do for this man. And for herself. She felt her heart thudding, her breathing deepening, knew that her cheeks were flushed, her eyes sparkling, her skin tingling with health. And she was not surprised.

It was only a matter of arranging the moves. Chess players and power brokers did it every day. Foote did it every minute of his life. How easy, how simple! You only had to let your own blocked-up power pour free.

In a slow, quiet voice she said, "Go and shut the door." Watching him as he moved immediately to obey, she contemplated the possibilities.

She possessed a slave. A wonderful possession! But it posed an unforeseen problem. She knew what *he* wanted—but what did *she* want? Love, of course. Climax with the *right* man. And this was hardly that. Love, climax, yes. And with the right man, yes. But on that road, towards that goal, what little needs lurked by the wayside, what thirsts, what number of gaping chickmouths?

Having shut the door, he turned around and waited. So craven, so complete was his submission that he made it clear he would not make the slightest move without a direct command. Still searching for ideas, for the right idea, she ordered him to flick the master switch, and looked around once more at the noise and lights and convulsive movements. After a while she had him switch it off. Nothing there. But she was into it now.

She ordered him to kneel before her. As he knelt she raised her right foot and commanded him to remove her shoe. Then the stocking? She froze in indecision. She could not tell him to take *that* off. Why not, if he was her slave? Because...she did not trust him that far. Not yet. She was alone in his apartment, in the basement, in a subterranean cavern—What if he went wild? He might be a slave, but she was a little afraid of him, too (as one is of slaves). It was part of the excitement.

"Take off my stocking."

This he did with the carefulness of a nurse. And held her foot, gazing down at it placidly, awaiting her commands. His utter placidity dazzled her. It was a kind of Zen-like reconciliation with himself, with his desires, his ambitions, his fate. She had seen it in Renaissance paintings, the faithful in prayer. Meditating monks.

It made her feel like the Old Testament God with a repentant rebel before her begging forgiveness, and ready to do whatever was commanded. So she said, "Kiss my foot," and the assiduousness, the abandon, the sensuality, the *love* that he did it with made her feel giddy with power, and the power built on itself. Her chronic insecurity melted in the heat of his surrender.

"Stop."

He sat crouched over her foot, gazing at the varnished toenails, awaiting her orders, and she marveled at the mystery, so alien to her, of total submission. Even in that mesmerized moment of surrender on the massage table with old Foote she had not done that. Not that.

"Go ahead," she said.

Her own voice impressed her with its tone of authority. She made him make love to her foot, the whole foot, with special attention to her big toe. When he came to a corn she instinctively drew back, but he clung to it with a strange insistence that made her relent, and he made hungry love to it too. Kit drifted between the polar sensations of sweet languor and fulfilling authority with their opposite needs.

After a while she moved him up her leg. She made him linger at the back of her knee. Her skirt rode at the very top of her thighs like the briefest of miniskirts. She watched him, wondering at her excitement. So many kissing lips and licking tongues had traveled this path while she had tried to feel something, desperately telling herself to feel something, something direct and honest and pure, something...transcendental, without ever a positive result. How was it possible that this strange creature was affecting her in this way, merely by submitting? They had *all* submitted.

No, they had not all submitted. With them, the submission was a means toward an end. With him, *it* was the end—all that he wanted. But, was that possible?

He kept moving up her thigh, not in a rush, singling out every square inch for special attention like a concerned craftsman. She thought she heard a low moaning, droning sound, like the hum of a bee. She smiled to herself, content to let him continue, until he reached around under her skirt and, with his hands under her buns, prepared to gather her up to his face like a peasant with a plate of soup and she said, in an alarmed, abrupt voice that surprised her, "Stop!"

But he did not stop. He went blindly on. She repeated "Stop!" and slapped his face, not hard, but smartly, and he stopped. Abject, breathing hard, unrepentant but obedient. She saw it all. This slave, her first, was going to be hard to control. A delicious challenge.

She told him to stand, and considered him. Then she sent him to the dummy that she felt was the key to all this. She made him switch it on and place himself across the ape's knees, and as the paddle rose and fell with its gears grinding and whirring his eyes rolled towards her in a plea that she understood, for she too knew this was only an appetizer. Then, her eyes wide with the fullness of this understanding she very calmly ordered him to switch it off and to bring her the paddle, which he did obediently as any willing slave, and to bare his bottom—"Take down your pants. Take down your briefs"—and after studying this erogenous package with its uncertain semi-erection that was hers to command and enjoy as she wished, she found she was unable to keep herself outside the scenario.

Parting the coat she unbuttoned her blouse, unhooked the bra and freed her breasts. She let him gaze at her for a moment, then ordered him across her knees. He obeyed without a murmur, getting across her knees like a small boy. She brought the paddle down, not hard, then harder and faster, counting to herself without meaning to, until she had reached six. But something was wrong. I don't care for this, she found herself thinking. Why do I want this man? I don't want him. I don't know what I'm doing here. Why am I doing this?

His buttocks were red, and she was bored and embarrassed. And he was too heavy. This is so stupid, she thought. "Get up," she said to the inert body.

Even that was awkward, he putting his hands to the floor to get to his feet. But then she saw his glassy staring eyes and a full erection now and felt she was on the right path. A tension crackled between them, exciting her beyond anything in her experience.

"Take off *everything*," she said, and was surprised at her voice, so calm it was, although her heart was beating very fast. Planning her moves with voluptuous delight at this sumptuous buffet of possibilities, she thought, again with surprise, that this was her moment, she had him exactly where she wanted him.

Those soft submissive eyes were passively watching her.

She slipped out of everything but her skirt. "Carry me to the bed."

His strength surprised her, despite the obvious muscularity of his neck and arms. It struck her that for all her amorous experiences she had never been carried to a bed. Or held more lightly.

Her head rested on a blue cushion, the red hair flaring along the headboard. She knew instinctively that it must make a lovely sight. "Now go on," she said, and closed her eyes as he made oral love to her, and dreamed and smiled, and love swelled inside her, and suddenly, "Beat me! Hit me! Spank me! Hard!" she cried. "Please! I want you to beat me!" So he turned her over with a simple motion and spanked her as she writhed under the smart blows. She turned over again and held out her arms. "Now! Take me now! Take me now! Fuck me! Fuck me now! Do it! Now! Yes! Oh yes!" Things were happening inside her that had not happened before, not even that one surprising time with Foote, unfamiliar sensations that told her she was totally ready as he fell upon her, entered her, their apposite movements making one harmonious rhythm. Her mouth opened in silent laughing anguish as the long awaited cascade started up—And then he stopped.

"No!" she cried, "No! Don't stop! What are you doing? Don't stop! I order you, I command you to come! Come! *Please! Why don't you come!*"

Wailing she beat him with her fist, pulled his hair, scratched his back. But she saw his face—the muscles working heedless of her commands and screams and pleas. He was fighting a private struggle—he too—with eyes shut tight; triumphing once again over the spasm that had threatened to shake him apart and leave him shattered, scattered, burnt out, dissolved. He choked it off with a fistlike grip of his loins, a grip stronger even than his need to prostrate himself before his queen.

* * *

Kit lay on her side, on the edge of the bed, almost off the mattress, with her back to Zudd. It was the way she lay in the solarium, but now she was not naked. Her skirt's hem lay across her hips. Her breathing had slowed, her fists were unclenched. She did not want to move. She did not want to think. The single most awful thing that had ever happened to her had just happened. She could not face thinking about that. The one person she most hated in all the world was there behind her. She did not want to see him, or think about him. But the thoughts came, regardless, and with them, inevitably, came questions. Questions requiring answers she had to have.

"Why," she said tonelessly. "Why did you do that."

And Zudd, propped against the wall on his elbow, said, "I had to."

"Why."

"I—I always—I have to."

"What does that mean, *you have to*."

"I can't...let that happen."

Kit raised her head a little. "What do you mean? Why not?"

"I just...can't."

Kit raised her head a little more and turned her head to look towards, not at him. "Why can't you? What do you mean, you *can't*? You were *there*, and you *stopped* it. You *stopped* it. *Why*?"

No answer came. She turned some more and looked at him. "I don't know where you're coming from. Is it some kind of problem you have? Has it ever been like...like *that* before?"

"Never."

"Yet you broke it off!"

"I had to!"

Kit sat up facing him, not straightening her clothes, ignoring the feeling of awkwardness. She thought, What kind of jerk am I? Humiliated, and by a janitor! And like that! Is that how he gets his kicks? By beatings and frustration? Is that *it*?

No. She could not accept that explanation. He looked too crestfallen. And he too had been so very close. She thought bitterly, He must be insane. How could he wait until the very last second, and still cut it off like that. What kind of an idiot am I, letting him do this to me. My *God*! What's the *matter* with me! *Humiliated*! By a *janitor*! And like that! Is that how he gets his kicks, this—this subterranean monster? This troglodyte? By tormenting women? Frustrating them—is that his thing?

But there, right there, was the challenge: If she got another chance she would push him over the edge, somehow she would do it. She felt robbed, violated. Her first orgasm, the first true one, was there, in limbo, in vitro, a happening waiting to happen. The bastard! But *she did have that power* over him . That was important to remember. She must not lose sight of that. She would have to learn to use it better.

One moment she hated him, the next she wanted to start over again and reach that place and wipe out the misfire—go to the edge and over. The sensation of being so close and losing it was more than she could bear. She had a right to that withheld ejaculation! It was hers! She still remembered her half-brother, when they were kids, yanking the soda away and leaving her with a useless straw in her mouth. Over and over. And laughing. Zudd, at least, was not laughing. He seemed as upset as she was.

She got up and straightened her skirt and added the rest of her clothing. She ran a small brush through her longhaired wig. Holding a mirror up to her face she applied the quick touches of makeup she had learned as a model. Then she lit a cigarette and sat down again with her drink. She swivelled to face the bed. She crossed her legs. She pulled deeply on her cigarette.

He too had got his clothes back on. He sat on the bed watching her, touching the welts her nails had left on his face and neck, waiting for her to say something.

Blowing out a hard curler of smoke, Kit took a good drink from her glass and gazed before her, licking her lips as she sought a foothold for a way out of the pit.

"You haven't told me why," she said finally.

He brooded his answer before releasing it.

"Because it's natural. It's Nature's way. And I hate Nature."

"You what? You hate Nature?"

Kit had never heard anyone say such a thing, except once.

"How can you hate Nature? Nature's all we've *got*."

"Not the way I see it."

Kit looked at him. "Is this some philosophy or something? Some kind of religious cult?"

"Just mine. There's nobody else. Not yet."

"So tell me about it."

Zudd fidgeted. He had never tried to explain it to anyone. He poured himself some Scotch and gulped it down and returned to the edge of the bed.

"Nature is like a mountain stream," he said. "Or a river. It starts out here and winds up there. Life, in other words. It's an unbroken cycle from birth to death. Like an electric circuit. Well, I break it!" He looked straight at her. "See what I mean? I *break the cycle*."

"You break it? How?"

"Every way I can. By not going along."

"But, what's your purpose?"

"To break Nature's hold. *On me*."

Kit was trying to make sense of these remarkable assertions. She already knew he was a kook, but how crazy *was* he?

"I knew a hippie once who hated Nature he said because he'd got his girl friend pregnant and she had an illegal abortion that nearly killed her, and he got so depressed he tried to commit suicide. He jumped from three stories up and it crippled him for life."

"The mistake was to get her pregnant in the first place," Zudd said.

"He hated condoms, too."

"That's not the answer," Zudd almost hissed. "The first law is to hold on to your sperm, keep it to yourself, inside yourself, don't let it go. The man who lets it go is killing himself the slow way. He might just as well go ahead and kill himself the quick way and get it over with, the way he did."

"Law? What law? Whose law?"

"Mine."

She could not help gaping at him.

"Is it really against your…your religion, or whatever, to have an orgasm? How can you make love that way? What do you mean he's killing himself? *Killing* himself? When he's having so much fun, such joy, such a celebration of *life*? You're not an unfrocked *priest* by the way, are you?"

"I'm not an unfrocked priest. Look. Every orgasm—I mean, I'm referring to the male, every ejaculation is a miniature surrender to death." He felt suddenly cold and started to shiver. "That's what they call it in Europe, you know—the little death. And I, I don't want those little deaths. That way I'll avoid the big one."

He watched her to see if she caught his meaning.

It took her a while. She had listened attentively, holding her cigarette beside her cheek with the wrist bent back in a consciously sophisticated way she had evolved. That hand now descended as astonishment sped across her face.

"Are you saying—you don't mean—you mean you want to avoid *death*? *Dying*? *Forever*? Is that what you're saying?"

He leaned forward excitedly, his passion now in full command. "If you can cut the river's flow, make it flow off in another direction—Don't you see?" He sat back. "I've done a lot of reading. I could talk about the World as Will, and Causality, and the will to reproduce, and male insects dying of exhaustion or else being eaten by the female right after fertilizing them, and *eternal recurrence in the circle as the symbol of Nature*. Don't you see? Schopenhauer, Nietzsche, Berkeley's system of perception, and a lot more, but what for? What I did was I took the best from everything and created a synthesis that I put into three words—*Smash the cycle*!

"Smash the cycle?"

"Smash it! Keep away from that finish line! After all, if you don't go to the wall you can't be shot."

"Of course you can. Random shooting goes on all the time.

Innocent people get shot just for taking a walk, or while sleeping in their beds behind brick walls."

"You know what I mean. It's just a metaphor. I'm talking about what we *can* control, not what we *can't*."

"I just don't think you can avoid it. I mean, everybody has to *die*." She couldn't believe she was having this discussion—with anyone, let alone the building's janitor. "Any scientist will tell you that. Any priest or philosopher. Any *any*thing."

"Who cares? What do they know?" Again Kit gaped. (It was a cool gape, that she had developed in her social and business adventures with New Yorkers. Her face simply went expressionless, even her eyes, especially her eyes, which stopped blinking.) This was strong stuff for her. Along with the upper crust and residents of Who's Who, these were her world's VIP's whose names he was tossing around. How could any sane person attack them? But Zudd charged on, "Do you think they really *know* anything? Those same scientists and philosophers will admit that nobody knows anything *for sure*. As for the priests, that's all fantasy and fable, and handed-down fantasy at that. But even if I can't avoid it altogether (this he tossed off as a dialectical concession for the sake of appearing reasonable), it can still prolong the journey to that finish line for a long, long time. If not indefinitely." He leaned forward again. "*If, not, indefinitely*. Because when you break a cycle, *you've broken it*. It is *broken!* Even Nature doesn't know what to do then."

His eyes beamed at her. The same eyes that had gone so utterly dull and soft with submission not fifteen minutes ago!

"Do you see?" he said.

Kit knew she did not possess the power of logic to enable her to follow his rationale, or the imagination that could adhere to his slippery metaphors. She was prosaic, practical. Sensible. She could respond to the imaginative—if it made sense; or if, lacking sense, it impressed others. Or if it overwhelmed her with science. But this guy was far out, there was nobody but her to impress—she suspected he had tried with others and failed; and it was down to science; and he was hardly a scientist, with a title before his name and half the alphabet after it. So what did he know? Precisely *his* question about *them*. Between the two she chose the scientists, and then delivered the only reasonable, rational judgment that came to her. "I think you're crazy."

His reaction scared her. He stiffened and lowered his eyes like a soldier being unfairly upbraided. His mouth tightened. He appeared to be struggling with an impulse to do something dramatic, and possibly violent.

"I'm sorry, Homer. What I mean is, it's so far *out*. I'm not used to hearing this kind of—I need some time to get used to it, you know?"

She saw him soften. It had been exactly the right thing to say. And she had called him Homer.

"Calling a man crazy doesn't make him crazy," he said with a child's petulance.

"I know that," she said. "I didn't really mean it."

"Others say it and they mean it. But it's like I said, nobody knows anything for absolute certain. You can't repeat that enough, you know. You can't! (His tone grew strident with the resentment of the chronically misunderstood.) They call me a crackpot but you should hear some of the crackpot ideas that come along. From responsible people. Scientists. Like those four scientists who said that people driving on the right side of the road causes tornadoes. Maybe you saw it in the papers a few years ago. And the TV anchorman smirked when he mentioned it, but the fact is nobody knows how they do start, so who can prove they're wrong? You can't! Well, nobody can prove me wrong either. But every time I would mention that to somebody—just a hint you understand—they would make some wisecrack. When people don't understand something, because they haven't got the information, or the imagination, they make a wisecrack. And that's if they don't rear up and reject it altogether, or even throw you out on your ear. But what do they know? They're fools, morons, ignoramuses! Let them laugh! Who cares what they think with their little bird brains. *I'm* laughing at *them*. At those... those *pigs*! Those *jackasses*! Those ignorant—"

"Stop it!" Kit said sharply.

She had it back. Her spirit. The quiet authority in her voice. It arrested him in mid-flight. He stopped talking, stopped gesturing. His hands fell to his sides as at a bugle call. Again he was alert only to her, a prisoner of her eyes, obedient to her voice.

"I can hear you," she explained quietly, "there's no need to shout." Her eyes gazed across at him, regally cool, and with, once again, the conviction that she and she alone held the key to his deepest desires. "Remember whom (she said whom) you're talking to." Zudd gave a chastened little nod, a scarcely visible smile of recognition. "Now go on."

He went on. It was easier now. The distorted ambience had been set right. All was back in place. Even an apostle of disruption like him needed this in order to function. All the great ones did. Was this contradiction the exception or the rule? For he might be the sworn enemy of Nature, but he reserved a role for Nature that would eventually thwart her and serve his own ends when he was ready.

Regaining his reasonable tone of voice he said, "Tell me this—Is Harrison Foote crazy?"

This startled her. It hit her where she genuflected.

"Of *course* not. What are you talking about?" But she wondered, Harrison Foote? The Foote Foundation? All that money and science and Progress with a capital P, the hiring and owning of geniuses, of people who either know everything or know how to find out fast, the toplevel movers of topsecret mysteries that you never hear about until thirty years later, all this at his fingertips while he remained the most perfect gentleman she had ever met—him crazy? This basement weirdo was the crazy one if anybody was. Yet…there was this improbable *intimacy* between the two. What did this privileged janitor know? And exactly how did he know it?

"What has Mr. Foote got to do with this…this kind of thing?"

"He wants to live forever too."

"Mr *Foote*?"

"Only he's going about it in a different way."

"But…He's at least seventy years *old.*"

"Seventy-three. So what?"

"Well , I mean, the Fountain of Youth is one thing, but—does he want to go on being *seventy years old? Forever?*—Why would he *want* to?"

"He doesn't want to give up all that money and power. And the importance. Think of it. People *like* him. He's worked at it. Politically he's on the side of the good people, the people with a heart—a liberal. But a liberal who votes Republican. So the liberals love him because he's an environmentalist and has compassion for the poor and the conservatives suck up to him because he votes their ticket and makes big campaign contributions to them too. Each side forgives what he does for the other side. Now that's not easy, is it, but he manages it somehow. The young like him because he comes out for them, the old like him because he's always joking and philosophizing about what it's like to be old. He takes care of himself. Do you know he works out every morning? And takes cold showers, and eats a low fat, low salt, low sugar diet? And takes his antioxidants religiously? And the way he dresses, in that casual but natty way, and combs his hair just right, and stays thin. Can you blame him for not wanting to give it all up? I've heard young women in the elevator gushing about what a beautiful face he has—what beautiful wrinkles, what a beautiful expression, what a beautiful *placidity*. God! It's a game, and he plays it with the skill of a master politician. So, naturally he doesn't want to hang it up. Do you blame him? How many seventy-three-year-old men have beautiful young models in their saunas? Why shouldn't he want to stick around as long as he can?"

"So what's his idea? If it's not like yours, what is it?"

"Did you notice all those red buttons everywhere, up there? It's a hi-tech intercom system with an alarm button in every room. At least one. Some rooms have more—one has three. The Finnish sauna, the Roman bath, the Hollywood solarium—there's even one by his commode. And they all connect to my switchboard and his clinic and his cryogenics company. I'm his backup system. He trusts me. And I live here. He wanted me to live here. I'm a kind of life guard. When that rings and if he's not on the other end telling me he's OK I double check with the Foote Clinic and the freezers *pronto*. One right after the other. To make sure they got the alert. And I mean pronto—He's tested me a few times."

"Cryogenics? You mean, they put him in deep freeze for twenty years or so?"

"Or thirty. Or forty. However long it takes medical science to find the cure for what killed him. He thinks it'll be his heart. So they revive him and fix that and he lives until something else goes blooey, then they either fix that too or they freeze him again until they find that cure too. And so it goes—forever. Don't laugh, he's invested a lot of money and a lot of faith in this. Anyway, it's true that nobody dies of what's called old age. They always die of *something*. Something that medical science hasn't found the answer to yet."

"Well, then, it's scientific. That's different. Mr. Foote must know what he's doing, he's a very smart man."

"But he doesn't know about mentis interruptus."

"I never studied Latin."

"I made that up. It's what I've been telling you about—the breaking of the life cycle. You do it in the general way but also in as many particulars as possible, so that you confound the whole fundamental system, the natural design. You interrupt the decaying process. You think I'm just talking? I've trained myself! Stopping yourself right at the moment, right at the climax of something isn't easy! You think it was easy to stop myself like that? But I did it! I *have* to do it. You see that, don't you? I've built myself up to this with injections, pills, powders, potions, you name it. I've been immunizing myself against poisons, insecticides, tobacco, exhaust fumes, smoke, poison gas—I'll be indestructible! Think of it! Only something external like a knife or a bullet or a bomb will be able to kill me. And I'm more than halfway there, a lot more. I grind up the plastic from all these bottles and frozen dinners and cigarillo tips and mix it in with my meatballs and hamburgers and a special roll that I bake myself. It was a risk, when I started, sure, but I figured if it didn't kill me it would immunize me, if I did it very gradually. It might produce a mutation! A mutation that would enable me to thumb my nose at death! And it hasn't killed me *yet*, okay? I feel *fine*! So what about that? *Mutatis mutandis*—change every little thing as you go along and pretty soon you've changed the whole ball game! That's where I'm one up on the old boy. He needs the freezer and the whole warning system, and me, and the technology, and the technicians. I don't need anybody."

"You need me," Kit said.

Gravely, he nodded.

"Why?" she said.

"I can't tell you," he said finally. "Not yet."

"Does Mr. Foote know about any of this?"

"I'd never tell him. What for? He'd think I was crazy. He figures he has the answer with his alarm buttons and his freezers. But when they warm him up twenty, thirty years later and give him the latest miracle drug that cures him and he comes back to his penthouse that's waiting for him with a new generation of staff won't the old bastard be surprised to see *me*, haha—still going strong, ha ha! And maybe you, too. Won't he be surprised! Oh, I'm looking forward to that!" Zudd was walking up and down, grinning and talking excitedly and giving little high-pitched giggles. "No deep freezes, no pneumonia, no hoar frost to brush off, haha! And the beauty of it is it's free! No depending on clinics and doctors and temperature controls. No liquid nitrogen—nothing! *Mentis interruptus*! The WILL!"

"Maybe me, too, you said?"

Suddenly he was serious again. Solemn. His changes were startlingly dramatic, almost theatrical.

"Yes! If it's what you want. Do you? Do you want that? Think of it! We could start a new evolutionary line, a race of immortals!"

Not knowing whether to laugh or flee, Kit said, "For that you'll have to stop interrupting the mentis, won't you."

"For that I would!"

She looked at him. He was the god now, Jupiter, hurler of thunderbolts, ready to hurl the thunderbolt that would begin a new race of demigods immune to the mortal attacks of man's ingenuity. Yet she knew that with her eyes and voice she could change him back into trembling servility, attentive to her commands.

"And when would that be?"

"When I know the moment has arrived."

He seemed unaware of the incongruousness of his words and his vulnerability, his terrible need. "I'll know when it's the right time," he said. "And that's when I'll do it. That's when it will start. What a beginning that will be!"

"If you mean I would have to start eating plastic and everything, forget it."

Zudd frowned. "I've considered that. It might not be necessary. Our child would inherit my immunity, or some of it. I don't know, I'm not sure. That's why I have to wait. I have to think about it." He brooded on that, then got excited again. "Don't you see how fantastic it would be if you could help? But you already *are* helping—more than you realize! You don't have to eat plastic or drink poisons. You've been taking all kinds of drugs for one thing or another, you smoke, you eat in restaurants and fast food joints, you drink wine made with sulfites and liquids full of cafeine and who knows what else—You're doing your share without knowing it, don't you see?"

She saw. She didn't believe him, but she saw. But now he was excited again. He lit a cigarillo. He took a swig of the Scotch. He ate a chocolate selected precisely for its sugar and lead content. Chewing it, he fell into reverie. After a while he realized that it was very quiet and looked around to see The Look—Kit gazing steadily at him, calmly and wordlessly subduing him, commanding him. The chocolate went down in a hard swallow. His heart was pounding again. He waited, cowed and trembling.

"Come here."

He went to her and stood waiting, the cigarillo at his side.

"Give me that." She took the cigarillo and laid it in the ashtray beside her cigarette and looked at him again. "Drop your pants." When he had done that she leaned forward and took him in her mouth. His head tilted back, his eyes closed, and the pain of the struggle between his pleasure and his will ravaged his features until, at the last possible moment, when it appeared he was lost, he broke away. He staggered out of reach and stood shaking with knotted fists, his chest plunging and rising, gulping air, doubling over finally in the ecstatic agony of his triumph.

Kit stood up, snatched her purse. Her eyes leveled a fierce smiling challenge at him.

"We'll see about all this," she said, hitting the switch as she went out.

Thirteen

After waiting more than an hour in the cold Tom had gone across the street to The Heavenly Haven for a drink.

He had one at the bar, then another, trying to figure out what was going on. He tried calling her, no luck, and finally went home, troubled and angry and frustrated. And tired. And hungry. He ate half a sandwich.

The time he had lost waiting for her would have to be made up. His plate was too full. Too many manuscripts to be read and decisions made. On top of it all he had made the Raines novel his crusade. There was opposition, and he was furious at the infusion of politics into what should have been purely artistic considerations.

His opponents on the editorial board countered that he was the one who was being political by wanting to publish a novel that seemed indirectly to attack affirmative action. His reply, that it was not attacking it but exposing a flaw in human nature, drew smiles and smirks. He was badly outnumbered. But he was the boss.

Well, not exactly. Foote was the boss. And he was unable to get him to take a definite stand. The editors thought he was on their side. Tom thought he was on his side but that he was afraid of a counteroffensive by the liberal left. For that reason he had been an early convert to the anti-capitalist and feminist and all the other politically correct stances. His switchboards and reception desks and executive positions were manned by African-Americans, Asian-Americans, Native Americans, female Americans, gay Americans—anything but straight white male Americans. His Foundation did not bother with Americans at all, but went straight to the Third World for its personnel. His commercial empire had not been harassed by a single ethnic or political incident in thirty years. He was not about to risk his happy alliance with the liberals for a novel.

On the other hand, it was a good novel. It had the ring of honesty, of truth. It was well written, and very moving. You put it down with a sense of having had an unusual experience, and an edifying one. You felt you had read something far better than the usual run of novels being published. So the old man dawdled, and kept Tom sleepless.

Sitting down to resume work Tom saw that he had left his briefcase at the tavern. He rushed back in a cab, found it, and went out looking for another cab and there across the street was Kit doing the same thing.

Shouting her name he rushed across, barely missing being hit by a car.

"Where have you been, for Christ's sake? Where are you going? What's going on? What's the matter with you anyway? What's this all about?"

Kit looked at him, confused, distracted. Tom? Here? Then she remembered. *Still here, still waiting for her.* She ricocheted from delight to wonder to gratitude to suspicion to compassion. And back to wonder: Waiting? For her? *All this time?*

Then came the question she had forgotten all about. Why had he been there, outside that door, in the first place? What exactly had Zudd done? And in what way was she about to be exposed, embarrassed, eviscerated? Well, she didn't care. What she wanted now was to stay inside the protective cocoon of her thoughts. Tom, delighted though she always was to see him, was an interruption. She was still in the basement with that crazy exciting man and his crazy ideas.

"What time is it?" she asked Tom in a surprised voice, the sleeping beauty that has been kissed awake.

"The *time*? It's nearly midnight! What kind of a fog are you in? Are you high on some kind of drug or something?"

"What's the matter, Tom? Why are you so upset? What are you doing here?"

All logic seemingly gone, Tom could only stare with the helplessness of the bereft. She hadn't heard a word he'd said. "That's what I'm asking *you*. *I'm* here because I forgot my attache in that bar across the street." Kit cast a dreamy look at The Heavenly Haven as if it were the explanation to everything. "I was here in the first place because of your urgent, I repeat urgent message to meet you here at seven o'clock. Right here. Across the street from the bar. I might remind you that you did not show up and neither did you leave any further messages."

With her most endearingly concerned and innocent expression Kit said, "What message?"

Tom looked far left, then far right, then at her again.

"Seriously, are you high on something?"

"No. A little whiskey." She thought, Why don't I just lie and say yes I'm on speed or coke and get out of this hassle, whatever it is, and go home to bed?

"You don't remember leaving a message—two, in fact, one at my office and another with my service?"

"I did not leave any messages," Kit, a woman with an honesty obsession, said with a degree of satisfaction.

"Well *somebody* did."

"They did?"

"I'll have to look into this."

"Look into what?"

"Sweetie, if somebody's playing games with me, and in your name, I want to know who, and why."

"Does it really matter?"

"Of course it matters!" Before she could ask him not to shout, not that he had actually shouted, he said, "By the way, since you didn't leave the message, why are you here? And at this hour?"

Kit regrouped: She must keep Zudd out of this.

"That was the message," she said sweetly. "To meet me here at midnight."

"You said you didn't leave any message."

"I…forgot about that one."

"Kit, this isn't like you." They gazed at each other. "Okay, why urgent? And why here in particular?"

"Did I say urgent?"

"Both times."

That devil, Kit thought, imagining Zudd at the closed circuit TV screen. He's the Devil. He thinks of the details. "It wasn't really urgent," she said. "I was just, sort of, depressed."

"Depressed? About what? I mean, what made you say it was *urgent*? I mean, I'm not trying to pry, but something must have *happened*."

"There's this old man," Kit ventured, and caught her breath at the mistake.

"What old man?" Tom glanced at the building. "You mean Foote?"

"No, I don't mean Foote! Why should it be Mr. Foote? What do you mean? What are you suggesting?"

"We happen to be standing outside the Foote Building, so, naturally…What old man?"

"An old man of…eighty. He's been running after me. You know, one of those old Greek tycoon types who like young women."

"What about him?" Suddenly, with Kit looking more and more distressed, Tom feared the worst. "Have you been seeing him? Dating him? *Having sex with him?*"

"Don't be ridiculous! What do you take me for? A man of eighty! Look, what is this, a third degree?"

"Sweetheart, it's my constitutional right to try to understand *what's going on.*"

"Well you're being too inquisitive. And I don't owe you anything." (She said out of habit).

"Okay, you don't owe me anything." (Same habit.)

"Right!"

"Right. So? Are you going to fill me in?"

Looking at him Kit realized she did not want to lose Tom. There were any number of reasons, but the most salient was it would be too great a loss. She thought maybe she loved him. And although it was not the first time she had had this thought, this time it hit harder. Because how many people could you love, and in how many ways? Only one, she decided. And that could be Tom.

"There's this old man. He likes me. In fact he's in love with me.

He's married."

"So, what do you do with this old man, exactly?" His tone, his expression said he was not going to believe her answer, but also that he was not going to be difficult. Indeed, he had already decided not to look shocked or skeptical at anything he might hear, for fear of losing the rest of the story. To get the whole truth he would have to play the confidant. Already he had heard enough to start an ulceration in his stomach. But he had to know.

"Hardly anything—I mean, he's an *old man*. All I do is sort of reach behind me and—well, you know—" She dismissed both the act and the rest of her sentence with a deprecatory grimace—"It's *nothing*, Tom."

It took Tom a minute to understand. Then he shut his eyes tight as the blade in his gut (forget the ulcer; this was a *knife*) made a half-turn. (The other half in abeyance: it could be worse— wait, it probably was worse.) "This is awful, Kit! *Kit!* This is *awful*!"

"He's very...gentle, and considerate, and discreet, Tom. It's not what you think."

"But how far does he go?"

She said archly, "*No further*."

"God!" Tom wanted to take her into the bar, but their conversation there would be too easily overheard. It was safer out here where passersby glancing over caught only a word or two. He tried to lower his voice. Anguish forced it back up. "And is there some kind of payment for this?"

Kit stared at him, speechless with amazement. He took it for outrage, and began to formulate an apology. Suddenly she was in tears.

"I'm sorry," he said.

"You make me feel dirty and—used," she said, recovering quickly, dabbing her eyes with a tissue. She took out a cigarette. He lit it for her. "It's not like that at all," she said, exhaling a stream of smoke. "It's related to art."

"What?"

"Oh, you wouldn't understand! He's an artist. And a very good one."

"You mean, he paints pictures?"

"Yes. He's a very serious painter."

"But what's that got to do with you?"

"I model for him."

"Why?"

"What do you mean, why?"

"For pete's sake, there are artist's models for that. Professionals."

"He wanted me."

"Why you? Is it a portrait?"

"Sort of."

"Do you keep your clothes on?"

"I wear something. *Look.* I'm not answering any more of your—"

"I'm just trying to figure out who it is. El Greco was Greek, but he's dead. I can't think of any eighty-year-old Greek—does he have to be Greek?"

"I've had enough of this," Kit said looking frantically for a cab.

"Where does he live?"

"None of your business. Not here."

"So why are you here?"

"I told you, I came to meet you! And I'm sorry I did!"

"Then why were you hailing a cab? And why were you so surprised to see me?"

Kit turned back to him. She waited a moment, and another. Then, a step shy of crashing in tears, she instead said evenly, "Keep it up, Buster, and you won't see me ever again. And I mean that."

Tom took this in—the level look in her eyes, the level tone of her voice—and realized that she was not the woman he had known. One, something was happening to her that had not happened before; two, possibly as a result she was a different woman.

Baffled, scared, he blew out his breath, along with the other questions waiting in the queue, and made an adjustment.

"You wanted to meet me. I'm here. You wanted to talk about it. We're talking about it. So why are you running away?"

"I'm not running away. It was a mistake. And I'm tired. I'm going to bed."

"Just tell me one thing. What does your therapist say about it?"

"He thinks it's my most mature relationship."

"Really? He said that?"

"He doesn't think much of my previous relationships."

"What about me? I want to marry you. Isn't that mature?"

"You're not the first man that wanted to marry me."

"Okay," Tom conceded, and waited.

"He says you're a butterfly. You don't stick to anything, or any place."

"I will, with you."

"He says people will say anything to get what they want. Then when they get it they don't know why they said it."

"Is that what you think about me?"

"He's the one who said it. I don't know what to think about anything anymore."

"FUCK YOU! YOU SON OF A BITCH!"

They swung toward the sound and saw only the door to the Foote Building in the act of closing. It was the door Kit had come out of. Startled New Yorkers continued on as if nothing very unusual had happened.

"Who was that?" Tom said. "It was somebody inside the building. Who's that over there?"

He peered after a figure in an overcoat and a fur hat walking away rather quickly.

"I think that's the guy he said it to," Tom said. "You know, I could almost swear it's Harrison Foote."

"Don't be ridiculous," Kit said in unthinking reflex. She had seen at once that it was indeed Mr. Foote.

"I don't know," Tom insisted, "I've been seeing a lot of him lately, and I could swear that looked like him."

"Can you imagine anybody saying that to Harrison Foote?"

"A fired employee. A frustrated creditor. I can think of possibilities."

"There's that novelistic imagination again. Whoever said it is inside the building. *His* building."

"So? It could still be the fired employee. He just hasn't packed up and left yet."

"Or it could be that it was not Mr. Foote."

"Well, okay. I've never seen him in a coat and hat, so I can't be sure."

An empty cab was coming. Kit raised her hand.

"You're going home?"

"I really am very tired, Tom."

"I'll bet!"

"What's that supposed to mean?"

"Go ahead and jerk off your ninety-year-old bag of bones! Watch out it doesn't break off in your hand!"

"Now *that does it*! You're a pig and I want nothing more to do with you, Tom Hutchins! I thought you had some European refinement, but I was wrong!"

"Refinement?" Tom yelled into her face, startling her. "Do I need a course in sensitivity training? Let me tell you that underneath this refined exterior lies a traditional masochistic Welsh git!"

The selfmockery confused Kit. Anyway what was a git? Opening the cab door she lowered her eyelids and replied with consummate dignity, "I prefer the American kind! Good night!"

Her remark puzzled Tom as much as his had puzzled her—and himself. The cab took off before he could say anything more, not that he had anything to say. When he did, he said it (in the form of a generalization, in the category called sweeping) to a bartender a few hapless blocks down the road who, leaning on the bar on crossed forearms with a toothpick in his mouth, nodded wise empathy.

Kit, though, in the cab, had just two very specific thoughts in her head: Fired? Zudd?

Because that had been Zudd's voice.

Fourteen

That most popular of democratic charades, Find A Culprit, as opposed to the totalitarian one of Pick A Victim, was in its most dangerous stage.

One team of reporters, from the New York Times, took the side of the dead Pakistani crew member. They claimed he had been sacrificed because he was a Muslim, discovered signs of racial profiling in the hiring system, and blamed the oil company's executives. But the attack was softened by senior editors who knew that the important Foundation sired by that oil company systematically gave money and grants to liberal activist groups and Democratic political campaigns.

Another team, from the New York Post, went after the marine insurance company for having cut corners, and thought it had a winner when it found out the owner was an Indian immigrant, but it seemed to lose interest after learning that he was a devoted family-values man with no known enemies and a record of being kind to his employees.

The companies blamed government bureaucrats and the economy. The bureaucrats blamed the inspectors, who blamed bad luck.

What had happened was the authorities, involving mayors and governors and borough presidents and departmental chiefs and superintendents all vigorously blaming each other and justifying their own actions, or inaction, had persisted too long in the effort to rescue first the oil from the tanker, then the tanker itself, before turning their attention to the crew. Saving the crew had then required acts of individual heroism, which dominated the headlines and the TV news and delayed the investigation. It was now too late to do anything but try to save the piers along the Manhattan and New Jersey shores.

And the shipping. The oil was now gushing into the river. You could see it from the piers and ferries and helicopters, floating in broad formless glistening patches.

Science rose to the opportunity. One system after another was tried, and finally all at the same time—detergents, chemicals, plastic foam, high-pressure hoses, channeling, scooping, pumping, even that of letting Nature take its course. Meanwhile there were the seagulls coated with oil. Groups of volunteers joined forces with government agencies, trying to save them.

Ordinary citizens went about with their usual baggage, carrying both the touchingly naive faith that science would come through and a thrill of fear, of pleasure-panic, that a devastating fire might break out that would kill thousands and change the city's topography forever. The news media were tireless in their vivid portrayal of the appalling possibilities. Experts mushroomed. Columnists outdid each other with moralistic sermons.

It was a good time for small business. Peddlers sold great quantities of oxygen inhalers, skin-protecting salves and ointments, antioxidant pills, syrups and face masks "just in case". There was an upsurge in the discussion of cancers internal and external and of respiratory problems. The discos and cocktail lounges were full. People flocked to the churches. Never were New York's priests, prophets and revivalists in greater demand, or more eloquent.

In spite of her frustration, Kit had felt in control upon leaving Zudd's basement. Her libido was on fire, her adrenaline still coursing. She felt vital, embattled, hopeful that her deliverance was at hand. His insane resistance had in a strange way acted as a solvent upon hers, prodding her towards the total surrender she had longed for yet fought against. She was impatient to resume the fight with her strange new lover. What a man! What a demon! What a playmate! That alternating current of slave and master. The way he fell into one role, then emerged from another, like a human shell game.

But was she up to it? Would she have the power? Yes! Because at the right moment she could command, and he would obey. Those soft brown dog's eyes, full of adoration and submission, were her security, the sign of his vulnerability, and the promise that she, only she, could push him over the edge.

She had had a breathstopping glimpse of that power. But she needed more—more knowledge, more skill in its application. More wisdom, in a word.

Tom had been a temporary interruption. And a bothersome one. But not a problem. Tom she could deal with. Tom was easy. Good old Tom. She would love to have a drink with Tom and tell him everything—Mr. Foote, Zudd and his weird ideas, everything. He would understand, and was sure to have a moral line on it all. And an intellectual stance.

But he had forced her to lie. She could not forgive him that. And he was jealous. She had seen that clearer than ever. What were his thoughts on prolonging life? Did he too want to live forever? Maybe it was a male thing. She knew of no women with this desire. Maybe, if they could stay young. But old, like Mr. Foote? She didn't think so. And she? Would she want to go on and on living? On and *on*? She had never really thought about it. What *would* Tom have to say about that?

And Homer Zudd. Was that really him, cursing out Mr. Foote? It couldn't be. It had to be someone else. Or else the man in the hat was not Mr. Foote. She couldn't wait to see Zudd again and find out. Circumspectly, of course.

Before falling asleep she had decided how to treat her new lover: a little bit as a boy friend, and a little bit as the custodian that he was. She would see him only in his basement apartment—in any case it was the only place she cared to see him. And only after visits with Mr. Foote. That was when she used that private elevator. She would stick to that. Of course, he would be waiting impatiently for a quicker visit. Well, good, let him wait.

She fell asleep smiling.

But when the very next day she saw him outside her office, with that yearning, persecuted look in his eyes, she suddenly changed her mind. Having already given him no more than a condescending smile of recognition and nothing more, she stopped and said "Four o'clock"

— surprising herself as much as him—before sashaying on past.

* * *

With that unexpected resumption, on an impulse, of an affair she had coolly intended to attenuate, to icily control, she became a different woman.

It was the start of her obsession with Zudd. She went to him frequently after work. She went to him on the weekend. On the days Foote summoned her she went to Zudd afterward.

And what a struggle was fought between these two—this Tancredi and Clorinda in their fearsome armor, grappling in their sexual night. She fought with all the power she now knew she possessed in her eyes, her voice, her manner—the manner queenly, the voice that of one who expected to be obeyed, the look that of a royal beauty. Like the pincers of a nutcracker, voice and look caught and held him powerless, shivering, ready to obey without question, seemingly willing to be destroyed and even to self-destruct if that was her wish.

But unlike the male spider he refused the role Nature had assigned him, refused to be devoured. At that moment, she lost her power.

Having lost the chief prize, she swept up all the rest with vicious fervor, indulging the imaginative employment of her powers, prodding her fantasies to new frights and fascinations, and finding in him a more than willing partner. No grovelling was too low, no flagellation too absurd, no oral adoration too wearying or monotonous.

This too turned against her. She grew addicted to his worship and his masochism. And each time he stopped himself at that last hurdle, robbing her of her orgasmic breakthrough and her power, she felt a despairing need to taste that power once more, to humble him yet again, to punish this balky slave. Thus did each frustration ensure that she would return.

She began to demand whippings for herself, and cried out for mortification. "Hurt me!" she demanded of him. "I want you to hurt me! *Please hurt me*!

She felt a pressure building inside her, felt caught in a triangular trap: Zudd wouldn't, Tom couldn't. Foote was past it.

She had always sensed that she needed exactly the right preconditioning, without knowing what that could be. Now she knew. And she knew that Zudd was its artificer.

Zudd, her slave who was destroying her, metamorphosing her. Indoctrinating her in spite of herself.

Yes, indoctrinating her, because in the exhausted truces between battles, they talked. Or he talked and she struggled to understand. And she thought she did understand.

In these truces he reverted to his previous persona. The yearning, worshipful prostration of his ego at the feet of his goddess was suspended. He behaved normally. At any moment she wished, a single command or a regal look (it had to be regal) would be enough to put him back under her spell, but until then they rested, smoked, drank, nibbled packaged junk snacks, and talked.

She learned a lot more about him, and at the same time was able to verify his boasts. She saw with her own eyes that he slept little, lived on his nerves, injected himself with poisons and drugs in amounts that horrified her and that would have killed an ordinary man on the spot. He ate biscuits he himself made from a blend of white flour and unnatural ingredients that included hard and soft plastics and soft metals and insecticides, ground and milled and boiled and blended into a fine meal. She saw him grind it, saw the mixture, sifted it curiously through her fingers, tasted it. She even ate it—tried a tiny piece of the baked biscuit, making a face as she chewed, and discovered with surprise that, despite its peculiar texture and flavor, it was edible.

"I hope I don't get sick from this," she said. "I can't afford to miss a lot of time away from my job."

"From that amount?" Zudd smirked. "Even when I was starting out I would eat more than that, and you see it didn't kill *me*. I did get a little queasy a few times, at the beginning. But it hasn't killed me. Nothing has killed me! Not the smoke I intentionally inhaled along with the usual smog everybody's always complaining about—those daily reports on air quality and all that crap—Kid stuff! Like those paltry amounts of chemicals and hormones and antibiotics in the food—amounts so small it's laughable. You've seen how much I take in, and I'm still here! Because I *use* it. I make it work *for* me. You see what I mean, don't you, Ms Harlow?"

That was another of his weird idiosyncrasies that she had somehow got used to. Bizarre though it was, it struck her as appropriate. She had invited him, with a strained laugh, to call her Kit, or Catherine. He did, sometimes, but it did not seem natural. He always reverted to the formal. He seemed to want it that way.

And it was true, whichever the sadomasochistic scenario they were in, it was his formality that seemed most suitably to go with queens and slaves and flagellation, with goddesses and haughty commands. Intimacy and informality, she had decided, would come later, with the orgasmic breakthrough. With the real pillow talk.

"Take electricity," he said another time. "Lightning. It hits something and turns it into something else. Fusion. Atomic fusion, for instance. Or just your ordinary house current. Touch a screwdriver to a naked wire, or poke it inside a wall outlet. So long as you take the precaution not to get yourself electrocuted, what happens? A short circuit. Which transforms the metal and everything else in contact with it—in a flash of sparks and fire and smoke! That's what I do. I short-circuit the so-called natural process and transform it and everything it touches, I change the symbiosis, I fuse the elements, I confuse Nature by defusing and altering her lethal design. The way you dig a trench and an earth wall and reroute a river. That little transformation can be enormous down the road. Introduce a change no matter how small into the chromosomes and who knows? Anything can happen! A mutation! All things are possible! Look, you don't have to invent life, or capture it—you already have it. Just eliminate the end result of the procession, that crazy parade, just eliminate death, and what's left? Life! Eternal life! Adam and Eve were supposed to live forever, but Nature interfered. And the human race just gave up! Surrendered! I say let's go back and start over, with a mutation that cancels out the original one that got us on the wrong track to begin with. Why not? Who can say I'm wrong?"

"An orderly anarchy! (he said). That's the best kind...This endless process of everything feeding everything and being fed everything in return, the neat rhythmic cycle leading to death—Disrupt it! Break it! Interfere! Not with just a few silly soaps and sprays and detergents and petty stuff like that, which everybody does, everybody who shops in a supermarket, and the powders and deodorants, the chlorine in the water and the food colorants and additives, the sulfites and sulfates—those practically harmless chemicals everybody squawks about, the bans against passive cigarette smoke—they make me laugh! You know what? They *like* the idea of death. Ecology and all that crap. One thing changing into another. Well not me! I don't want to change into anything else. I don't *want* to be part of the organic whole. What for? *I want to be me! I want to do it my way!*"

"So," Kit mused, "all along I've been doing what you're doing, without knowing it?"

She was impressed in spite of herself by his pseudoscientific approach. Like he said, who was to judge what was pseudo and what was not?

"Sure you have! But not enough to do you any good. And think about computer technology and its exponential growth, how right at this moment people are hammering away at their computers sending humanity into the stratosphere with advances in science whose powers double every five years—voice recognition, genetic mutation, pill-size medical microcameras taking pictures inside the body, interplanetary flight. Great dreams, right? And at the same time other Great Dreamers with the same computers and expertise are trying to find a way to destroy humanity unless it surrenders to their particular religious faith and goes back to Old Time Religion—the Islamic version. The jihadists. People who don't care how many people they kill, including themselves. God and the Devil. Both working away at the same tree of Mankind—one to make it grow and blossom out in all directions and the other to cut it down unless it agrees to stop growing. And whose voice is it, yammering in both their ears? Nature's! Well, I'm putting a stop to the whole insanity. Nature is behind the whole shebang, and that's where I come in. See what I'm saying?"

He paced in his excitement. Always. He had that energy. At some point she would level one of those looks at him and watch, with barely concealed awe, the change that instantly came: that softening in his eyes, that distracted, dazed rounding of his pupils, that strange tranquility (while his heart, she knew, pounded—she had felt it pounding against her body). And if she went on to whip him with the rope thongs he always made sure to leave within reach there would follow the throaty cries to beat him harder, humiliate him more, always more: "Harder! Harder, my queen, oh my goddess, yes! I'll do everything you command—anything!"

He seemed immune to the realization of how ludicrous he sounded.

And she imitated him, demanding sharper and still sharper pain from her master, her flagellator—despising herself for it, then demanding it again.

Yet always he drew the line at orgasm. He would not ejaculate. No amount of whipping or commands could do that. Always he fought it and won, withdrawing just in time.

And she accepted it, because it made a perfect fit with his ideas, ideas she was unable to refute, and because the glimpses he gave her into his life, of loneliness and ostracism, of feeling himself different from others, aroused her compassion and gave her the illusion that she understood him.

Then there was the mystery of his birth. Her own father was a scoundrel who deserted his family, but at least she knew who he was. Zudd, as far as she could tell, did not. He hinted at things: illegitimacy, shadowy manipulations, a lobotomy.

"A *lobotomy*? On *you*?"

"On my mother. They did that to her. She showed me a scar. She told me that's what it was."

"Do you believe that?"

His favorite expression was "I'm not sure." He used it now.

Like his story about how he got his job, and his peculiar relationship with Mr. Foote.

"Why does he trust you? Why you, in particular?"

"He likes me," Zudd said with a smirk.

"Come on, why you?"

"I'm not sure. We have a kind of…relationship. He treats me like a kind of godson."

"Why?"

"I don't know."

"I think you do. Why won't you tell me?"

"There's nothing to tell. After Vietnam I sort of, you know, moved around and didn't know what to do with myself. I was drinking and doing drugs and feeling very low and angry about, well, just about everything and one night in a bar I met a guy who told me about the Foote Foundation and how it helped people like me, giving them jobs and getting them straightened out. He even told me where to go, if I was interested. So I went and...here I am."

"You said godson."

"He took a liking to me."

"Why? How? What did you do, spread your coat for him to walk over a puddle?"

"He interviewed me."

"Foote personally interviewed you? For custodian? Isn't this a little unusual? Are you telling the truth?"

"It surprised me too. He told me sometimes he took an interest in young people, especially if they were Vietnam veterans. And so on. To go to him with any personal problems."

"And did you?"

"No."

"But he trusts you."

"I guess. At least with that red button."

"I'd call that a heck of a lot of trust! He's trusting you with the whole rest of his *life*." Kit felt sure he was leaving something out. "How did you say you met that man in the bar?"

"He was sitting on the next barstool and we got to talking."

"Who started?"

"I'm not sure. I guess he did."

"What was he like?"

"Oh, jacket and tie, good haircut, glasses, some kind of company inspector. What are you getting at?"

"Coincidences. Especially lucky ones."

Zudd furrowed his smooth brow for a moment, then resumed his previous and by now chronic expression of incomplete disclosure. Kit was not satisfied. She already knew that his submissive state was only good for actions, not speech. She could not make him say things with that look, only do them, and anyway it had to be sex. She decided to try startling him into revelation.

"Why were you swearing at Mr. Foote the other night? And like *that*."

It worked. She now had all his attention, and without any need for regal looks.

"What do you mean?" he said with nervous eye movements.

"I was there. I saw. I heard you."

"You were still there, outside?"

"I was having a quarrel with Tom Hutchins, trying to explain that I hadn't left any messages, and why I happened to be there at that hour."

"What did you tell him?"

"Lies. (Zudd nodded solemnly.) I don't want him to know about you. (This time Zudd did not nod.) Or...the penthouse."

"He's going to know about me sooner or later," Zudd said.

"He is? Well, then the later the better," was all Kit could manage. So often she found herself wanting to tell him off, and refraining. Well, she knew why. He reached inside her in a way nobody else had been able to do, and made her doubt. Equals hesitation, equals second thoughts. He was right, one day it was going to come out. He was not threatening to tell, he was forecasting. He was reading entrails. Her own could only agree.

"Why is he so important to you," Zudd complained.

"He just is," Kit replied, as if it had been a question.

Zudd was silent.

"So, how *is* it you can curse at your boss and get away with it?" she asked. And when he stayed silent, she went on suspiciously, "Is it some kind of gay thing?"

"What are you talking about?"

The rejoinder was so vehement and so out of character that they stared at each other.

"It's all right," Kit said gently, "you can tell me."

"I'm not gay," he said angrily.

"Is he?"

"No...Not that."

"What, then?"

"He's just, you know, old. He likes to look around, try to keep up with the times. He likes to see the mannequins and pictures and stuff."

"Mr *Foote?*" Kit needed some time to absorb this news. "So, I'm not your only visitor." Zudd looked down. "You know?" Kit said with a fluttery laugh, "you had me fooled. I was actually working towards the conclusion that you were his son. A bastard son, or something."

After a moment Zudd said in a low voice, "I'm not his bastard son so much as he's my bastard father."

"You're his *son?* So I was *right!*" She was astounded. "But why are you here in the basement? Why are you a custodian? Why doesn't he...?" The questions trailed off.

Zudd took a deep breath that was like a sigh. "My mother's mind wandered a lot. She did drugs. And alcohol. You couldn't always believe everything she said. So when she told me what happened I wasn't sure she was telling the truth. Or that she wasn't, you know, fantasizing. You couldn't tell. She would give you that sincere look and tell you stories that...Well, one of them was that he was my father. But she changed the story—or the details—and it sounded, it was a little different every time, a detail here, a detail there. I never could be sure. One time she implied it was his brother Jeffrey. And she was a militant radical. Her lovers were all activists who hated the rich. So did she, but she was one of them. There was always enough money—it would just show up in her bank account. I could understand her anger, but I also felt I couldn't believe everything she said. You know, she was an extremist. She could say anything. So these stories about her and Foote—well, you know, it could just as easily have been a Black Panther, except I wasn't black. But you know what I mean. There were just too many contradictions. When she died I didn't know what to do with myself. The money dried up. I was at Berkeley. Everybody was screaming about the Vietnam War and burning their draft cards. So I signed up, and went to Vietnam. I was always a contrary type. Then when I came back, there was this guy giving me shit about being a Vietnam vet and killing babies and we had a fight and he pulled a knife, and I killed him, with his own knife. I didn't have to, I had the knife, but I was mad and I killed him. Stuck it in his throat. I hated the bastard. You know, what's a pacifist doing with a knife? And why's he trying to kill me? I really hated the son of a bitch. They're still looking for me for that. But not by my name. That's when I became Homer Zudd. It's a nom de guerre. And I came to New York. What the hell, to get lost but also to see if there was any truth in my mother's ravings. She always wanted them to do a paternity test, but they kept giving her psychiatric exams instead. As far as I know they never went ahead and did that test."

"Then how do you know he's your father?"

"I can tell. His expression. Body language. The way he looked when I came right out and asked him, even though he denied it. I think he wants to come clean and make some kind of a deal with me, come to some kind of understanding, but they won't let him. Family, family counsellors, lawyers, the whole structure. Gerald McCord was a weak link. Another few talks and I'd have got it out of him. Besides, why did he give me the job? Why does he keep me on? I've cursed him. I've called him names. I'm still here."

"And he wants to see the mannequins being spanked."

"I guess. I'm never here. He kicks me out. I hate that. I have to go out and walk the streets for a couple of hours, whether I feel like it or not."

"So that fight, when you swore at him, was over that?"

"Hell no. It was over you."

"*Me?* He *knows?*"

"He's not sure. He suspects something."

Kit needed to think.

"Do you care?" Zudd asked her.

"I don't know. Yes, I do care. I don't want him to know."

"Why? What do you owe him? You don't owe him anything. He's using you. He always gets what he wants."

"I generally get what I want too," she said, without much conviction.

"Not like him. He has too many things going for him."

"I think I have a few things going for me, too."

"I know, but with him...Anyway he's going to find out. If he wants to find out he will, we can't stop him. Nobody can."

Kit sighed. "Everything's getting so complicated," she said.

"Not for me. For me they're getting simpler."

"Simpler?"

"For me." He gave her a patronizing smile. "You know how Marxists thought that capitalism would get the world ready for communism, and the Nazis thought Western democracies were a preparation for the New World Order? Well, my bastard father, Harrison Foote, has got the human species ready for me. It's a window of opportunity. And I'm the...some would say prophet, I would say activator."

"They both failed," Kit pointed out.

"Don't be too sure. What about the neo-Nazis? The New Left? The KKK? The Taliban?"

What she could not dispute, finally, was his individuality, his flying in the face of the established rules and conventions. And his unexpected obeisance. At parties she longed to introduce his ideas, to see what the reaction would be. After a few drinks people were always coming up with some shocking theory or other, but it was not the same thing. They tended to be cute. Zudd's ideas were anything but cute.

How she wished she could talk about him with somebody.

Fifteen

Sitting in her office a week before Christmas, fiddling with an account she knew would be handled by someone else anyway, Kit found herself thinking of Tom.

He had not called in over a week. Could he have found someone else? Her heart fluttered with an unfamiliar anxiety. It occurred to her that she had not been treating him well. She was spending too much of her free time with Zudd. Still, it was not like Tom to ignore her like this.

She dialed his office and learned that he was home with the flu. She called him.

"Is that nice?" she scolded. "In bed for a whole week and not letting me know?"

"I thought of it, but...."

"But what?"

"I kept falling asleep."

"Well how are you? You don't sound so bad."

"Oh no, I"ll be back in a day or two. I'm okay."

"Well I'm coming over to see you. What shall I bring?"

"I'm running out of fruit juice. And aspirin."

"Okay. (Fruit juice was out with Zudd, but aspirin was a favorite, he ate it like popcorn.) Fruit juice and aspirin." Then, disturbed by his composure and feeling a need to reestablish herself on the familiar basis, she said playfully, "No serious conversations, okay?"

He did not answer right away, which surprised her. "I will be serious for no more than three minutes, Catherine."

Another flutter. "Sounds scary," she laughed. "And depressing. But I think I can stand three minutes. Provided you say something funny right before and right after."

"I can't promise that."

"I think you've lost your sense of humor, darling," she said. "I'll be over at eight. Is that all right? Why don't I bring some sandwiches from a deli, and some beer?"

"If you want."

Things were slipping out of control. Her job was unstimulating and had the feel of a...sinecure, Mr. Foote, polite and considerate as ever, was behaving like a young lover who felt he had her right where he wanted her and was vexingly contented withal, with Zudd it was a perfectly frustrating stalemate, and now here was Tom sounding alarmingly self-possessed. Was that why she had called him darling? She never had before. Not him, not anyone. It was not her style. She felt a migraine coming on. Thank God for Tylenol Extra Strength. (Zudd would approve of those, though not of her need.)

To complicate matters, she had a note from Foote asking could she pose for him later in the day, as he would be out all afternoon. Would nine o'clock be all right? If not, no need to call and not to worry, he would understand.

Before going home to change she dropped in to see Zudd.

There was a certain thrill of excitement in going to the basement from her office, rather than from the penthouse, because she had to use the common elevators, and there was the risk of being seen. She could not think of a reason to give for being there, if she were asked. Sometimes she heard a door closing, and once she saw a custodian—who, fortunately, had not seen her.

This time she was earlier than her usual time. She found Zudd working on something that it struck her he was being secretive about, a little package with protruding wires. She did not ask him about it. Anyway he was always fiddling with something. They had exhausted themselves the evening before in an orgy of sexual tyrannies and there were no demands today, so he was not surprised that she was not staying.

She had a drink and a smoke and watched him puttering. She had something on her mind, that she wanted to say to him—either that or burst.

It was that she could not go on like this.

"What's that," she said, "a bomb?"

Zudd grinned, "I wouldn't fool around with a bomb. That's one of the things that *could* kill me. Anyway bombs aren't in my program."

He put it away finally and made himself a drink and lighted a cigarillo and sat down with her in the living room area. The apartment was quiet. The ape (in the orgy area) was headless, the mannequins lying scattered around and the cushions on the floor. It all had an air of disuse, like a spoilt child's playroom.

"You've got something on your mind," Zudd said.

"What if somebody saw me coming here? What would I say?"

"Is that what's on your mind?"

"No—but what *would* I say?"

"That we're secretly married."

"Don't be funny."

"Why not? People marry their chauffeurs, their housekeepers, their nurses. Why not their janitor?"

"I want a serious answer."

"How about I fixed something for you and you needed it, like a watch or a bracelet or a handbag or something. I wasn't around so you went looking for me. People know I fix things."

Kit sighed, "I suppose I'll think of something. A handbag isn't bad. *Can* you fix a watch?"

"Sure. Does yours need fixing?"

"Not at the moment."

"So what was it you wanted to talk about?"

She wasn't ready. "It can wait."

They sipped and flicked ash and gazed at each other neutrally.

"I guess you're doing something special tonight?" Zudd said.

"Why special?"

"You're not staying."

"So?"

Zudd shrugged, "I just thought."

"I don't come every day."

"No, but you've never come to tell me you were not coming."

Kit smiled, touché. "The point is," she said, "I'm not staying but that doesn't mean I'm doing something special—your word. If you must know, I'm going to see a sick friend."

"Tom Hutchins?"

"Yes. You knew he was sick?"

"There's a lot of the flu around. It was just a guess."

"I notice you have a way of making these very accurate guesses."

"So, you're going to see him tonight."

"Yes. Why? What's so strange?"

"I didn't say it was strange."

"But you're upset. Does it make you nervous?"

"No," he said too quickly.

"I said nervous, not jealous," Kit said. Zudd bit his lip. "Anyway I haven't seen much of Tom lately."

"Does that matter to you?"

"What do *you* think? Go ahead, make another one of those guesses."

"I know it does. I just don't understand why."

It was her turn to be silent. And it was the kind of silence, the leaving crucial questions unanswered, that haunted Zudd. It was the only time, sexual bondage apart, that he felt, acutely, painfully, the failure of his mastery over her. There was that withholding. She was not entirely his. Would orgasm do it? Maybe. For a while. Then she would fly that full-sailed boat into other harbors, in search of all those orgasms that were out there. So it was good that he too withheld. It was yet another excellent reason for doing it.

He liked that, the having another reason. One reason was rarely enough motivation for him to commit himself to a course of action. Two made it irresistible.

They sat smoking in a troubled way, looking absently at some object.

"I know you're not entirely happy with me," Zudd said.

"I'm not, how could I be?"

"You don't really understand me, do you."

"I think I do, but then—no, I don't. I don't understand why this 'little death' business of yours has to go that far. I mean, the *absoluteness*. I think it's some kind of block, and you've made up your theory to include it. I mean I'm not an analyst but if you really loved me it seems to me—"

"You know I do!"

His eyes held hers with a bright, guilty, stubborn ardor.

"Do you, Homer?"

"You know it!"

"Then, say it."

"Say what? I've said it a dozen times!"

"Say it now. In cold blood. Without the sex, without the, you know, my commanding you to say it. Say it all on your own."

"I—" He gagged, breathed hard, seemed to suffocate, and jumped up in exasperation. "I hate those kinds of statements!"

"You don't hate hearing them."

"Not when it's in the context of...what we do."

"Yes I know. Then it stops. Then *you* stop. Say it!"

"You know I love you!" he barked, turning aside.

Kit smiled a sad, resigned smile. "You can't say it."

"Why are you torturing me with this? You know what you mean to me. How I feel about you. I couldn't be without you anymore. You know that. That look you give me sometimes. Those commands. Your whole manner. Without you I'd be...."

"Lost?" said Kit with a sudden insight she was not sure she could trust. "Because you'd have to start over? Have to go looking for another queen bee?"

"You're my queen bee, Ms Harlow. Kit. It's you. It has to be you."

"Up to a point. Then you take over. That's the problem. Ms Harlow becomes Kit. The queen becomes the commoner."

The look he now gave her was slow and long and brooding.

"You're going to quit," he said.

"I'm thinking about it."

There! It was out. What would he do? She had always thought him dangerous to a degree, without knowing the degree.

"Don't, Kit." He was the piteous custodian in the hallway, before anything had happened. "Look. The fact is...I mean...I want to tell you something. I haven't mentioned this before because, well, I'm not really ready yet, I'm still working on it but one day soon, very soon, there's going to be a big, important change. The whole future. It's the start of something...important. Really important.

Momentous. It's what I've been talking about all this time. Do you read me? My vision of the future! I see it all the time, in front of me, and you're in it! A necessary part of it! But I need you to be patient, Kit. I need that."

"A future? You and me? And what else? And junior makes three?"

"Yes! What did you *think* I was talking about all this time?"

"That was talk. But then you have this problem, you know? *You stop*. And now you're telling me you want to have a *baby?*"

"I can't talk about this! I just can't. Not yet. But I'm...You know, you can plan and prepare and train yourself for something, and then the moment arrives...You have to know it when you see it. And you have to act when that happens. I think I'm there. I think it's starting to happen. But you have to understand, Kit, it's the hardest decision I've ever had to make. Just please wait and be patient. I've trained myself to be what I am right now. To change that, even for one glorious moment, will be very hard. Very hard, Kit. And I—I'm just not ready yet. I'm getting there, but I need a little more time."

The appeal in his eyes, so intense, softened her. "All right," she said. "Except that I don't want any babies." She might have added, 'especially yours,' but held it back.

"That's okay," he said craftily. "I'm not there yet."

He knew she forgot to take the Pill for days at a time. When he was ready he would surprise her, overwhelm her with his passion, reduce her to— no, *elevate* her to seminal glory.

* * *

Kit arrived at Tom's apartment with a bag stuffed full with rye-bread sandwiches and pickles and olives and a six-pack of beer. He was dressed in slacks and slippers and a burgundy satin smoking jacket she had bought him. She saw he had been straightening things, especially the piles of books on every surface, which now were stacks. She took off her coat and straightened a few more items, to establish her presence, and they settled down on the sofa to the food, and to safe gossip—their jobs, the incessant Christmas caroling, the commercialization of Christmas, the weather, the oil on the river.

She could see his three-minute speech being refined behind his eyes.

"Mozart?" she said bending an ear to the music coming from the surround sound music system he had set up at great expense when he was still underpaid.

"How did you know?"

"Isn't it always?" she said and Tom had to laugh.

She had brought far too much. He had half of the pastrami and she half of the corned beef, which still left two halves and a whole chopped liver sandwich and most of the kosher pickles and Greek olives. Kit made the instant espressos while Tom got out the Cognac and glasses and they lighted Havana cigars and it was happy hour. Or should have been—always had been, in the past. But now there were those three minutes.

Get it over with, Kit thought, staring into the ashtray as she carefully placed a butt of gray ash before it was ready. Turning back to Tom, her eyes fell on the olive pits.

"Shall I clear those things away?" she said sweetly.

"Don't bother."

That left them with no more buffers. Even so, she parried to postpone the expected.

"So you'll be back at work tomorrow?"

"I have to be. I want to be. I have an appointment with Foote and that writer I was telling you about."

"The black novelist?"

"Rodney Raines. Foote called to wish me a speedy recovery and said he wanted to see me about that manuscript. I'm not sure, but I think he's read it. I don't want to put that off. But I really am feeling much much better. So, a good night's sleep and…I was pretty run down."

"Me too," she said.

"You?"

That changed the venue and the mood. It was as if Tom had been waiting for just that.

"Hard day at the office?" he grinned, his eyes a little too bright.

"Well, you know."

"Yeah."

For the first time she noticed he was losing his hair. A bit of a widow's peak. The thought endeared him to her and provoked a fantasy scenario of domesticity, of husband and wife. She had never really thought of him in that light.

"Kit," he said, his voice changed, "I've been thinking about us and...I'm giving up. I mean, I'm giving you up. I mean I'm giving up the fraction of you that I flatter myself I still have—though I'm not sure even of that. I want you to know I'm a quitter. If I think a person doesn't want me I quit."

Quietly, so quietly that it seemed she too was unsure of his importance to her, she said, "Fraction? It's...more than a fraction, Tom."

"I can't believe that," Tom said, the conviction in his voice ambushed by a tremor. "You keep reminding me that you don't owe me anything, which is true, and that I've no right to question you, which I suppose is also true. But what are you hiding? What's wrong with answering a question, unless you're hiding something? But okay, you have a right to yourself—provided you're keeping it and not giving it to someone else. That's my problem with this. I'm not sure I trust you anymore. I realize my job has been keeping me very busy lately, but even taking that into consideration you certainly don't seem to have any time for me, except for the occasional drink between appointments, and this surprising visit. So, what's left?"

Kit did not seem to want to answer, and he was about to go on in this agitated tone when she said, "I'm going through something, Tom, I'm...I'm working something out."

This was a phrase hallowed in cinematic and television melodrama, phrases like "I love you" and "Don't shut me out", and it should have softened Tom the way it did audiences. Instead it tore into him like a harpoon, because it meant she was suffering over another man. For her to have simply lost interest in him would have hurt enough; to have lost her to another man would have hurt even more; but for her to be *suffering* over another man was the cruelest thrust of all. It left him not just diminished but dissolved, disintegrated, soiled, an especially insignificant detritus: rejected by the rejected.

"But it's not with me, is it. It's with some other man. I don't know who it is, maybe it's that old man you were telling me about, maybe it's someone else—but it's not me. What puzzles me is that for a girl who is hooked on someone you haven't been looking very happy about it. You look pale and tense and nervous. And you've been so very secretive of late, which isn't like you. And circumspect—all that lying and faking me out that night. I suppose you were very pleased with your cleverness. But women in love don't behave that way. I know from experience. They *look* different. They want the whole world to know they're in love and how happy they are, including the poor sap of a presumptive boyfriend who has lost out. The only explanation I see is that you're hooked but not happy. Which puzzles me because I didn't think you were the kind of woman to languish and suffer with the wrong man. But then of course I obviously don't really know you, do I. I knew a different Kit Harlow. I *saw* the outside woman that everybody sees, the tough hardnosed ambitious intelligent selfcentered beauty, but I didn't believe her. I believed in the inside woman that I also saw, *and that I know is there*—warm, soft—a woman who had suffered. I saw that suffering. It was clear as day. It was there in her beauty—in her eyes, in those pronounced laughlines—"

His face working with his pain as he touched on the traits that enthralled him and moving his lips as if even in the act of renouncing her he would press them to those very features he looked away, turning his whole head like the romantic lead in a silent movie, and sighed.

"That was the woman I loved," he said quietly, turning halfway back, "and still love. But that woman I don't see anymore."

Kit didn't either, although, sitting here like this with Tom it seemed absurd to imagine any change in herself. She felt as she always did when she was with him—heckled but safe. This fancy, though, would vanish the moment she re-entered the street. She knew that. And that it would happen regardless of anything she might tell him. And that her life would never be the same the moment she walked out the door. She was caught in a vortex. And though it was excruciatingly her turn to speak, to deny, to refute his argument, to win him back, knowing he wished for nothing more, she could think of nothing to say.

If it were Zudd, she thought despairingly, she could give him a *look*. But with Tom? Even if it worked a little bit it would not be in the same way and it would not be the same thing. If it were, all things would become possible. Certainly Tom would not deny her, he could never hold back like that, not Tom. She tried to imagine him with Zudd's dull passive expression in his eyes, that submissiveness. No, not Tom. He would make some joke and ruin it.

This thought made her smile. It was a smile of affection.

To Tom it was something else—another sign that she was indeed a changed woman, a woman inexplicably indifferent to what he had just told her and to his pain.

"Well," he said bitterly, "that's my three-minute speech. I'm afraid it took a bit longer."

Kit sighed. How could she explain everything? After an uncomfortable minute she rose on weak legs and he saw her to the door. The way he looked, his heart was broken but he was resigned to dealing with it somehow. She felt close to tears.

"Goodbye, Tom," she said, her voice catching. She kissed his cheek and went out. The door closed slowly behind her as she went down the flight of stairs. Only then, with the door shut, did she understand that he was really not going to call her back.

In the street, looking blindly about for a cab, she thought, It's over.

She was fifteen minutes late for her modeling date with Foote. Riding there in a cab she found herself biting her lip to stop the tears from coming. They came anyway.

"Is it all right if I smoke?" she asked the driver as she lit up.

"Yeah, gawhead," the cabby said, having seen the tears in the rearview mirror.

A few puffs and she was all right again. What must be must be.

Then she noticed the people in the street.

They were moving in a strange, uncoordinated way. The choreography was wrong. Strangers seemed to be talking to each other. They gestured, and pointed westward, and craned their necks to see something that was not there to see. They broke into a trot, and slowed to a walk, and trotted again, all the while scanning the skyline.

As they turned and drove west to the Foote Building she saw the gaptoothed sky over the Hudson River illuminated by a glow, and was struck by its beauty.

"What's that?"

"Must be a fire," the driver said following a red Fire Department car through a red light. "I hope it ain't the erl."

"Do you think it is?"

"Well it ain't the aurora borealis, that's for sure."

Sixteen

For the first time, Kit took the Bis elevator to the penthouse. Until now she had only used it when leaving. This meant Zudd might be watching. She ignored the TV camera's eye. Let him see where she was going. Let everybody see everything. She smiled to herself. You really thought you were going up to visit God in this capsule.

"I wasn't sure you'd come, my dear. I'm so glad. I thought you might have a previous engagement. Of course I would have understood perfectly if you hadn't been able to make it."

"You made that clear," Kit said. She felt a sudden impulse to slap his face and say cut the bullshit. Instead she let him offer her a cigarette, and smiled, and slid back into his cocoon of propriety and refinement and indulgence as she carefully blew smoke up over his face, instead of into it.

"Time is growing short," he explained. "I'll die if I don't finish that painting in time." He smiled and she smiled with him. "I'm free this evening, unexpectedly. I took a chance. I'm so glad you were able to make it."

What was different? It was that he was not just being courteous. He really wanted her there, and did not care if it showed. What else did he want? The usual? Not this time, Buster, she thought. She felt out of control.

"There's a fire on the river," she said.

"I know! Come and see."

The flaming river inflamed her. Even as she looked down at the excitement on the river her thoughts and fantasies stayed red-hot. She was thinking, I could slap him, and he would like it. As long as it was sexual, he would like it. I would give him commands, like with Homer. He'd love it. As long as it was sexual, he'd love it. Looking at the flames and fireboats and copters she thought, Should I? Most of her egged her on, but one wise little voice said, Then what? You make *him* your sexual slave and what have you got? A very old slave? What would you do with him? Await his next incarnation? He's very nice the way he is. Keep him that way.

She listened to it, then went through with the whole silly ritual—the posing, the nudity under the Grecian robe, the early break that became, as she had somehow divined, a closure. Then the sauna while he waited, she now knew, in the solarium, confident and scared, with his talcum powder and scented oils and colognes, for her to come out and lie under the lamps.

Everything the same—But when she emerged from the sauna she walked up to him and tore his towel away so that he was naked too and took his face in her hands and kissed him with her tongue.

She had studied him while posing. And thought about him in the sauna. She was tired of being in his control. She had noticed the compensatory characteristics. There were wrinkles, but they were well placed. It was an old face, but a good one. The eyes had lost some luster, but had gained understanding—an understanding that was real, not the fake understanding of the young.

Now, having kissed him the way she kissed her younger lovers, she drew back and looked at him, at his body, and smiled.

Yes, he was not husky, but there was no flab, either. He had biceps, discrete muscles that were used and useful still despite the flaccidity, muscles formed by sailing and tennis and skiing and golf and polo and all those sporting activities of the country gentleman. He was certainly not bad looking for a man over seventy.

So she lay down and let him make oral love to her until he was truly tired and they were content.

For a time she lay with her eyes closed, smiling to herself. The old guy, while no Zudd, still had unsuspected passion. Like Zudd he had satisfied her desires with what became a mindless lasciviousness, an intemperate delivering of himself to whatever was desired, with the difference, in his case, of those red buttons on the wall.

There was always that about him. The buttons. It could always be the last time. Cryology, for pete's sake. The thought made her shudder, until she opened her eyes and looked at him. He was happy. When was the last time she had made a man *happy*? He was more than that—he was in love. She saw it on his face clearly.

But there was that final insurmountable climb to the summit. What about Viagra? Maybe he was past it, maybe not. Maybe she *and* Viagra could do something about it. Could she revive an impotent seventy-something man? The challenge seemed deliciously irresistible, almost as good as the one in the basement.

"I'm hungry," he said, his countenance fairly oozing love. "Are you hungry?"

"I already had some dinner...Maybe a little something."

"We'll go out," he said.

"Out?"

"Yes, why not? Do you care? If we're seen together?"

"No," she said, and thought about it, and repeated more convincingly, "No." If it got into the papers and Tom saw it, good. Serve him right for giving her the gate. Zudd too—he already knew everything else, he might as well know this too.

Of course, there was his side of the equation—his wife, his grown children, his family (and who were they to talk, with those reports and rumors of scandalous behavior by the various Footes, the occasional lawsuits and settlements?) and their socialite peers. He could deal with it, as he did with everything.

"Me neither!" Foote had the wild-eyed smile of the fool—of one who has thrown caution to the winds. She thought him foolish but sweet, and, for the first time, vulnerable and lovable. She had a sensation of security different from any she had ever felt before. This was power! This was safety!

"How about The Four Seasons?" he said.

"Why not?"

What else was out there for her? Hunks? Was there such a thing as a happy marriage, a successful marriage, with a hunk? Complete with children? Maybe she was old fashioned, or disillusioned, or desperate, but she *wanted* children. She wanted a house, a husband, children, her own little family, God save her! Screw the hunks and the hotshots and the losers, like Hutchins. Here she had a winner. Wait a minute. Children? With a seventy-year-old man? Slow down.

"You really must call me Harrison now."

"Harrison."

"Please say it again."

"Harrison."

The way he beamed, you'd have thought she had just told him he was going to be a father.

They went to The Four Seasons in his chauffeured limo, riding through smoke clouds and admiring the view of the red skyline over the river. At the restaurant they behaved sedately, enjoying their secret.

At the same time, his eyes pondered. His mouth might be a perpetual smile, but the eyes were wise with doubt. Several times, there and on the ride to her East Side flat, she asked him why he was looking so serious. "Oh no, I'm very happy," he said finally. "I can't remember when I've felt like this. But you know, I am seventy years old. I would seem to be too old for you. Wouldn't I?"

His eyes implored her to disagree.

"Why think about it?" she said with a gay mindlessness. "If we like each other who cares about all the rest?"

"Exactly my sentiments!" he said. "*Do* you like me?"

"Of course I like you. Can't you see that?"

"At my age, one doesn't trust one's eyes," he said with a sad smile.

"Keep on like this and you'll turn me off," she said sweetly, and meant it, although she made it sound like a joke. She kissed him and got out of the limo. Tony the doorman, with his hoodlum background, was impressed by the limo. She almost told him who was in it, just to watch his face.

* * *

The best witnessed, analyzed, reported, photographed—and the worst prevented—avoidable calamity in New York's history had started under a pier on the Manhattan side of the Hudson River when an arsonist's spark caught hold of some floating debris and prospered. Soon the oily surface was aflame. It licked at pilings and speedily gained the open river in the general direction of the marooned tanker.

Fire boats on the river and fire engines on the piers hurled water at high velocity. Aircraft too were in action—monoplanes, biplanes, copters—, but in spite of their brave sweeps that dropped plastic foam and liquids and chemical powders the flames continued their march toward the tanker like columns of soldier ants. Shortly before noon they reached it. Shortly after, came the explosion and a field day for all the photographers, professional and amateur, gathered on both banks. Bits of hot twisted metal fell from the sky and were pounced on for souvenirs, burning hands in the process. It was a moment of intense excitement for the residents of New York and New Jersey and their lucky guests as they watched and recorded the massive effort by an army of firefighters to save Lower Manhattan and Hoboken. A climax of sorts came with the second fiery explosion, when the tanker began its gentle slide toward the river bottom.

Then came the smoke. Burning oil gathered into a heavy black cloudbank that covered the area like a putrescent mattress, blotting out the sun. A puff of wind blew it over Manhattan where, with criminal mischief, it left it.

The polyphonic choir of squabbling authorities harmoniously vituperated at this trick of fate. First off, they demanded to know who had ignited the oil. Like authorities everywhere they had been hoping that the corruption and deceit and buckpassing and favor swapping that had accompanied the emergency from the beginning would pass unnoticed by dint of the emergency's simply resolving itself. Politicians understand each other, but, with no time for classical literature or theater, they do not understand fate.

It exasperated them that the crisis did not providentially work itself out in the usual way. That little gust of wind could just as easily have left the smoke over New Jersey, for pete's sake, or blown a little harder and sent it to Connecticut. It could have turned around and sent it out to sea. But no! With an apparent predilection for ethnic diversity, for gorgeous mosaics and, it would seem, for mischief,

Somebody up there—or down there—had chosen The Big Apple for its theater, and there the smoke stayed.

The authorities turned on the hapless pilots who had been in charge of the two vessels. They in turn blamed the faulty equipment, which incriminated the owners. Everybody blamed the pyromaniac who, "with monstrous disregard for human life and private and public property", etc., had applied the fatal spark.

Accordingly, the word went out, and, inevitably, down, to find this malefactor. A black ragpicker with no family or friends was pulled in. He confessed. He had found a pack of cigarettes in the street, had settled down in comfort at the end of a pier, lighted one up, smoked it halfway through, and then, smiling, dreaming of an earlier and more prosperous time, flicked it into the river.

The police figured they had their man, but a militant black organization got interested, black congressmen joined in, and the ragpicker was released and the arresting officer arrested instead after the accusation was made that he had once been overheard using the N-word to his wife, who was African-American.

Then the eager mea culpas started pouring in. Everyone who had thrown down a cigarette or match in the vicinity of the river confessed. In the end they were all sent home. The disgraced cop, after a tearful public apology, was fined and sentenced to a course in sensitivity training, before being reinstated.

The news media, having alarmed the public with vivid journalism, now tried to reassure it with interviews of experts who said the danger was more apparent than real. They said winds from the southeast would soon blow the smoke away. TV weather reporters with dryblown hair and contact lenses showed how and why, thanks to Northerly winds and the various lows and highs, the desired change would take place.

It did not happen.

The awful cloudbank simply sat there, defying every prognostication.

One moment there would be some improvement, then the air would turn black again.

There was no sun, no moon, no stars. There was no sky. Strangers asked each other if this was the end. "This is it!" cried

Revivalists. In the churches and temples, man's representatives to God prayed for wind like becalmed sailors.

Expert theories proliferated. Bearded physicists said it was the beginning of an ice age. Mustachioed cosmologists spoke darkly of anti-matter and black holes in the universe.

Trying to calm the people, the same TV screens and newspapers that fed them a daily ration of dead birds, dead fish, dead plants and prostrated octogenarians also showed them the mayor in a hardhat, glaring out over the river with a gas mask buckled to his belt, conversing meaningfully with a retinue of officials, his face grim but confident, when he was not visiting a victim in one of the city's hospitals.

This time it did not work.

As the tanker settled under the flaming surface after the second explosion, the city too exploded. All the gaseous sociological pressures ignited. Juvenile gangs went shouting and looting through the soot darkened streets—black gangs rampaging south, white ones north. At upper Central Park they collided and fought each other with every available weapon, but chiefly with automatic rifles and handguns. On the first day there were two dozen dead. Impressed by so many casualties, both sides fell back and resorted instead to foraging and mugging, with only the occasional skirmish.

Cats vanished into backyards, dogs cowered in dark corners snarling at every approaching footstep. Police cruisers, paddy wagons, fire trucks and ambulances raced around with their sirens and flashing lights, crashing into each other in the smoke.

Never had New Yorkers been so confused and frightened. Left wing extremists planted a bomb in City Hall, injuring a night watchman. Right wing extremists looted an armory. Everybody wanted a gun. Contradictory reports by journalists with a political agenda gave the impression that awful facts were being withheld for political reasons, and this in turn led to wild rumors of atomic leakage, radioactivity, poison gas attacks by terrorists. The impression gained ground that everything, the whole system, had broken down, that Progress had got out of control; that in some unpredictable (or anyhow unpredicted) manner, past and present had combined to foul the future. And in fact, diplomatic observers hastening from the city talked to interviewers about the strange phenomenon of people swearing mindlessly in the streets, laughing aloud like lunatics, shouting to perfect strangers some personalized version of "I told you so!"

It was as if everyone identifying with New York City, be it residents or settlers, critics or lovers, even those wearing I LOVE NEW YORK teeshirts, with a red heart for the L-word, had all along expected something terrible to happen and were only surprised at its character and genesis. And its timing. It seemed nobody was actually ready for what everybody had expected.

Zudd too laughed, with a deep, selfcontained satisfaction. He was in his element—his amalgam of elements. He went around looking and listening, his senses thrilling with voluptuous pleasure. Here an injured pedestrian, there a gasping asthmatic. A flaming fireman leaping from a high ladder. Sightseers caught in a gust of smoke and running in panic like rats. Cars speeding into chain collisions in the smog as they tried to leave the city. No one had time to die a natural death anymore. He felt gigantic, powerful—the incarnation of an idea whose time had come.

He alone was able to breathe the smoke and smog without coughing his lungs out in the street, without need of the pitiful handkerchiefs and tissues and even gas masks others clung to. It was the final proof of his progress—of his achievement. Kit would be impressed.

More, she would be convinced. Her last doubts would dissolve. What more evidence could she want than this, that he alone had no need to run in search of pockets of uncontaminated air, or to go about with (increasingly expensive) oxygen tanks strapped to his back? Or to agonize over the food supply and fresh water? That these conditions, far from alarming him, excited and stimulated him! That he, at least, was on the right track for surviving this apocalypse. Nature herself would now be confounded, outmaneuvered, violated! O, bliss was it for Zudd in that dawn to be alive!

But Kit had a habit of scoffing at things she did not understand, and he felt that something was still missing from his exposition; that she still doubted, and would continue to doubt, in spite of his performance in the smoggy streets. He needed something more.

He did not think he had any serious rivals. Tom Hutchins was too soft, Foote was too old. Even in the streets he saw no competition. Everybody went around like a scared rabbit, ready to run from the first sign of a swirling cloud of smoke, coughing and retching even when there was no reason for it. Thanksgiving came, and the eve of Christmas, with no improvement in view.

The driver of a van, heading for a store front, spat black on the sidewalk and said something angry to Zudd that he assumed was about the pollution.

"Excuse me?"

"An owner oughta pick himself a manager and let him manage. The manager picks his own coaches. Where the fuck does the owner come off picking the manager's coaches? That fuckin Steinbrenner oughta be shot. Where does he come off?"

The driver, a small man, looked at him with that argumentative ratty expression one saw in sports-oriented bars where they drank beer from the bottle and argued sports strategy and criminology. The arguing was traditionally done in a loud garrulous voice, with expressly minimalist vocabulary, every idea a passionate affirmation accompanied by violent gestures. Zudd always expected fisticuffs or worse to break out, and felt frustrated when they did not.

"Stuyburner?" Zudd said.

The driver gave him a strange look.

"Steinbrenner! George Steinbrenner! The owner! Of the Yankees!"

"Oh, the Yankees, yes, of course."

The driver looked at him. "Yeah, the Yankees, George Steinbrenner, the Yankees—What are you, from fuckin Mars or somethin?"

He went into the store.

One day I will make even you immortal, Zudd thought as he walked on.

A street between two Village avenues was blocked off by police barricades. What would this one be about? Others too had gathered out of curiosity. Holding dirty cloths and tissues to their faces they craned their necks to see what was happening. Laughing his high-pitched giggle but keeping it carefully internal, Zudd looked down the street and saw the usual fire engines, ambulances and patrol cars. Thick smoke, thicker than the surrounding pollution, rose from a wrecked building.

"Another fire?" Zudd asked his neighbor.

"The post office was bombed!" the man said, clearly excited. "Terrorists! There's some dead in there! They're still digging 'em out." As he spoke they saw a body being carried out on a stretcher. The man shook his head, his face sickly with slobbering pity. "Whoever he is that guy probably has a wife and kids, y'know? He went to the post office to mail a Christmas card, forfucksake. Now he's dead. And on Christmas Eve, too. These people got no respect for nothing, you know what I'm saying?"

The good man, having removed the handkerchief to say this, replaced it and glanced at Zudd for the expected commiseration. What he saw was a smile.

"What's funny?" he demanded.

Others turned toward them—a plump woman coughing softly into a tissue, a large man in a plastic raincoat, a thin round-shouldered youth with a scraggly brown beard and glittering eyes. Zudd saw this could get ugly.

"I was thinking, usually they blow *themselves* up."

"Oh, yeh," the man said, mollified.

All but the skinny youth turned back to the street scene. Zudd felt his gaze.

A reporter came out. The cop at the barricade asked him about the one on the stretcher. The bystanders strained to hear.

"It's a girl. She's dead."

"Oh!" said the plump woman with the tissue. "The poor thing."

"How do you like that," Zudd's informant said, shaking his head.

"They think she's the one that did it. It went off too soon."

"How do you like that."

"The poor thing."

"Pretty, too."

"How do you like that."

The trouble was, Zudd liked it. He was happy! People blowing each other up, and themselves too! It doesn't get any better than this. He decided to leave before his glee betrayed him. That keen-eyed scarecrow especially disturbed him.

As he went along, absently gazing down at the usual decor of newspapers, dog turds, colorful blobs of expectoration, discarded tissues, candy wrappers, cigarette butts, tiny broken glass containers and the syringes that always accompanied them, and the doomsday handbills, one flyer caught his attention.

> MUSLIM TERRORISTS ARE NOT THE REAL ENEMY! THE REAL ENEMY IS THE GOVERNMENT! DESTROY THE CAPITALIST IMPERIALIST PIGS! LIBERATE THE PEOPLE! FIGHT WITH US FOR FREEDOM! ROUT THE RIGHT WING FASCISTS! UNITE FOR A BETTER WORLD!

The organization's name had been smudged and stepped on and he could only make out enough of it to suggest that it contained the words "Love" and "Humanity".

"Hi," said a voice behind him. Zudd knew even before turning around who it was. The glitter-eyed youth came up to him, grinning amiably with his mouth. He came close and spoke in a low voice.

"I saw you back there. I've seen you before and I just remembered where. At the river. I'd just thrown something in—you know—and I looked around in the dark and there was this guy throwing something in too, and it was you! And that river starting to burn, man! Maybe it was mine, maybe it was yours—who knows? Cool it, man, we're on the same wavelength, you know? Hey I'm no pig. I dug you there and now I dug you just now. What I can't make out is what's your scene? I dig you're a loner. Hey, man, you got the right idea and the wrong way to go about it, you know? Like you can't do it by yourself. The pigs will crush you. You got to have a backup, a team, a family, a safe house—you need things like that. Wise up, man. They'll get us too, but we're a family, so we can help each other out and maybe one or two of us gets through, you know? Like there's no other way. We can get all the shit we want—explosives, guns, ammo—it's the logistics that's the problem, and for that you need family. You can't do it alone."

The ambulance sped past, its siren sounding languidly. The activist turned and watched it go. His face showed nothing. That fact appealed to Zudd.

"That was a great chick," the young man said. "Rich parents. Pigs. Motherfuckers. She up and told 'em that to their face. They thought she was crazy, tried to get her to a shrink. They just don't see. You got to wake people up, you know? Show 'em what they are, what they're doing, how they're raising their kids to do the same shit they're doing. She gave her life. We need more—we need you, man. Hey, if you're interested come to that luncheonette on the corner tonight at nine. I'll be there. And like, make sure you're not followed, uh?"

The smog swallowed him up.

Dropping the leaflet Zudd walked on. He was not a political person. He saw no need. Why bother killing people when all you had to do was outlast them? Mulling this over, he produced an answer: Because they keep coming. You are one and they are many and they have guns and bombs. You keep to yourself but one day you are in what's called the wrong place at the wrong time and you get it accidentally, from an explosion or a shootout. Besides, they live too long. Even the sickest ones drag on for years with their swollen livers and ulcerated stomachs and arthritic joints and pacemakers and surgeries and chemotherapies. Yes, it might be necessary to kill the bastards.

This was a new concept for Zudd, and it had a narcotic effect upon him. This man and his little group did not interest him, but something in them did—a specific quality: Idealism.

It struck him that his own concept was incomplete. Something had been lacking, and it was idealism. The particular notions of the various causes and movements left him cold, but that element, idealism—that was something else! How was it he had never seen this? It was not for himself that he would create his new superspecies, but for the world! For homo sapiens! The human race! If necessary he would sacrifice his own life—not that it *would* be necessary—to that end. To a son.

That, he now saw, was the reason why Kit was holding back. He had described it as his private war against Nature, and she wanted something more—that missing component, altruism. You don't get far with a theory that does not include altruism. Now he had it. And he had his green light. Gentlemen, start your engines!

It was true—you had to have family! He was ready to start one.

His very own. The time had come to found his new species, his immortal race of men and women. With Kit to be the founding mother. This would be his gift—his Christmas present—to Kit, to himself. To humanity. Even if it cost him his idealistic life.

He rushed back to the Foote Building imagining how pleased she would be at his decision—his breakthrough.

He decided to say nothing beforehand. At the climax, he would simply let himself go! What a surprise for her! What a consummation for both! What a rebirth for the human race!

Seventeen

The Foote Building had so far staggered relatively well through the crisis.

The worst was during the Thanksgiving Day dinner, on the eve of the holiday, when the air filtering system broke down. People filled with turkey and stuffing and pumpkin pie ran gasping and vomiting from the cafeteria in search of a breath of unpolluted air. It took that whole day and the next to fix it. (The penthouse, with a separate system, and a backup besides, was not affected.) After that people began keeping oxygen tanks in their desks. There was some agitation in favor of asking the executive officers to hold regular smoke and smog and fire drills, especially smog. The executives were against it on the ground that it was unnecessary and would lose time and an equivalent amount of money, running into the millions. Finally the idea was shelved, temporarily, because the Christmas season was approaching, and, anyway, people had got used to the crisis.

By Christmas the office trees were all in place, the bunting and streamers and mistletoe had been strung, imaginative crèches were on display. From CEOs to office boys, everybody was busy with rush work, with personal plans for the holiday and preparations for the office parties.

The custodians were in great demand. Zudd got back to find everybody asking for him. With no superiors to have to answer to—he was responsible only to Mr. Foote—he ignored them all and went straight to the seventeenth floor. And found himself in the middle of an office party.

All the computer work stations on their casters had been rolled aside. Connecting doors stood open. Tables were set up with bowls of punch and canapés. From CD players came Sinatra and Rock and jazzed up carols.

People stood around holding their drinks and talking, for all the world like honest churchgoing provincials, about the weather. And with reason. There was exciting news. Some weather forecasters had predicted rain or snow—in fact a sprinkling of black rain had occurred that morning in Staten Island and Queens. It was snowing in Connecticut and Massachusetts. New Yorkers who hated snow were praying for it.

Among Kit's Christmas cards were three that were unsigned.

The "Rokeby Venus" by Velasquez was undoubtedly from Mr. Foote and Constable's "The Haywain" had to be Nature lover Tom. The third was more difficult—simple, banal, but with a subtle message for her alone. The three kings, the infant Jesus, the Virgin, the manger might be straight from Woolworth's, but the hand-written message added to the printed greeting read "The naissance starts tonight. Tonight it's for real. Please come. I promise I will." Her heart tripped. She looked up and saw Zudd standing just inside the doorway, his eyes like lazers, and it tripped again.

And yet she did not really want to go to him tonight. Not tonight. Not Christmas Eve. But she had little more to choose from, unless she wanted to give Katz a call. For all her popularity, Zudd was her only concrete offer.

Tom's card clearly predated recent developments. Things were moving too fast. She wondered if she would see him, or Harrison. Harrison had said nothing about the holidays. Was it because he thought her dance card was full? He never presumed. As a result, she alone in this whole building full of people had no Christmas plans. The thought brought a sting of tears that she fought off with a long belt of the punch.

* * *

Zudd kept trying to make eye contact with the woman who happened to be the one outstanding beauty in the crowd. But so were a lot of other men and a couple of women, and they had the closer proximity.

He had been invited to stay on and join in the fun while keeping an eye on the electrical connections that had caused some trouble. He kept out of the way, drink in hand, cigarillo in mouth, content to receive the occasional look, discreet, conspiratorial, from a Kit surrounded by men of all ages and waistlines, and to savor the momentous fruition awaiting them in the basement, provided she didn't get drunk and wind up with somebody else.

He wondered, while a silly typist chatted to him about office life, if she had taken the Pill today. But he reassured himself that she was careless about that. He squirmed with impatience—and anxiety. What if she had decided she was fed up with his intransigence and his far-out ideas? What if she did in fact get tight and fall for one of those cool, wisecracking, ponytailed narcissists? Or that body-building black who never passed up an excuse to roll his shirtsleeves right up to the shoulder?

Groups coalesced, couples vanished then reappeared, everybody was half tight and poking fun—some mild, some bitter—at the controlling influences of their lives, beginning with their jobs and ending with, not just the oil fires, but with earnest questions as to whether their civilization would survive to see the next century. Human nature quickly reasserting itself, the general conversation turned more prurient. Good cheer returned, accompanied by the words that TV and Hollywood had rendered socially acceptable: fuck, ass, penis, prick, motherfucker.

Kit was sentimental with thoughts of futility, the sense of her life being wasted. What did she have? A weirdly attractive basement dweller who wished to father a new human species, no less, and judging from his Christmas card was ready to start, although you could never be sure with him; and an uncompromising loser who for some reason was impotent with her although not with other women (she knew of one, first-hand), and who anyway had dropped her; and an interesting very rich but impotent old man who seemed to be saying the age difference was insurmountable even while trying to mount her every chance he got and falling more deeply in love with her at every failed attempt.

All this and the pollution and the new intimacy with Harrison Foote was bad enough, but at this time of year she always thought of her family. Christmas terrorized her, New Year's Eve was around the corner. Last year she had got suddenly tired of the round of parties and gone home for New Year's Eve, and during the Auld Lang Syne at midnight kissed her high school football star half-brother so incestuously, all boozed up as she was, that it produced nervous laughter and embarrassed jokes. Poor Ken was terribly upset. She wasn't sure he had recovered from that. His high school sweetheart was appalled, and they broke up soon after. What came over her when she did things like that?

"Just then Sweeney comes in and says, 'What the bleep's going on in that department, anyway? Do I send the memo or not?'" A pained expression representing laughter at this punch line gave Kit, who had not heard a word, her cue, and she laughed.

She saw Tom Hutchins come in and stand chatting with a former associate while surreptitiously, as surreptitiously as she herself observed him, looking around for her. She made sure to be deeply enthralled in conversation with an accountant. Unfortunately he was only telling her a smutty anecdote, and there was not much for her to say, so she just kept on laughing, at the same time wondering if Tom would come over in spite of himself. Of course he would. Why else was he here? Another woman? To make her jealous? Tom did not do things like that. Nonsense—everybody did things like that. And sure enough, there went pretty blonde Carol Zimmerman over to him. To his group, but it was clearly to him she went. Prearranged? A date? Kit wondered how she would take it if they left together. The thought disconcerted her enough that the smutty anecdote fell flat, and the embarrassed raconteur left her to his rivals. What bothered her was her suspicion that there had once been something between them, which he had denied. Was this a reprise? Just then his eyes swung to her and she looked away.

To Zudd.

But he was gone.

Probably fixing something.

* * *

Fed up with his own office party in the East Wing, fed up with everything, with his life, Tom had succumbed to the desire, suddenly overwhelming, to be with Kit, if only in the same room.

Drink in hand he chatted absently, answering questions about his new job as best he could, given his own ambivalent feelings, at the same time making sure *she* would only see him laughing, talking with animation, listening attentively to whatever it was he was listening to. And hoping it would somehow come to pass that they would meet, and speak, and reconcile.

She must know he had already lost his struggle to renounce her; that he would not be here otherwise. She had to know he was now Sam Katz: forlorn, pitiful. Annulled.

And frantic. Who was that new lover of hers? Was he here? He searched for clues.

His only wish now was to win her back—to win back the part of her that had been his. But his instinct (What else could it be? His brain had turned to mush, he could not think, instinct was now his lonely hope) was to craft a path back to her without seeming to crawl. To crawl, the instinct told him, would only lose her altogether.

So he fell back on his old standbys, patience and stubbornness. He would wait for her to come over to him. Of course she would taunt him by carrying on with everybody else first—with all those swinging, wisecracking, selfsatisfied jokers trying to get her into an empty office. He reckoned her lover was not here—no clinging, no steamy looks. It gave him a shard of hope. In any case what could he do but wait it out? Once he left the building it was all over. God knew when he would see her again—after the holidays, at the earliest. By then she might be forever lost to him. And whom could he blame if that happened but himself? Had he not released her, sent her packing? Bloody fool! To have thrown away his one weapon, his patience! Even sadsack Katz had not done that.

Couples had started dancing. Removing their shoes, dimming the lights, they moved in tight embrace slowly to slow music. Already jackets were off, ties loosened, blouses half unbuttoned.

The gambit was to laugh at first grab, until the sensuality took over. Waved hair fell voluptuously between faces. Holding on to a cigarette or a drink and to their partners, they trod the fallen streamers. Kit looked at them and laughed benignly at the increasingly bold badinage of her court.

Zudd was back, still discreetly in the background. The typist rejoined him. She had decided he was interesting, and that he was dying to join the party but reluctant to rise above his station. She kept trying to assure him it was all right to dance with her, and he kept refusing with an embarrassed smile she thought adorable. Finally he walked away. She shook her head, convinced she had failed him somehow, not handled it right, and went off to bestow equality on someone more receptive.

The taped music changed to salsa. Alas, there was only one Latino, and he was of the demure kind. Couples tried, spilling their drinks, and quit. The music was loud and hard. An important departmental head drunkenly talked shop with his married secretary, a loyal worker who had been trying to seduce him for years. One heard his voice intermittently.

A young woman started dancing by herself—the Latino would not join her—and was okay for a while, then flopped into a chair. A very young man started up. Everyone encouraged him. They wanted one good dance. He was good enough, though his rhythm was not quite right. It would not have mattered about the rhythm had he compensated with sensuousness—but he did not have that either. Then he was joined by someone who did—Kit.

They danced separately. Soon the young man saw they were not doing the same thing. He was dancing, she was doing something else. He preferred to watch.

Her long reddish blonde hair swishing about her shoulders, her eyes half closed, Kit did seem to think she was alone. She felt violent. What was a girl to do when she felt violent? She started unbuttoning her blouse.

Some gyrations later, with the blouse on the floor, she unhooked her black lace bra and let it drop. Then, with her breasts jouncing to the movements of hips and arms and her hair flying about, utterly bewitching her audience, she began to unzip her skirt just as a tall bald potbellied executive in shirtsleeves took uncertain steps toward her. She saw him, ignored him, began pushing herself free of the skirt—and stopped, stopped everything, stopped dancing, undressing, stopped moving as her eyes alighted on Zudd across the room.

"Come here, Homer!" And when he hesitated, when the submission in his eyes quivered on the brink, she said again, in a tone so confident and imperious it actually softened, "Homer, come here."

And still he hesitated, although she saw—only she could see—that he was trembling. Now her eyes widened a little with delicious threat, and her voice, after so many basement trials, grew testy. "I said come here."

And Zudd went.

Just as in the basement, he went. Blank faces moved aside, letting him through. He stood quivering before her.

"Take off my skirt," she demanded. "Get on your knees."

In his mind Zudd had already started to collapse to his knees and to reach for her skirt. He had already forgotten, or had accepted, that there would be an audience this time. But before he could move, the executive interposed himself, facing Kit with his arms opened wide.

"Here *I* am, baby! Try *me*!"

Kit laughed and held out her arms and they embraced and began dancing together—a slow dance, ignoring the salsa beat. Kit lay her head on his chest and he, encircling her with his arms and closing his eyes, began with her the loveless, erotic pseudo-copulation of the dance floor, moving with as much unctuous undulation as their respective contours permitted in this love of two strangers, two homeless, motherless children in comatose union.

Zudd went quietly back to his corner, and was immediately joined by the outraged typist. "How dare she do that! How dare she treat you like that! You're as good as any of us! What a nerve she has to treat you as if you were a…a *slave*, or something!"

Zudd looked at her with a quizzical smile, not really seeing her. He was thinking of what had almost occurred, and was excited up to the very limit of endurance. She was achieving her perfection at the same time that he was achieving his. She had been spectacular! Without that interference he was sure he would now be grovelling at her feet, obeying every command, right to the end! To climax! And all these people watching be damned! And a new species to be born! It was even better than the privacy of the basement. He had not thought of that. Her liberated instinct was better than his orderly plot. He admired, adored her more than ever.

* * *

Seated on the edge of a desk, Tom stared from the dancing couple to the carpet, and back to the couple. Uncomprehending, furious, devastated. Convinced that he had not known her at all. He had sensed the wildness, but had seen also a pride, a dignity—or had that been a contrivance? Women had always been a great mystery to him, and when he had achieved a rapport with one and gotten to know her, to know her answers and her questions, her depths and her heights, her ins and her outs, her kind of humor and the reaches of her intelligence, it had always turned out in the end that he had not known her at all.

Again and again he had found himself wondering, with Freud, What do women want? He watched Kit making love with her hips and naked breasts to a man she did not know and could not possibly care about, and the hurt went deeper than jealousy because he could not understand it, and because he had the disemboweling sensation, once again, that he never would. And in an act of sudden rebellion, of casting off the chains, he threw down his glass with a cry that was a sob and rushed to the door with the intention of hurling himself like a galley slave into the shark-filled sea, into the polluted night, into the acid of his loneliness and despair—And there, just entering, was Harrison Foote.

"Hello Hutchins. Visiting old friends?"

Foote peered round the semidark room smiling his wincing public smile even as the sound of his name rode the air currents.

"I hope you are all having a good party here on seventeen?"

The group around the dancing couple broke apart and revealed the executive making an awkward move to kiss Kit on the mouth, and when she pulled her head back laughing, or perhaps teasing, the executive, being righthanded, went for her left breast, just as a dance movement pulled it away from him. It made him look foolish as well as graceless and he began remonstrating and pawing at her. At that moment a hand gripped his arm and a voice urgently whispered to them both, "Mr Foote! He's here!"

They staggered apart. Someone handed Kit her blouse She slipped it on, lining up her thoughts. Why should Harrison frighten her? She had done all this, all but the dancing, enough times in the penthouse. She buttoned a couple of buttons and swept her hair back. What, she wondered, would be his reaction? How much had he seen? Why was he here, what did he want? This was no place for him to be—he belonged in his penthouse, or at some distinguished club, exchanging the season's greetings with other First Families and VIPs. He had not said one word, not one, about their getting together during the holiday. Paris, the Costa del Sol, Istanbul, Rio—everything had got mentioned except whether they would be seeing each other during this Christmas holiday.

Nevertheless, he had caught her in an embarrassing posture. With an expression that was part I don't care and part I can explain this (I think), she turned and made her way to the makeshift bar for another glass of the surprisingly strong punch, trying to order her thoughts, and her priorities.

Having arrested Tom in mid-flight, Foote, without moving very far from the door, was in amiable conversation with some revelers, giving the others a chance to straighten their clothes and demeanors. Lights went back on, one after another. Someone stopped the tape. At this, finally, Foote looked up.

"Please don't stop the music. Please carry on as if I weren't here, after all this is a party, not—I'll be leaving in a minute. (Cries of No, stay, Mr. Foote!) I only wanted to pop in and say hello, merry Christmas, see how you're all getting on in these wretched conditions...."

Someone handed him a glass of punch.

"Well, yes, all right, I will have one small drink, thanks very much."

He really did not seem put out, and everybody relaxed. Several couples resumed dancing, very demurely.

Flustered, Kit wondered what she had been about to do with

Zudd had the fat executive not interfered, and then with the executive had Harrison not come in. She wondered what exactly he had seen. And what about Tom? He might be through with her, but was she through with him? So immersed in her own tangle of confusion was she that when her drink, that she had left on the bar, was handed to her she emptied it like a glass of water. There was Tom, hesitating beside the door, there was Zudd, biding his time beside the tree, and there was Harrison with a drink, very adult, very debonair, smiling and chatting. She took a cigarette from an office boy who told her what a terrific dancer she was, and inhaled deeply, as if trying to blow a hole through the web.

Foote's voice rose a little and the room fell silent except for the music, which someone stopped.

"I don't want to forget why I dropped in," Foote said. "It's to give you some good news, for a change. Of course, I want to say 'Merry Christmas!' to every one of you (voices returned the greeting) and to thank you personally, all of you, for your faithful service to our organization, of which every single one of you is an important part, especially in this unpleasant emergency, which I'm most pleased to say is just about over now—That's my good news: it's *snowing*!"

With happy cries men and women started for the windows before realizing there weren't any.

"I'm afraid you'll have to take my word for it," Foote laughed. "It's true. It started half an hour ago and the smoke is lifting—It should be gone soon. The river fires have all gone out. Now *there's* something worth celebrating, wouldn't you agree?...Ms Harlow, have you a moment?"

Instead of waiting, as the boss, for her to come to him, he went to meet her and then turned toward the wall so that none but Kit could see his face or hear his hissing voice.

"How could you! How could you do such a thing!"

Taken aback by the change in his voice and the anger on his face, Kit went on the defensive and became a child—and, like a child, her first thought was to deny everything, then to explain it, then to apologize, then to win back his favor.

"What? What thing?"

"Behaving like a common—! With your colleagues! When we'd

become so…so close! How could you?"

"I, I don't know. Something…came over me."

"I thought you were so much more than that!"

"It's, it's that awful smoke and, and the fires and all the panic and everything."

"I thought—I had hoped you were happy here." He saw Kit's eyes lose focus, heard her silence. "I think of you as clean and, well, pure, and then I see you…."

"I *am* pure," she blurted, close to tears, "I *am* clean."

"Catherine, what is it you want? What do you need? I'll do anything I can, but you must tell me what it is. I can't help you if I don't know what it is you want."

She struggled, biting her lip. "What I want," she said finally, "I can't have, and you can't help."

"Are you sure, my dear? I have means. And I'm fairly open minded. And flexible. My dear Catherine, what is troubling you? I want to know, I *need* to know."

"Know what?" Kit said half to herself. "Everything?"

"Yes! Everything!" said Foote, his eyes alight with the security of the well informed. A smugly discreet smile went with it. Seeing this, an alcoholic anger rose in her.

"Well," she said with stilletto understatement, "there's your son. Do you want to know about that?"

The eyes frosted over. The whole face sagged.

"My….Did you say…my son?" he said weakly.

Kit waited, thinking, What have I done?

He faltered, "I have children…."

"The one in the basement."

"The basement? You don't mean…."

Looking as if he might fall, Foote turned by degrees and sought out Zudd, and just as slowly turned back, his mouth open.

"Who…told you that?"

"He did. Was he lying?"

Foote looked away. "He should not have done that…He should not have done that." He looked at her. "But, are you saying….?"

Kit just returned his gaze, unwinking

"My God!" Foote said. "Homer Zudd? And you? You? My God!"

I've lost everything, Kit thought. Sure enough, the old man turned and staggered to the door like a dying broken field runner through the crowd of dancing couples looking at him, at his face with concern as they made way for him.

Well, that's it, Kit told herself. You've done it. You'll be out in the street by morning, looking for a job. Stupid! Why did you have to do that? She saw Zudd and Tom watching her with intense interest, and turned away. *Idiot!* Close to tears, she looked for her glass of punch. *What got into me? Why don't I ever know when I'm well off? Why do I have to be such a damn fool? Why must I always go too far?*

Finding someone's drink on a desk she drank it down, then looked around for a cigarette and found Harrison Foote standing in front of her.

"I want to see you," he said. "Can you come?".

"You mean, *now?*"

"I can't order you. It needn't be for long. You'll be able to keep your engagements."

"I'll come."

"In, say, a quarter-hour?"

"Yes, all right."

This time he went out walking very straight.

* * *

Having failed in his attempt to get out the door, Tom languished on the edges of conversations, with his attention wholly directed towards Kit who, with Foote gone, was again surrounded by admirers. Every time he thought of going on over another man would join her group and he would refill his glass instead. He kept challenging himself to leave—snow on the street! clean air!—and chickening out with a projection of the terrifying emptiness of that street without Kit.

He should have spoken to Foote, talked to him about that novel. But the old boy was doing his Father Christmas routine—the bearer of good tidings, having a sip of punch, peeping at the goings-on (where was Kit? Here a moment ago. Probably in the washroom or off in a corner, necking, or worse—Fuckit! Why am I still here?

Could her lover be one of these guys? They don't look like much...But then when did that ever mean anything?), making his charming little speeches, probably looking in all the supply rooms hoping to find a couple in the act so that he could go back upstairs and wank. Wonder if he does manage to get somebody up there from time to time...Why the fuck am I still here, with this stupid glass of punch in my hand? That I don't even want? Can't even get drunk anyway. So why don't I fuck off? Better idea, why don't I just walk out of here and quit the whole stupid fucking farce? *Really* take off? And tell him off, while I'm at it? Yeah, why don't I? *Well why don't I*? What's to stop me? By God, I will! And right now! Quit the whole rotten sick frustrating castrating fucking circus!

And that was how Tom decided to go upstairs and visit Harrison Foote in his penthouse and tell him to stuff his Fiction Editor job and all his other jobs too. That he was quitting as of now—*now! this minute!* And merry Christmas!

Now, how to get up there. He had been up once. You change at some halfway point. Fortieth? Fiftieth? Can't remember. Have another drink first. Might as well tank up—snow in the street, must have turned very cold. Yes, Mr. Harrison Fuckhead Foote, get yourself another Fiction Editor puppet. If you had any balls you'd publish that novel, and you know it. If *I* had any balls I'd have told you that. Well, I'll tell you now! And quit, too! I don't need this job. Too many winners around here. Not enough honest men. Well, get stuffed! I quit! Right after this drink. Tell Catherine Harlow off too while I'm at it. Where is she? Probably having it off in a broom closet standing up, the drunken slut, with the mops and brooms and bottles of detergent—God! I'm well rid of her. *That dance*! Christ, what if Foote hadn't walked in? *Why does she do these things*? And that custodian. What was that all about? The poor bastard must be in love with her! And she knows it. And she was about to humiliate the shit out of him. God! I don't know her at *all*! She's every biblical and historical tart rolled into one! And I wanted to *marry* her!

Eighteen

Foote was waiting for her in front of a Christmas tree, a natural tree of beautiful symmetry ten feet high and stunningly decorated with colored bulbs and faceted lights that flashed and glowed.

Surprisingly, there were signs of departed guests. Quickly and quietly, even as they entered the main room, cups and plates and liqueur glasses were removed by vanishing servants.

Except for his shining eyes, Foote was back to normal. He welcomed her with his habitual courtesy and restraint. (A little too restrained? she nervously thought.) He had a bottle of champagne cooling in a bucket, and her favorite filtered cigarettes, and the usual tray of gourmet canapés waiting on a silver tray, and something new. Small. Gift wrapped.

A private party, just for the two of them?

Kit thought she should be feeling happy, or anyway good, now that all was going well again, with her expectations again rising on all sides. But there was a noise inside her, a volcanic rumbling, a visceral impatience. The private party she wanted was in the basement.

She sat back blowing smoke.

"Cheers," said Foote, raising his glass.

He drank to a happy Christmas and the coming year—This one, he told her, smiling meaningfully into her eyes, had been marvelous.

Kit chose her rejoinder with care. "For me too," she said.

The package was a gorgeous brooch, from Cartier.

"It's lovely!" she said. "Thank you, Harrison!"

She went over and kissed him and sat down again, crossing her legs.

"Would you wear it, just for now?" he said. Then, the brooch glinting at her throat, he gazed at her with a beatific smile as if she were the Madonna, and he the one privileged beholder.

They did not talk. It was nice, with the music playing—"Vivaldi, The Four Seasons," he informed her when she thought it sounded familiar. And the quiet otherwise, despite the revelry they knew was going on in the rest of the building and in the streets. It was like being in your own private chapel.

She waited for whatever it was he had on his mind, sorting different responses to the proposals, like posing, that might keep her from the basement. She had decided not to pose. Not today. Today it had to be Zudd.

Foote put down his glass and said, "I have got to know what there is between you, Catherine."

"Well, Tom likes me," she said, knowing he meant Zudd.

"You know who I mean. What could a beautiful intelligent sensible young woman like you find to like in someone like that."

Her silence was worse than anything she could have said.

"So. It's like that," Foote said.

"You said you understood about my personal relationships."

"Not with him. Good God! Not with *him.* Have you seen his apartment? Yes, of course you have. How could it happen? How *did* it happen? A *janitor*!"

"It's a long story. It's...complicated."

Foote's voice changed. "You don't want to disappoint me, Catherine. Not really disappoint me."

That got her attention. His eyes were suddenly in low gear. And suddenly she was afraid.

"Why should that happen?"

"I don't want it to. You must not see him again."

A life flashed before her eyes—that of Homer's mother, with secret crimes and machinations and lobotomies.

She said uncertainly, "All right."

"You will avoid the basement," he stated as a fact.

Kit nodded.

"Thank you, my dear." He had changed back, all smiles and deference again, just like chameleon Zudd. "I'm drinking to that." He raised his glass. "Oh, and to my picture. A friend of mine who was here this morning is on the Board of Directors of the Museum of Modern Art, and he's going to suggest it for the Museum. Isn't that marvelous?"

"Absolutely," she said, thinking, I must get to Homer, but how?

She did not want him coming to her apartment. Not there. Not Zudd. But she had to get to him. "You'll be an important artist."

"Well, you know, it will go straight to the Museum's basement for the time being, I'm sure. If they do want it. Of course, I would offer it as a gift."

"That's wonderful, Harrison."

"I knew you'd be pleased."

"Oh I am."

There was an uncomfortable pause, then Foote's tone of voice changed again.

"He's crazy, you know. Not altogether right in the head. An inherited gene, I'm afraid. From his mother. Then there's Vietnam and all that. You must not see him again."

"Well, I'll have to see him once more."

Again the eyes focused hard. "No, Catherine.You must not see him ever again. You must stay away from that basement. I sincerely mean that, Catherine."

"Just once more. It's something I have to finish up with him, then I'll say goodbye and that will be that. I don't like loose ends. It's all right," she cajoled, seeing his face, "I don't care as much as you may think."

It didn't work.

"I'm so glad to hear that but I'm afraid I must insist. You must not see him at all, Catherine. Ever."

"Not even once, to say just that?"

"Absolutely not."

Kit felt a rush of heat to her face. "I'm not your *slave*, Harrison."

Foote looked at her. "Are you *his*?"

"What? I—No…What do you mean?" She heard her own voice wobble.

"My God!" Foote's eyes went dull with lucidity. "My God! You *are*!"

"It's—it's not what you think." It occurred to her she could get up and walk out. Escape. "Look, you said yourself, you've no right. If this doesn't stop I'll—I'll have to leave."

"No, no, don't do that!"

"It's my personal life," she said.

"You're absolutely right. Please forgive me. I had no right to interfere."

Kit took a Sobranie from the silver box, and the gold lighter, blew a stream of smoke, and relaxed, sort of.

"I'll see him one more time. That should do it. But I'm not promising anything."

"I understand."

"I don't know that you do. It's sort of...*weird*. An aberration. Anyway nothing happened. I mean, nothing *real*."

"Well. I'm so glad to hear that."

They sipped champagne, she, completely relaxed now, thinking of the coming final encounter with Zudd while smoking and listening to Vivaldi, and Foote, his usual expression of approval stained with doubt, watching her every gesture.

This was now a Harrison Foote she was unfamiliar with.

"I do have to go," she said on impulse.

"So soon?"

"I did have plans."

"I'm sorry, and, well, disappointed. I was rather hoping—It's not the picture. That can wait of course—It's, I don't know how to put this, it's...the dancing."

"Dancing?"

"I wish you would dance for me."

"Dance for you?"

"Would you mind terribly? You know, the sort of thing you were doing downstairs. For me. Just for me. Would you?"

"I'm not really...I mean, I'm not really a dancer. I've never studied dance."

"From the little I saw, that's of no importance. Dear Catherine, let's do something really *exciting*. You were so beautiful and so exotic and so, dare I say, erotic, dancing almost as if you were alone—Would you do that for me?

"I guess…All right." The idea pleasured Kit. And he had given her the gorgeous brooch. The basement could wait a little.

"I thought you didn't like it," she could not help saying.

"Not in public," he said, and added reproachfully, "it's not the same thing, is it."

"What kind of dancing do you mean?"

"What you were doing when I dropped in. I might draw some sketches. I have the appropriate music here…."

He pressed a button on a remote. From the surround-sound speakers came North African strains interpreted by a jazz combo.

"Are you talking strip?" Kit got up, emptied her glass of champagne, and started to dance.

"I beg your pardon?"

"You want me to take it off, as in strip tease? Is that it?"

"That's the general idea, I suppose. I hadn't thought that far."

"How far had you thought?" she said dropping her shirt as she danced, topless.

"I don't know." He grinned uncertainly. "I'm not sure I understand the question."

"Do you want me to dance and strip for your *sketches*—or for *you*?"

"Does it matter?" he said, his brow furrowed with an introspection so intense he seemed almost frightened.

"Not to me. But to you." She unzipped her skirt.

"I don't know. What are you getting at, Catherine?"

That sort of question, in that tone of voice, would have intimidated her before.

"You're seventy years old, Harrison."

"I'm afraid so."

"If we're going to have a relationship, *any* relationship, you have to be honest with yourself, and with—"

"I am honest with myself."

"And with me."

Silence.

Then, tearfully and yet comically holding out his hands like a character in an Italian opera, he cried, "I don't know what to do!"

For the first time Kit felt on even terms with him. It was a nice feeling. It stirred her blood, and whipped her thoughts toward her obsession, her man in the basement who did know what he wanted to do.

"Think about it," she said, "while I dance. Would you like me to swing into Arabian nights, like the music?" Picking up the shirt, she used it as a veil.

"Oh yes. That's so exciting." Seizing a sketch pad he began drawing. After a while he dropped it and sat staring at her.

Kit had no idea what he was thinking, or if he was aroused, physically aroused, by her dancing, and decided she didn't care. She liked doing it, loved the music, loved fantasizing that she was a dancing girl in a harem and this was her one veil. What did she need another six for? She teased him, taunted him, growing ever more erotic—undulating, shaking her shoulders, planting her legs wide apart and grinding her hips, smearing her hair over her open mouth. All the things she had seen in movies and would never have dared do with her usual retinue of lovers for fear of being ridiculous.

Foote sat slowly moving his head from side to side as if saying no. What he was saying was, what am I to do? Saying it silently and with a kind of pain. Saying it to his ruthless, vengeful god of parameters, who answered him as he felt in his heart he deserved. This is your punishment for your hedonism, for presuming to grow old too pleasure-bent. There are laws, to which you must bow. Did you really think you could *have it all*?

"No, no," he agonized, so loudly that Kit heard it and froze.

"Something wrong?"

"What? Oh no, it's not you! Please go on!"

"You said no. You looked unhappy. Don't you like my dancing?"

"Oh I do. It's beautiful.You're absolutely ravishing. I haven't seen anything like it since—Please don't stop."

She tried to go on, but it was not the same, and she stopped again.

"I've lost the mood."

"I'm sorry. It's my fault."

Why am I doing all this? she asked herself, sitting down again with her shirt on her lap. Still no answers came. Except that she'd had a lot of punch. And eaten nothing. She could hold her liquor—that was always her problem.

A change in the music caught her attention. Classical again, slow and intangibly melodious. It broke her heart yet made her feel strangely happy—almost. (Was this a definition of art?)

"What music is that?"

"That I believe is the D Major string quartet of Haydn, the andante." Again he gave her that look of surprised approval. He was always rediscovering her. "So you like that, too?"

"Oh yes. Very much. It makes me want to cry."

Foote gazed at her while she listened with closed eyes. When the movement ended she opened them and looked around as if wondering where she was.

"I have to go," she said.

"Of course you'll want to shower, after all that dancing."

"Yes," she said, for she knew she would be too impatient once she had got through that basement door and had Zudd in front of her.

Foote turned to watch her go. He seemed physically unable to take his eyes off her They were even more naked than she was. She felt them sucking at her like leeches.

In the solarium she chose the sauna. She shut the door and relaxed in the steam, in her sanctum, and sweated, and smoothed her skin with her hands, and recovered her senses a little. And then, surprise (why had she not expected this?), he came in, wearing a towel, and sat down too and started talking as if to no one in particular.

"I have to admit, I'm confused. Seventy-three years old, and confused! I was settled into my life, the endgame phase of my life, or so I thought, and now *this*. You know, I used to require beauty like yours. Movie starlets, fashion models, young ballerinas.Then I got older and other things became more important....But now you've come along.You're beautiful, intelligent—but you're terribly young. I've fallen for you, Catherine. God help me, I'm in love with you."

Kit watched and listened in silence.

"My children are grown and living their own lives. I used to get crushes, I even fell in love once or twice, but I wasn't free, and I always did the right thing, even if it hurt. You never read about me having an acrimonious divorce with highpowered lawyers fighting each other and broken-hearted children and visiting rights. Then marrying again a year later some divorcee with more children, more acrimony, more broken hearts and prenuptial contracts. I played by the rules. I made the necessary sacrifices. One of them produced a bastard son whose very existence is a constant torture to me. And—I admit it—I hate him. What an awful thing to say, isn't it. But it's true."

"You really hate him?"

"I hate him, because I can't *do* anything about him. I can't even help him, do anything for him."

"You can't?"

"Not discreetly. Overtly is out of the question, you understand. And he resents that. Oh he doesn't say it in words, but it's in his eyes, it's in the way he dodges around my overtures. I never know what he will accept and what he will reject, and especially what he will demand once he does get around to asking for something. It could be my life. It could be my *soul*. He has an insane pride. Sometimes I think he wants me dead—even to kill me with his own hands. But then sometimes I think no, he wants me to live on with my guilt. Or to humiliate me terribly. Yet he never does anything to harm me. He doesn't ask for money, or special treatment. He seems to *want* to be where he is, to be the way he is. He's my skeleton in the closet—one of them—the worst one—and I really think that, that in some perverse way he *enjoys* that. That and his position. The hold he believes he has over me. Well, he's mistaken. There is just so much I will take. The next time he swears at me will be the last."

In the fraught silence he now looked at her with a fresh allbeit disconcerting appreciation.

"You know, Catherine, at this point I'd have to say you know me better than... (shaking his head with slow wonderment) *anyone*. You know *everything*."

It was that slow speculative shaking of the head. Once again Kit asked herself if her life was in danger, particularly if Foote went ahead and actually did something about his thorny bastard son who dared to swear at him in the street.

"We do have a rather...intimate relationship," she said with care.

It brought the emotion back into his face.

"How ironic that you should have one with...with *him*, as well."

Kit had nothing to say. There was a taut silence. Foote broke it.

"Why him, Catherine? Of all people? You must know many men, why him? What do you want, Catherine? *Really* want? What about us, you and me? Do you think we make a fit? My people have always let me...indulge my fancies, without raising too much of a fuss, as long as I stayed in control, played by the rules—But I'm losing that. Do you think, is there some kind of, could we have some sort of—of union? of some sort? do you think? I could give you a very nice place to live, and clothes, and, and anything you wanted."

She saw his helplessness. It was right there on his face. Naked male vulnerability had always moved her, but on this level—this was beyond her experience "I need to think," she said.

"Of course," he said in a dreamy voice. He seemed to hesitate—then, as if forcing himself to commit an unnatural act like eating insects for survival or drinking a bitter antidote to a poison, he rose and ran out of the sauna clutching the towel around his waist.

And Kit, left alone, sighed.

Some sort of union. Why not? She was already having it. And she liked it, sort of. She liked him. He fascinated her. How could a man so old still be attractive? Was it his money, his power, his social position? Yes, but it was more than that, it was his urbanity, his manners, his classical education, his European culture. But then... Oh, damn Harrison Foote! She did not want to think about Harrison Foote now—not right now. The alcohol and the heat and sweating and all that dancing and strip teasing and nudity and the very narrow escape from what she had been about to do with Zudd in her office with all those people watching was still simmering away inside her, gaining in intensity what it lost in the reduction. That Christmas card from Zudd was what was on her mind. She had to get down to the basement.

She bounded to the door. But Foote was waiting for her with the oil spray and the scented talcum powder. Seeing him, she knew

Zudd would have to wait. She could not duck ritual. Not classic, refined, mannered ritual.

Foote had recovered some of his composure. Her nudity was now so much an accepted thing, so much a part of the ritual, that she felt no selfconsciousness, and he, for his part, scarcely directed his gaze to her body. It was her eyes that he sought as he tried to read her disposition.

You have to play this right, she told herself.

Instead of lying down on the massage table with her back to him to wait for the shock of the oil spray and the massaging caressing touch of his hands, she sat on it and smiled at him. She wanted to be kind. She did not want to lose him. She had to get away without antagonizing him.

"Harrison," she said, "I'm going to get dressed. I'm not in the mood for a massage right now. I hope you understand. I want to think about everything. I need more time."

"I understand.You know," he said in a low, probing voice, as if to himself, "I was not all that crazy about sex. I *wanted* it, but, well, it had to be the *way* I wanted it. I ignored my wife. I hired prostitutes and escorts. I satisfied my needs of the moment, such as I perceived them, felt them. Sometimes I didn't want to—you know—fuck. Excuse me, only, everybody says that nowadays, don't they? But sometimes that was all I did want. Now that I want it more than ever, it's too late. I've tried Viagra. I've tried everything. Maybe someday they'll—I never really had the whole experience—you know, everything together. With tenderness. And love. And now, I thought—I thought...."

He stood up and whipped away the towel, revealing a semi-erection. "Look," he said, like a child with a clay sculpture. "It's the Viagra. But even with Viagra no one else has been able to do even this much for me in ten years. Only you."

Kit was impressed and distressed. This old man was not going to give her what she wanted. Only Zudd was going to do that. Only a Zudd brought to the right pitch, driven by her, commanded by her, loved by her, slapped and scratched and clawed by her, only Zudd letting himself loose, setting himself free from his insane restraints could do that. Zudd was waiting for her in the basement and she had to get to him, but there stood Foote blocking the way with his pitiful creation, seeming to implore her to do something, not knowing himself what to do, what to ask *her* to do. And she thought, The quickest, sanest, simplest, most pragmatic way out of here right now is to do whatever it is he wants and do it fast. So she lay down on her side with her back to him as always, and left it up to him. And he came and lay down behind her as always and touched her. But not like always.

There was no oil, no gentle, timid caressing. His hands felt tense. His breathing was louder and closer. A heat radiated from his body. There was an urgency in his fingers. Not content to caress they called to her with a pleading insistence, urging her to turn on her back. She turned, closing her eyes, and felt his mouth hot on her throat, her shoulder, her breasts—the nipples tingled against her will, sending delinquent thrills through her body. She opened her eyes and stared at the ceiling and asked a silent question of, of all people, Tom, who came to her at just that moment: What should I do?

The hot mouth moved to her belly, the tongue went into her navel. Seduced in spite of herself, she prepared for the full onslaught of oral sex, when what she wanted was the straight hard masterful head-against-headboard-thumping liberating seismic fire hose of Zudd.

Trying to seize hold of her thoughts she took his head in her hands. That at least stopped his downward migration. But it brought a face transfigured with passion up close to hers, an aged wrinkled face with feverish eyes and a helpless distorted mouth .

"Please my dearest, my darling Thaïs, my Lady de Winter, my Salomé, my Delilah,—my Bacchanale!" He lay on her, his breath a deluge of panting champagne-scented gasps at her ear as a middling hard something poked at her crotch with increasing urgency. "You can't mind, my darling, my Catherine de Winter, don't be cruel, Milady, my love—Take my life afterwards cruel woman but let me have this now, what harm can it do, with the pills you take nothing can happen—Oh Salomé! oh my duchess, my queen! Catherine the Great! Cleopatra! Oh! Milady! My love—!"

"Pills?" said Kit, "pills? I haven't taken one for days!"

The words froze him.

"You haven't taken—but—*WHY?*" he choked out.

"I don't know—What's the matter?" she said as he rolled over on his back with a groan.

"It's too late!" he gasped clutching the towel to his genitalia. "Quick! Do what you always do—anything!"

But Kit, reprieved, only turned away. She rolled off the table to her feet. That's enough of this, she thought. This is crazy. What am I doing here? Where are my clothes? Trying to get her head together.

Foote appeared to have dozed off as usual. Though nothing had been usual about this. Definitely he was getting too ambitious. She would have to think about that. She looked at him and felt contradictory impulses—tenderness, and indignation. The poor old dear. The satyr!

She decided to let him sleep. She would get dressed and leave. And go to Zudd. And then think about all this, size everything up—something she felt she was good at doing, once she actually got down to actually doing it.

Then Foote groaned, and it was not the sound of a man sleeping. It was a sound of distress. His eyelids fluttered.

She thought he was waking up, but the eyes failed to open—a flash of white and no more. The lips moved sluggishly, exposing the front of his tongue in mongoloid thickness. Spittle formed in a corner of his mouth.

"My God!" Kit said aloud.

He was trying to talk.

"The...button, push...button," he mumbled. Kit put her finger on the red button on the wall and pushed and pushed and pushed, thinking ambulance and doctors and save him, is he going to die, thinking I've got to get dressed.

But he kept making noises as if trying to speak. She tried to hear the words. He wanted something or somebody.

"I've pushed the button. I pushed it. Do you want something? Can you talk? What should I do? Can I do something? My God!"

"Tell—Homer—I'm—sorry..."

"Homer? Homer Zudd?"

"I—loved her...Tell him...Tell him...I want him to have...Tell him—I want…"

Breathing in drawn-out gasps he was unable to produce another intelligible word. His eyes closed and he fell silent, while Kit, not knowing what to do, listened for whatever guidance he might yet give. She was still bent over him when Zudd rushed in.

He stood inside the door staring at the old man, then at her nakedness, then at her.

"What happened? What's going on? What are you doing up here? I've been waiting for you."

Kit shook her head.

"Is he dead?"

"I don't know. I think he's breathing. I pushed the button."

"I know. What went on? The usual, I suppose?"

"What?"

Just how much *does* he know? she thought. She had never told him the details, only that they did not have sex. Feeling that was more or less the truth.

"We'll have to tell them what happened," he said.

"Who? They don't have to know."

"*I* do."

"No," Kit said, "you don't." Then, relenting, she added, "He got very excited. Excited and…aroused. Is he dead?"

Zudd went over and felt the old man's pulse.

"So he wanted it all, uh?"

"Shouldn't you call that place?"

"You already did. Anyway he's not dead."

"Are you sure? He looks dead."

"He's not. Oh it's not so easy with those people. You have to shoot them. And drown them. And poison them. And throttle them. They don't die. They're Rasputin, you can't kill them." He stood looking down at him, his cheek muscles working the way they did when he was overwrought. "For a long time I wanted him dead. But I want him to *know*."

"Know what? What are you talking about? Why do you hate him?"

Zudd made no reply, as if he had not heard. Sweat glistened on his face in the overheated solarium. He kept staring at the old man on the massage table with the rumpled towel over his loins.

"So he tried to do that, uh?"

"He didn't though. He said he was sorry."

"Sorry he tried to fuck you? Or sorry he couldn't make it? Sorry about what, exactly?"

"He said to tell you that."

"Me? That he's sorry?"

"And that he loved her. I think he meant your mother."

"He should be sorry, the rotten son of a bitch."

"He admitted he's your father."

"He did, huh? Big deal."

"He was talking about you. About how guilty he feels and how he's always wanted to have contact with you but you wouldn't let him."

"Why should I, for what he did? And did over and over. Fifty years from now he'll wake up and they'll fix him up and he'll start over again, right where he left off. So he tried to fuck you, huh?"

"I didn't let him. And that's enough of that language."

For the first time Zudd seemed to realize who it was he was talking to. His expression softened.

"You didn't let him?"

"I didn't help him."

"Really?"

"Well, why are you so surprised? What do you take me for?" Suddenly she was angry. "I don't just go along with every—What are you trying to say?" The anger turned to fury as she realized that this was Zudd, *her* Zudd, her man in the basement, and that all she needed to do was give him one of those Dragon Lady looks and he would dissolve before her eyes and fall to his knees trembling.

But this was not the place. She sat down on a footstool with her knees together and her hands clasped demurely on her lap. She was in that no-man's-land of feeling at once inflamed by alcohol and sensitized to the fact that she was a bit drunk and might not know what she was doing.

"Shouldn't we be doing something for him?" she said feebly.

"After all these years, somebody balked."

"What?"

"You refused," Zudd said. "You said no."

"I...."

"I *knew* you would, when it came to it! And you did! You said 'fuck you!' to him. (Excuse me.) God! I admire you more than ever! I'm sure nobody ever said no to him before. I'm sure of it! Oh Kit, you really are my queen! You said no to him—and now, right in front of him, you'll say yes to me! Let him know! Let the bastard know! Let him be a witness! You'll conceive our child right here, right now, right in front of him—him watching! I want him to see!"

"He can't see!"

"He can! He sees everything! He sees!" Zudd released an abbreviated form of the soprano giggle he normally uttered at the sight of human viciousness. "He knows I'm here! Let's do it right here, right now!"

"No, no... We can't."

"Why not? In front of him! Right here! It's perfect!"

Kit said with a sigh, "Oh, God, no, Homer, not now, not here."

"Then let's go downstairs!"

"We can't just leave him here like this, Homer!"

Zudd sprang at her and seized her by the throat. "*Now*, damn it! *Now*! We have to do it *now*! *Right now*! *Why are you taking his side?*"

There was a noise outside. Zudd fell back, looking at the door. Kit gasped for air, fingering the red marks of his hands on her throat.

"Somebody's out there," Zudd said, himself again. "Kit! Forgive me! I didn't know what I was doing. I'd never hurt you. Forgive me!"

The look she gave him said, Never.

There was another noise, and a voice that seemed to be muttering to itself.

"Maybe it's them," Zudd said. "But it's too quick—they're all the way out in Queens." He went to the door, hesitated, and opened it when the doorknob rattled.

"Is Mr. Foote in there?" Tom Hutchins said.

Zudd tried to step outside without letting Tom see in, but Tom had already seen Kit. He put his hand on the door for a better look. "Kit?" he said and pushed into the solarium. "Kit?" he repeated, as if truly not believing his eyes. He stared at her, and at Foote, and back to her, and at Zudd, and back again to her.

"What's this all about?"

And at Foote, and at Zudd. His eyes found no resting place. "What's going on?"

"Oh God," Kit said. "Tom, it isn't what you think."

"So it *was* him! What is this, a goddamned orgy?" He turned to leave, but remembered the reason for his coming. "What's wrong with him?" he asked Zudd.

Zudd took a deep shuddering breath. "He...he must have passed out."

Tom turned to Kit. "How low can you sink? Or is that what you're trying to find out?"

Kit, on her footstool, staring blankly before her, drifted between Chirico and Munch—between desolate urban freakout and senseless shriek.

"There's no keeping up with you," Tom said. He put his hand inside his collar and pulled it with an anger that broke the top button and jerked collar and tie askew. It was the most violent thing Kit had ever seen him do. She could have laughed, were she not still drifting. Tom's voice rose in wonderment. "I come up here to quit my job—and here *you* are! I was *wondering* where you were. I never saw anybody move so fast! Wherever I go, there you are, eithed naked or getting there! Old Mr. Foote's latest...what? What are you? His latest what? Mistress? Concubine? Call girl? And *look* at him! Congratulations! You wore him out!"

"My clothes," Kit said looking around in distraction without moving from the footstool.

"Your *clothes*?" Tom shouted. "Why bother? Think of the time you can save!"

Kit jumped up and shut her eyes and opened her mouth wide as if she had decided on the shriek. Instead, a terrible composure settled on her face and her eyes narrowed on him, ice-hot.

"Do you want to know how far I've sunk, Mr. Hutchins? Well I'll *tell* you! Into the *basement*! So there! *That's* what I've sunk to, if that's anything to you! Up and down—up to the penthouse, down to the basement. Like a yoyo! And I *like* it!"

"Basement?" Tom said, disoriented at the unexpected attack (by a naked woman yet), and by the shriek that wasn't, "what basement? What are you saying?" He looked at Zudd.

"What am I saying? I'll show you! You want to see what I'm saying? *Here's* what I'm saying! *Homer*! Come over here!"

Zudd looked at her, once again, like the dog that does not trust its master's tone.

Kit's voice lowered, sharpened. "Come here!"

Zudd went, marched up to her like a little boy.

"Give me your ruler," she said looking not at him but at Tom. "Drop them!"

Zudd handed her the ruler from his back pocket.

"Drop them!" she said, threatening him with the brightest and most irresistibly beauteous hazel-eyed look she had ever yet given him. Rendered defenseless, Zudd let his pants fall to his ankles. Plainly fully aroused, he awaited further instruction.

"Take them off. Off! And your briefs—off! And your shoes and socks—off!"

He stood before her naked from his shirttails down.

With idiotic incredulousness Tom stared at them both, wanting to look away, wanting to rush out, unable to.

"Get over that table."

As Zudd obeyed, laying himself on the second rubbing table, Kit swung the ruler with practiced crispness. Four times she swung it with an angry energy reborn for each blow as four broad red stripes sprang up.

At each swing Tom winced with indignation and made as if to leave. Each time a glance from Kit, naked Kit, gleaming-eyed Kit with that metal ruler in her hand held him motionless.

Now the ruler clattered to the floor. Zudd turned to look at her. Her color had deepened, her eyes seemed to lose focus. Her bosom rose and fell noticeably.

"Now!" she gasped. "Homer! Now! Are you ready?"

"Yes!"

Smiling, Kit said, "Are you sure, Homer?"

"Yes! Yes! I've been ready for hours!"

Kit said to Tom, "Do you know what love is, Mr. Hutchins? *This* is love, Mr. Hutchins. Feast your eyes, Mr. Hutchins. Feast your libido."

Speechless, Tom watched her lie back on the table and raise her knees to welcome Zudd upon her.

"I don't have to watch this," Tom managed, not quite to himself.

"Yes you do!" Kit said.

And it was true, he could not move. He watched as the coupling commenced, and heard the lovers at their verbal minuet.

"You're going to give me what I want," she breathed to Zudd.

"Yes, my queen, I'm ready now."

Queen? Tom's brain echoed. Queen?

"For me."

"Yes. For our new race."

Race? New? Our?

"I've waited so long for this moment."

"Me too. Oh how I've waited."

"Oh! oh! Now! Come now!" she cried out. "Yes! Yes! Now! Don't wait!"

"Yes! Now! Now!"

Foote's arm flopped over to his side with a thump and a loud groan, and Zudd froze.

"He's alive!"

"What?"

"My fucking father—he's waking up!"

"I don't care! Don't stop! Come! Come!"

"Yes!" Zudd resumed his thrusting. "Watch, you, you bastard! Watch!"

But the rhythm was different, uncertain.

"You *want* him to see!"

"Yes! Yes! I do! The bastard! I do!"

"Then come now! *Now!...Ohhh, God!*"

It was a cry of despair, because for all Zudd's exclamatory yesses, and for all his thrusting and sweating self-exhortation, the moan he at length uttered was not in ecstacy but in pain as he slowed and stopped, finally inert. With a terrible groan he rolled to one side, fell from the table to the floor in a frightening thump, and lay there, a crumpled fetal heap with his face in his hands.

Kit turned away. She threw an arm across her eyes and lay on her side without a sound. And Tom looked at her and fought with himself.

The exposed shoulder blades, the helpless spine, the terrible nakedness, the fetal position, the hugging herself in misery. It broke his heart, and he went to her.

"Kit."

Getting no response, he touched her arm in a plea to help. She shook him off. But it was a shaking-off that broke his heart further—a pathetic little movement of her arm that on the surface seemed to reject him but underneath needed, asked pitifully to be petted and hugged and reassured.

He sensed that, but was afraid that the symbolic rejection of that arm movement might metamorphose into a real one for his having witnessed her mortification. Some sort of lese majesty had occurred in his presence, for which she might not forgive him.

"Kit."

"Go away."

"I won't go away."

Surprised at his own tenacity he plunged on.

"Kit," he said, "I don't know what you're into. I know you want to experience orgasm, that it's a problem. I don't know why it's so important to you—but it is, and I understand that. Your problem has become my problem. You wanted it so bad that I started to want it bad, and your impotence became my impotence."

It was Foote who spoke up, surprising them. "Gallantry, chivalry, respect," he said in a low, slow voice. "The forgotten magnetism. Forget your British mysogeny, man. Indulge her."

The suddenly alive old man had managed to turn his head to look at him, at Tom, ignoring, for once, the beautifully astonished eyes of Kit.

"Forget yourself, for God's sake! Go to her! Offer yourself to her! Give yourself up! Surrender!"

Out of the stunned silence came a reply from somewhere.

"It won't work."

It was Zudd, on the floor. "She won't meet you halfway," he said without removing his hands from his face. "You have to force her to come to you, to want you, to beg. You have to hold back and make her beg. The experts never got anywhere with her. They were too dumb. They were weak."

Tom shook his head like a wet dog. Save yourself! his inner voice bellowed, let the devils fight it out! Leave her to her fortunes! You don't know this woman! She's not for you or for anyone! Go, already! Get away!

It was no use. He could not walk away from Kit. Not Kit.

So he listened to them, to the two devils. Trying to understand her, he listened, and found Foote reasonable but wrong. Out of sync. Passé. The janitor too sounded right—but crazy. They were both right, they were both wrong.

And me in the middle, he thought. Paralyzed. Always paralyzed.

Nothing to fall back on. No philosophies or religions. Just doubts. And desires.

But Kit was still there, he had that.

"Kit, do you want me to go away?"

If she says yes, I'll go, he told himself.

She turned around and looked at him with a soft expression that said no.

He said, "Everybody seems to know what you need except me." Kit smiled a little. "I think what we both need is dinner," he said. "What do you say?"

She was silent. Then she gave a sarcastic laugh and said, "Dinner."

He leaned closer. "Yes, Kit, dinner. I know what you want. Do you think I'm blind? Of course I know what you want. But not here, Kit. Not in this place. Not with these people here. And not with a whip in your hand."

"Whip?" Kit said, sitting up. "I don't want a whip in my hand."

"But that's what you've always had. Don't you see, you've created a will o' the wisp. You can't run after it—it just slips away. It will always be just outside your reach, as long as you chase it with that whip in your hand. That's what the janitor is saying."

"Homer? He has his own ideas. He couldn't care less about that."

"Are you sure?"

Kit looked away and thought for a while. "I've made too big a deal out of that, haven't I."

"I think so. But how can I judge?"

"Give her your all," cried Foote.

"Make her beg," cried Zudd. "It's what she wants."

"What I really want, more than anything else in the *world*," Kit said, "is my *clothes*. I want to get *dressed*."

"And then?" Tom asked her with a twinge of apprehension.

"Then, all right, dinner. Then we'll see."

Tom blurted, "I love you, Kit."

With a sad smile she reached out and caressed his cheek with her fingers.

"I really do," he said helplessly, simply stating a fact.

"Love!" Zudd said with a groan, moving in and out of consciousness on the floor.

"Love," said Foote, in a voice that grew faint even as he enunciated the word.

"What about them?" Kit said. "We can't just leave them."

"Where are his servants? Where's his valet?"

"I don't know where they are. I never see them. But I've pressed that red button. They should be here any minute."

"Who? The servants?"

"The doctors. I don't know for sure. I think it's his cryogenics company. Or his clinic. They're taking a long time."

"Cryogenics? You mean they're going to freeze him?"

"That's what I was told."

"But he's not dead! What he needs is a *doctor*. A *hospital*." Then he saw that Kit's eyes were not on Foote but on the janitor, and filling with an even greater concern—more like horror. "What's wrong with him?" he said, following her stare.

Zudd had dragged himself into a corner like a dying bull in a bullring.

"Hey, man," Tom said to him, "it happens to everybody at one time or another, you'll get over it."

Kit took some steps towards him. "Homer! What's the matter?"

Zudd's face was gray and twisted with agony. He writhed and shuddered and seemed unable to breathe.

"He's in real trouble!" Kit said, horrified. "Look at his face. He's in pain."

Tom went over for a better look.

"This man needs a doctor!"

Zudd gasped, and gasped again. His hands moved like a silent film actor's rendition of sorcery, carving pirouettes in the air. Then, in convulsive movements, they sprang to his throat, his heart, his liver, his gut. It was as if an army of jagged lightning bolts had leapt from a lumbago advertisement to attack his flesh while paranha chewed him up inside.

"What's happening to you?" Tom asked him.

Zudd gasped, "It's no use."

"Get the Foote Clinic," Kit said. "There's a number on the wall."

Zudd began to breathe with slow care, as if nursing a dwindling supply of oxygen. "It's no use," he said between spasms of breathlessness. "It's in my guts, my lungs, my kidneys—it's everywhere. I know what it is. They won't be able to do anything for me. Not for me."

"But they can make you more comfortable," Tom said. "They have miraculous drugs. They might cure you."

"You don't understand. Drugs are what got me here. I'm immune to drugs. I went too far. Or not far *enough!* I missed. I wonder by how much? Maybe by only a hair!"

"Missed what?"

"The mutation," he gasped. "The genetic mutation."

"Mutation? Whose mutation? What are you talking about?"

"Mine! But it went wrong somewhere. You can't do it in one generation. Maybe two.You just have to hit the right combination. It was a gamble, and I lost. But what if I'd won? Pulled the lever at just the right time? In spite of all your scientific snickering it's what you all want, isn't it? You try by laboratory inches, I went for the theoretical mile. And I almost pulled it off! Kit! Our son would have had my resistance—but greater than mine! Think of it! I didn't miss by much! We almost did it! Kit, my queen mother, my Eve! We came close!"

"What's he talking about?" Tom said. "A child? With you? What was all that about a new species or super race back when you were...you know, trying to...."

The reply, again, came from Zudd.

"Yes! A super species! Not a race—a species! Super-resistant, an alternative to Nature—immortal!"

"What's he talking about?" Tom kept asking Kit. "He's daft. He's raving. But you, Kit, were you actually going along with all this?" Kit looked away.

"Look, suppose I make you more comfortable and get a doctor here," Tom said to Zudd, bending down and touching his arm.

"*Don't touch me!*" Zudd screamed, actually screamed, and Tom recoiled in alarm from a body he now saw was shiny with sweat. "It hurts! It's like fire!"

"Okay, okay, it's all right, I won't touch you. But I will call a doctor. God, Kit, I don't know what weirdness went on between you, but—Kit?"

She was gone. He hoped, prayed she was only dressing, and would come back.

"What's *not* weirdness?" Zudd said. "Her and old Foote? Her and you? Her and anybody? Anybody and anybody? I'll tell you something, we understood each other. And we still do in a way that you don't, and never will! Let her deny it all she wants. We had something. But there was this soft sentimental female core. I knew it was there, more than she did. But we needed each other. Let her deny it!"

He was out of breath. He lay on his forehead, panting.

Tom, at the phone, dialed the Foote Clinic number printed on a laminated card fixed to the wall. It had an extension, which he had no opportunity to ask for because after a long ring the receiver was picked up by a woman who said hurriedly, "Hold on please," and then gave a shriek of laughter. There were noises of the phone bumping against something then clattering onto a hard surface, and scuffling and running and scraping chairs and a male voice laughing along with the playful female shrieks. Tom hung up.

"What kind of clinic is that? They're playing grab ass! I couldn't get through to anyone! Is that his cryogenics place? Christ, he'd be better off in a tub of ice cubes."

That brought a cackling laugh from Zudd. "Ice cubes!" he gasped. "Better off with ice cubes!" His laugh ended in a coughing fit wrapped in pain.

"What can I do for him?" Tom looked around hopelessly. Kit came in, dressed. Wearing the brooch.

"Kit, thank God you're back. I'll have to call 911. His private thing isn't working. And it's both of them—your friend's in a bad way too."

"God," she said looking at Zudd. "Let me try that number again."

Tom rushed over to Foote and felt for his pulse.

"I can't feel anything."

"Hello?" Kit said into the phone, "hello?"

Tom went back to Zudd. "Do you want anything? Is there anything I can do?"

"Is he dead?" Zudd said. "Is that old bastard dead? I've got to outlive him! At least that!"

"I think so," Tom said. "Why do you want to outlive him? Is he really your father? What makes you think you're going to die? We're getting help. You'll be okay."

"You're wasting your time," Zudd muttered.

"Why? What have you done? If you've poisoned yourself, tell me what you took, it will help them find the antidote."

"I told you, it's too late."

"You said you had a secret for immortality." Tom was crouched beside him. "What is it? There must be an antidote. Tell me what you did."

"Immunization. I immunized myself."

"What do you mean? You mean, some sort of injection? Anti-viral? A homeopathic herbal tea? Some sort of multi-preventative? Against what? Every known disease?"

"Against death!"

New York had taught Tom to be cool in the face of outrageous declarations, and his reaction to this was in the nature of a reflex. "I understand that," he blustered, "but how? You mean, a sort of somatic missile defense system?"

"Against *Nature*. By confusing her. You have to break the life cycle that leads straight to death. Old age and death. Do you see?" Zudd was excited by this apparent opportunity to gain a disciple.

"I think so…Go on."

"By confounding the cell structure. By doing everything wrong. You have to frustrate Nature. Why is Nature always right? Because *she* says so? She set the whole thing up, and tells us how to proceed, and our reward for doing everything right, the way she says to do, is we get to die—Big deal! Get old and arthritic and die. Why not change the rules, change the whole process, screw up the works and see what comes of it? Who made Nature the big boss, anyway? God? Don't make me laugh! Anyway God moves in mysterious ways His wonders to perform, right? So, maybe mine is the mysterious wonder! Maybe He planned my intervention all along, haha! You do it with frustration. You avoid orgasm. What good are all the hormones and pills and injections and trying to stay young, only to ejaculate yourself into the grave? The old buzzard is over seventy—and he's dead! Trying to fuck one last time! The stupid sonofabitch. She was his *niece*! My *mother*! His *niece*! She couldn't make a scandal—she had to run away and hide, and invent a whole story about who my father was. An officer who died in the Korean war. Of course. She made him out to be a hero, too. Why not? Once you're imaginary you can be anything! And now the son of a bitch is dead. I outlived him, haha! He's dead because I didn't call the clinic. Fuck him. Why should I call them? You called them, and what did you get? Grab ass, hahaha!...I depended on myself. I trained myself to breathe smoke and fumes and eat anything, drink anything—chemicals, drugs, insecticides, additives, plastics, who gave a shit? Whatever was in the supermarket. You should have seen me in the crisis!"

"Hello?" said Kit, "hello? *Please!* This is *urgent!* Hello?"

"Why cooperate with that tyrant, Nature? She's the enemy! It's a trap, a sucker's game. Love's an even bigger trap. *Love*?" he scoffed. "That's the biggest sucker trap of all! You can't break any cycles that way."

"But if people don't die, the world will be overpopulated," Tom tried to reason with him.

"Don't kid yourself. They'll kill each other off like never before, and that's saying something! Holocaust will follow on holocaust. Every backyard will have its crematorium. The ashes will make a terrific fertilizer. And a great cleanser. They'll probably find a way to run machinery with it—a fuel, a source of energy. Whole industries will depend on it. Their stocks will go through the roof. *Then* watch the killing that will go on! Open your mind, man! Get the whole picture!"

"He's raving," Tom mumbled to himself. "The man's insane."

Still he felt he should be able to reason with him. He wasn't frothing at the mouth or anything. He must be reachable. "You say you want to frustrate Nature," he said. "Yet you wanted a child. Wasn't that cooperating?"

"I had to. Science hasn't caught up with me yet. It was a momentary cooperation—with a purpose. I used cooperation and threw it away like a plastic container. Because it's a trap. You put your head—both your heads, hers and yours—inside those jaws, then you snatch them out again quick. You do it for just that moment you need to achieve your goal, to get what you want—a son to carry on your purpose. A Siegfried, immune to everything, carrying your genetic mutation forward to the goal of immortality."

"Without love."

"Definitely without that stupid sentiment, that fatal glue that gathers our powers, our vital energies, and runs them down the sewer into the grave."

"How can a man seem to be talking sensibly, using everyday words, offering seemingly sensible thoughts, yet be crazy as a coot?"

Tom was talking towards himself, but was intercepted.

"Crazy?" Zudd said. "Or just ahead of the rest of you? Why won't you open your mind? You can open it when you want to, as long as it suits you, jerks you off, but when it doesn't fit your preconceived ideas your brain shuts like a clam. How many cigarettes do you smoke in a day? How's your lungs? How's your liver? What was in the food you ate today? You *better* start changing those genes, man. Look, all it needs is a good start, a big push. That fire I started—I started that fire, you know—Did you see how many waves it made? All those psychic convulsions just waiting for something to make them go—a starting pistol. Then they all go off like popcorn. Try it! You might hit the lucky mutation!"

"Listen," said Tom, "if you started that fire, then so did three hundred and fifty others, at last count. It was on TV. Seems everybody and his sister was on the wharves and under the piers throwing lighted matches and cigarettes into the river trying to ignite a Götterdämmerung. That's how people get their rocks off around here—didn't you know? The cops finally had to let them all go—there were too many."

Zudd said bitterly, "I had a reason. I had a purpose."

"So did they," said Tom. "Kicks. Rebellion against something—anything. That's reason enough around here. Hey, did you really think you were the only nut in New York?"

"I'm not insane!" Zudd gasped.

"And by the way, it was Mother Nature that brought the snow that put out the fire and moved away those black clouds, wasn't it? You know what?" Tom ran on, "You're a bunch of nuts. That's why I don't think I can blame Kit for anything, whatever she's done."

"You like being trapped? a slave?"

"What are you talking about? She's what protects us. From people like you. I'll stick with Nature—if I can find any part *of* her in this town."

"It's your funeral," said Zudd. At that instant a spasm jerked through his whole body, from the hair on his head to the toes of his bare feet. Yellow flushes alternated with red ones. A final convulsion left him apparently paralyzed. There was a last raucus gurgle, and he lay motionless, his mouth and eyes wide open.

Tom straightened up and stood looking down at him.

"Hello!" said Kit. "Listen what *took* you so long, we've been trying to get you for *ages*! I have a mind to report you to Mr. Foote—or anyway his family. Nobody minds your having some fun but this happens to be an emergency. It's life and death! Mr. Foote is dead I think and his son, I mean the janitor, I mean the custodian is dying too and, I mean, get *over* here, right *away*. What? Who am I?" She looked at Tom in alarm. He shook his head violently. "The cleaning woman," she said and hung up.

"They're coming," she said to Tom. She saw him looking down at Zudd. "How is he?"

"He's dead."

"Oh!"

She went over and looked down at him. "Poor Homer. How he must have suffered. Couldn't you make him more, you know, presentable? I mean—you know...."

Tom rolled Zudd over on his back and straightened his legs and arms. He closed the eyes and mouth, pulled down the shirttails. Kit brought the brown pants over and covered his legs.

They stood there looking at him.

"He said you understood each other," Tom said.

"He said that?"

"That and a lot of other things."

"He understood me better than I understood him, I think. We had power over each other. I don't know if that's the same as understanding each other."

Tom sighed, audibly, fighting off the questions that boiled in his head.

"He looks more peaceful now," Kit said. "What exactly did he die of, I wonder."

"Fulminating everything."

"What do you mean?"

"What I mean is instead of immortality he hit on a brand new sensational form of multiple death, or anyway death from multiple causes. His genetic mutation sure did go wrong. In his terms, he pulled the wrong lever. So they're coming over? I don't think they'll ever figure out what killed him. Some sort of toxic poisoning, I suppose. What can we tell them? Should we even bother?"

"Tell them what," said Kit, "that he ate plastic and drank chemicals and smoked the foulest weeds and took every pill he could get hold of? They'll find all that stuff in his kitchen anyway. And a lot more."

"Yeah," Tom nodded, "they wouldn't believe us. Who would believe anything so simple as a man waging war against Nature? I mean, don't we all, to some extent? The term has no meaning when you're as advanced as we are."

Kit said with a shiver, "Let's get out of here. We can't do anything for them now."

"I think you're right." They looked at each other for confirmation.

"Foote's people will be here soon, doing whatever they do."

"Yes, let's go."

"Please!" came a feeble voice.

Foote?

"Don't leave me alone."

"Tom! He's alive!" They went to him. "We thought...."

"Do you want us to wait until they get here?"

"I want you to call them back and say I'm all right, not to come."

"What?"

"But you need a doctor!"

"No. And I don't want to be resuscitated."

"You don't?"

"I forgot about the memories, the regrets, the selfloathing. They'll never cure that, no matter how many cures they discover or how hard they try. I can't escape my past."

"Regrets? That's what's bothering you? *Regrets?*" said young Tom.

"They start out as nothing. But they fester. You get older and older and they get deeper and deeper. You can't sleep. And while I was lying there frozen they would increase, and intensify. And the mental pain with them. And I can't face that. Piaf sang 'Non, je ne regrette rien,' but she was a sparrow, and sparrows can fly. Sinatra sang 'Regrets I've had a few, but then again too few to mention.' That's not a sparrow, that's a liar. Of course, being Italian, and Catholic, they are so good at covering things over—I envy them that. If only I could forget my past! Or at least live with it."

"Maybe what you need is a religious conversion."

"I've decided to accept death, that's my religious conversion. Catherine?"

"Yes, Harrison."

"I have a last wish only you can grant me."

"Yes, Harrison, what do you want?"

"Would you stand over there nude, where I can see you? Just that? Would you do that?"

"Nude?" Kit said. "Nude? I've just put my clothes *on*."

"That's how I want to die. Looking at you. I beg you."

"I guess you're not exactly ready for a religious conversion," Tom said.

"I want to die looking at her. That's all. Just that."

"Sorry, you'll have to look at her the way she is." Tom was trying not to get angry.

"I can't see her."

Blushing, Kit moved to the foot of the rubbing table.

"Raise my head a little more," Foote said in a voice so marked with suffering that Tom, in spite of himself, out of compassion obeyed what sounded like a command given to a servant, and he added the pillow from the other table to the one under the dying man's head.

"Ah, yes! Now I see her. Ah, yes. What a lovely creature. If only I could see her naked, one last time. Catherine, my dear Catherine, Milady, my own Venus de Milo, wouldn't you consider...? I beg you."

"I'm sorry, Harrison, I just don't—I'm sorry. And I'm not Milady or Venus de Milo, I'm Kit and I have arms."

"I've felt those arms around me. I have felt them! Oh, Kit! Oh, Catherine! Oh!"

Tom wasn't sure if the old man was coming or going—dying, or having an orgasm—and for once did not know what to say. Foote's eyes rolled in his head and he appeared to be gasping for breath at the same time as the white towel across his loins rose a little, resembling an igloo. He was trying to steady his eyes enough to keep looking at her. And it was Kit who moved.

Impelled by a force that bonded her to the old man and rendered her impervious to extraneous protests she began removing her clothes—"*What are you doing!*" Tom shouted—until she stood naked again so that he could see her—his Venus de Milo with arms, his Milady, his Delilah, no longer blushing, but radiant, smiling a little.

Her eyes held the same look she had given Zudd, but instead of imperious, now it was quiet and wise with a secret understanding, and with a sense of power—the power, this time, not to command and reduce, but to nurse, and give sustenance.

Foote sighed, "Thank you! thank you! thank you!"

Even as he contemplated her his smile faded, his eyes filled with sadness. Then he startled them both yet again by opening them wide with a sudden urgency.

"Forget what I said!" he cried in a hoarse, gasping whisper. "I didn't mean it! Let them come for me! It's all arranged! I want to live! I want—"

His mouth jerked to one side as his eyes squeezed shut. He

shuddered, then relaxed, and they realized he was dead, really dead this time.

"What now?" Kit said after a while, strangely calm.

She reached for her clothes.

"Why did you do that?"

"I don't know. I suddenly wanted to. I can't explain it."

"Christ you're so different from what I thought."

Having buttoned her shirt, Kit cleared her tresses from its collar with her hand and a toss of her head and said, "I'm getting out of here. Now."

"What about them?"

"I don't care. Stay if you like, I'm leaving. Look, his cryogenics people will be here any minute."

"Right, let's go."

Suddenly Kit thought she was going to faint. She leaned against Tom.

"Are you okay?"

"I thought so but...I need a drink."

"So do I." But something still troubled him. Then he saw what it was. "Look!"

Instead of falling and lying flat, the towel across Foote's middle had risen and was actually higher. The igloo had become Mount Fujiyama.

"Are you sure he's dead?" said Kit.

"Christ, how can you ever be *sure* around here? He's *dead*. Let's just go!"

With a last shivering look at Zudd, Kit went with Tom to the door.

"Just think," She said at the door, gazing back at her employer, "they'll bring him back and he'll go on, and on...with his money and his institutions and his painting young models and his massages and saunas and cuddling up behind them and his graceful aging...At least Zudd was trying to improve the species. This man was just about pleasure. His own pleasure. He talked a wonderful game. But I wonder if he wasn't, sort of, the Devil."

"What I'm wondering is if he'll come back—you know, be brought back—in our lifetime," Tom said. "Think of it."

Kit gave him a look of consternation.

"In our lifetime?" she echoed.

She had not thought of that.

In the spacious anteroom the Christmas tree still sparkled, the bottle of champagne was still in its bucket, the flutes waited. Kit stared at it all, stared so long and so blindly it made Tom uncomfortable. He wanted to snap his fingers in her face like a hypnotist. The elevator did it for him, arriving suddenly and disgorging a team of five men, three in white medical suits, two in designer casual wear. They rushed out carrying a stretcher and bags of medical equipment.

They hesitated, looking around.

"Where's Mr. Foote?" one of them asked.

Before Tom could speak Kit said, "He's gone. They've taken him away."

"They? Away? Who? Where?"

"A team of doctors," Kit said, her face pale, feeling Tom's eyes on her. "I think Bellevue."

"Bellevue!"

They rushed back into the elevator pushing frantically at the buttons and leaving behind a heavy odor of whisky.

"Why'd you say that?" Tom asked. "I notice I keep asking you why you do things."

"And I never have an answer. I guess I just don't want him to come back. He's dead, let him stay that way." After a pause she said, "Does this make me a murderer?"

"I haven't the foggiest. It's playing God, in a way. But then, what did you do, except misdirect them? I honestly don't know. I mean, how can you kill someone who's already dead?"

On the ride down in the smaller, private elevator, when for the first time they were safe from being overheard by anyone living or dead, they remained weirdly silent. Tom sensed a fulcrum in Kit that might tip her away from him. Staring at that table in the anteroom she had seemed to be summing things up, maybe her life.

He had always felt that if she would only do that, all would be well. She would see him as her savior and companion and turn to him. Now he wasn't sure. He had always been eloquent on the subject—but now, if she were to ask his opinion as she had often done, he had no ready answer. Too much had happened. He only knew that he wanted her more than ever.

Startled by her pallor he gave her a cigarette. She pulled the smoke in deep, throwing her head back as if gasping pure oxygen.

"The one thing I'm not going to do," Tom suddenly blurted, "is I'm not going to try to understand you. To understand a woman, she must be diminished, reduced, robbed of her freedom, made into a programmed mannequin. I don't want that. I'd rather have you fully evolved and mysterious, with all the doubt and pain that comes with it, even if...."

"Are you sure?" Kit said, so quickly it interrupted his thought.

"I think so. Yes...I'm a modern male masochist, I suppose. I don't see any alternative, not for me anyway. I want you the way you are."

"Do you, Tom?"

It sounded like a refutation.

"I just said so," he replied, blinking uncertainly.

Equally uncertain was Kit's smile, and as unconvincing.

"The question is," he said with a quaver, "do *you* want *me*."

Kit leaned against him with her face against his chest, and Tom put his arm around her and rested his cheek on her hair gratefully, even while inhaling the hated penthouse perfume. He decided to feel relieved, even almost happy, and to ignore for now the troubling fact that his question had not truly been answered.

They landed. The doors opened and they stepped out into the foyer.

Tom looked up at the chandelier and down at the thick carpet.

"Ah, the basement," he said with an unnatural cheeriness. "And that apartment would be through there. What's that over the door—a TV camera. Right. And this is the street door."

He opened it and was showered with snowflakes.

"God! Isn't this gorgeous?"

"It's beautiful!"

They went out into the snow flakes and clean air, drawing deep breaths.

Tom stood looking around. He stared across the street at The Heavenly Haven. In spite of his resolution, he turned to her with a look of reproach.

"This is where you were that night."

"Homer did that," she said. "I didn't know. But, does it matter?"

"Of course it matters!" His face showed it was a cry from the heart, untouched by human thought. "Everything matters!"

Kit nodded slightly. She seemed to be appraising things he said in a new light. To Tom it meant she had opened her mind and was willing to understand his feelings better.

He could explain them now. It meant she was listening. How could she not have seen that everything mattered? If only he could make her see, oh how eloquent he would be then, and how happy to be able to explain it all to her.

"I saw you as I was leaving—I'd been modeling for…Well, you know."

"Modeling. Right," Tom muttered.

He couldn't help it. There was a bitterness in him, whatever his resolutions. But not to worry—he would explain and the scales would fall from her eyes. And he would feel better. They both would. And they would be happy. Truth was the best way, the *only* way.

"There you were, walking up and down. I couldn't leave. I was trapped. I wound up going in there. I was looking for another way out."

"Are you sure you were only looking for another way out?"

Kit sighed.

"And what you found was—what? Sadomasochism?"

"Kicks."

"Kicks? You mean, self-debasement?"

"That…was part of the bargain."

"Debasement a bargain?"

Kit gazed at the street, where cars skidded by on the snow with revelers shouting through open windows and laughing patrons went barging into The Heavenly Haven.

"On the surface I suppose it was a bad bargain. The penthouse and the basement both. I've heard of bargains struck with the Devil, and with witches. I guess Homer was my Devil and I was his witch. Harrison too, in a way." She turned to him. "I don't want to think about it right now, you know?"

"You don't want to think about it."

"Not right now. Look, your tie is still all twisted," she said straightening it a little.

They studied each other in the lamplight, with its halos and rainbows.

"When?"

"I don't know. When I'm ready."

"I need to talk now," Tom said. Kit was silent. "I have to talk about it. I can't help it. I can't put it out of my mind."

"Merry Christmas!" a group of teenagers yelled at everybody as they ran by.

After a moment Kit said, "You'll always see me in that solarium."

"I don't *want* to, I'll *try* not to, but…."

"I know. *But*."

Tom's desperate eyes sought a refuge between snowflakes. And Kit, looking at him, studying him, studying everything in the past weeks and months, reached a conclusion.

"Tom." He looked at her and she said, "It's no good, Tom."

"What's no good?"

"Us. We have to say goodbye, Tom."

"*Goodbye*?"

"They didn't want to die. You don't want to live. I need somebody who wants both. I'm starting to see a light at the end of—I'm starting to like myself a little."

"I do want to live, I do! I love you, Kit! I want to marry you and put all that out of my mind forever and, and marry you and, and have kids and, and publish that Raines novel and other rejected novels that deserve publishing, and settle down here in New York because it's a city of rebirth and renewal and—For us, too. We'll start over, I'll put that right out of my mind and…and I'll never think of it again, any of it and…and…."

He put his face in his hands.

"Goodbye, Tom. We both need that. Rebirth. But not in the same cradle, you know? Go ahead and publish those novels and get on with your life and settle down and I wish everything good for you, Tom, I really do. And if you ever do get really free of all this baggage…."

"Baggage? Baggage? You said you wanted those things—marriage, children, a home."

"I do, but I want to be free, too. And to *feel* free. Free from questions and criticisms and moral scrutiny and sermons. Maybe it's the wrong way to go. Maybe the priests and preachers and mullahs and you are right, but it's too late, I can't go back. I'm not sorry I did what I did. Because I've survived it. I feel as clean and as pure now as...as these snowflakes. I'm sorry, Tom. I really am, but I have to do this, I really do."

"Priests? Mullahs?" said a bewildered Tom. "Me? What are you talking about?"

"I like the excitement!"

"What excitement?"

"The excitement of liberation, of freedom, of the *sense* of freedom."

"Freedom? With Foote? With *Zudd*?"

"Well, yes. I know it sounds crazy. I have to feel my way, Tom."

Tom could only move his head from side to side in total bafflement.

With a light kiss to the lips Kit walked away, homeward bound and happy, to her apartment in the darkling shower of those clean, pure snowflakes, while Tom, as puzzled as ever, helplessly watched her go.

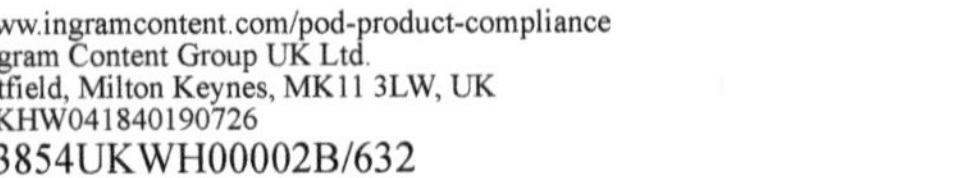

www.ingramcontent.com/pod-product-compliance
Ingram Content Group UK Ltd.
Pitfield, Milton Keynes, MK11 3LW, UK
UKHW041840190726
13854UKWH00002B/632

9 780977 956142